D1012826

"With a cast of monsters and madmen, psychics and government spooks, ghosts and (yes) gods, *River Runs Red* is a thriller of apocalyptic proportions. Mariotte's latest reads like a clock-slamming game of fast blitz supernatural chess played out on a board stretching from the dungeons of Iraq to the deserts of the American Southwest. With an endgame fought on the dark rivers of the human soul, it's a battle at once mythic and personal . . . and a surefire checkmate for readers everywhere."

—Norman Partridge, author of *Dark Harvest*

"Mariotte keeps you entertained and gives your gray cells something to chew on while they're helping you manufacture monsters in your mind's big-screen, surround-sound theater . . . Don't let this horror fiction escape from you."

—*The Agony Column*

MISSING WHITE GIRL

"*Missing White Girl* takes us on a police-cruiser-speed journey through the intense four days following the kidnapping of a teenage girl . . . Mariotte hits upon some fascinating topics . . . He throws in just enough grit and gore to appease action junkies . . . But his true masterpiece is Buck Shelton. In his hero, he's crafted one of the finest new sleuths in fiction: a very real man who finds solace in the challenges of his job when things get rough at home, who isn't so hardened that a dead family of four can't still shake him to the core, and who isn't afraid to make solving a crime a little bit personal. It would be a pleasure to see Buck again."

—*Tucson Weekly*

continued

Jove titles by Jeffrey J. Mariotte

MISSING WHITE GIRL
RIVER RUNS RED
COLD BLACK HEARTS

COLD BLACK HEARTS

JEFFREY J. MARIOTTE

JOVE BOOKS, NEW YORK

THE BERKLEY PUBLISHING GROUP
Published by the Penguin Group
Penguin Group (USA) Inc.
375 Hudson Street, New York, New York 10014, USA

Penguin Group (Canada), 90 Eglinton Avenue East, Suite 700, Toronto, Ontario M4P 2Y3, Canada
(a division of Pearson Penguin Canada Inc.)
Penguin Books Ltd., 80 Strand, London WC2R 0RL, England
Penguin Group Ireland, 25 St. Stephen's Green, Dublin 2, Ireland (a division of Penguin Books Ltd.)
Penguin Group (Australia), 250 Camberwell Road, Camberwell, Victoria 3124, Australia
(a division of Pearson Australia Group Pty. Ltd.)
Penguin Books India Pvt. Ltd., 11 Community Centre, Panchsheel Park, New Delhi—110 017, India
Penguin Group (NZ), 67 Apollo Drive, Rosedale, North Shore 0632, New Zealand
(a division of Pearson New Zealand Ltd.)
Penguin Books (South Africa) (Pty.) Ltd., 24 Sturdee Avenue, Rosebank, Johannesburg 2196,
South Africa

Penguin Books Ltd., Registered Offices: 80 Strand, London WC2R 0RL, England

This is a work of fiction. Names, characters, places, and incidents either are the product of the author's imagination or are used fictitiously, and any resemblance to actual persons, living or dead, business establishments, events, or locales is entirely coincidental. The publisher does not have any control over and does not assume any responsibility for author or third-party websites or their content.

COLD BLACK HEARTS

A Jove Book / published by arrangement with the author

PRINTING HISTORY
Jove mass-market edition / June 2009

Copyright © 2009 by Jeffrey J. Mariotte.
Cover photograph of "Ghost Town" copyright © James Nazz / Corbis; "Ominous Storm Clouds" copyright © Dick Reed / Corbis; "Polisario Front" copyright © Jacques Haillot / Sygma / Corbis.
Cover design by Rita Frangie.
Text design by Kristin del Rosario.

ISBN: 978-0-515-14626-4

JOVE®
Jove Books are published by The Berkley Publishing Group,
a division of Penguin Group (USA) Inc.,
375 Hudson Street, New York, New York 10014.
JOVE® is a registered trademark of Penguin Group (USA) Inc.
The "J" design is a trademark of Penguin Group (USA) Inc.

PRINTED IN THE UNITED STATES OF AMERICA

10 9 8 7 6 5 4 3 2

Acknowledgments

I'd like to thank everyone in Hidalgo County, New Mexico, who helped out with this book, in ways large and small. Special appreciation also goes out to Cindy Chapman, Dianne Schlekewy, D. P. Lyle, MD, Howard and Katie, and the wonderful people at Jove, especially Ginjer, Susan, Jodi, and Amy.

1

THEY were dead, all of them dead, and so was she.

As the brilliant flare faded from Annie O'Brien's eyes and the roar faded and the hail of debris tapered off, all she could think was that her father had always told her to look for the silver lining, and while for her that lining often turned out to be aluminum foil, cheap and easily torn, this time she was able to console herself with the realization that there was indeed silver, polished and pure: At least the bomb had taken care of her Christmas shopping predicament.

The date was the nineteenth of December. Annie and four fellow cops were closing in on a murder suspect (Annie's case; the dirtbag had killed two high school girls, and she had been working it for a couple of weeks, with their pictures taped up over her desk at work and on her bathroom mirror at home), having ascertained that he had holed up in a third-rate trailer park near Buckeye and Forty-third. One of the four cops was Ryan Ellis, with whom she was sleeping in spite of both the Phoenix Police Department's regulations and her better judgment. He was so gorgeous and so good in bed that she couldn't help herself. She'd been looking for a way to break it off, but maybe not looking as hard as she might have. It was, after all, almost Christmas, and it seemed heartless to break up with someone at the holidays. But she had to get it done. Ryan seemed to be falling hard. She knew he had shopped for her. He had already mentioned making plans for next summer. She hadn't shopped for him because she'd had every intention of being broken up by the holiday, and why go to the trouble if she knew she'd be returning whatever she bought on December 26?

But she hadn't managed to let him know her intention, and he hadn't picked up on her subtle hints. Too subtle, she supposed; too nuanced. He was gorgeous but not that smart. The best present for a guy like him would be a clue. Or maybe a full-length mirror, because he was all surface, with nothing inside.

When she had learned where Trey Fairhaven was hiding out—he had ordered digital cable in his own name, dumb even for a criminal, a class of people not generally known for feats of intellect—she told Lieutenant Carson and Carson assigned Ryan, two uniformed officers, and Will Matson, a detective who had just transferred over from Vice, to check out the place with her. Annie drove, Ryan riding shotgun, Matson in the back. The two unis took a squad car.

"Annie O'Brien?" Matson said on the way. "With that red hair and those emerald eyes? You must be pure Irish."

"No cigar for you, Matson. My dad was a mutt, but mostly a British Isles mutt—Irish, Scottish, English. But Mom was French. Not French-American. French. They met when Dad was stationed in Frankfurt and vacationing in Paris. I'm not sure what they saw in each other, but they stayed together long enough to have me, and then for her to get really tired of living in the States. She's back where she belongs now, a stone's throw from the Seine. If you've got a good arm."

"And your dad?"

"Gone. Five years now; I'm used to the idea. He was on the job."

"I'm sorry, Annie."

"Don't be. And it isn't really even Annie. It's Annicka. I just go by Annie because it's easier for the cops and other Neanderthals I usually hang around with."

"I know I have a hard time with more than two syllables," Ryan said.

How I wish you were joking, Annie thought. But they were pulling into the Frontier Town RV Resort, her unmarked Crown Victoria in front, the squad car behind, so she shut up and focused on scanning the trailers for any sign of Fairhaven. If the trailer park had ever resembled a resort in any way, it didn't now. The road was paved but crumbling like dried-out cookie dough. The trailers were bleached out by the sun to the point that everything had a kind of pale grayness to it, including the ceramic gnomes and deer and rabbits standing sentinel around some of them. A few spindly ocotillos and a half-dead saguaro cactus, spines drooping from a split up one side, passed for natural beauty. Last Resort might have been a more appropriate name for the dump.

"Pretty place," Ryan said. "Maybe I should move my grandma here."

"What, and lose her spot under the freeway?" Annie said. "Look for space fifty-seven."

Curtains fluttered in the window of a mobile home that slanted awkwardly toward one corner, where the cinder blocks that supported it seemed to have disintegrated. The curtains had daisies on them and moth holes lacing them, and the hand that Annie glimpsed holding them back, then releasing them, was brown, pudgy, and female. Trey Fairhaven was a white guy, thirty-three years old—a year younger than Annie—and built like a tweaker, like he hadn't eaten a solid meal in a month.

"We're being watched," Matson said.

"Since the second we pulled in the driveway," Annie said. "You'd almost think there were lawbreakers about."

So far she liked Matson. He wasn't as attractive as Ryan,

so she wouldn't feel compelled to sleep with him. And he seemed smarter. Not hard to achieve, but still, bonus.

"This is forty-four," Ryan said, pointing to a wooden sign poking up from the gravel beside a trailer bedecked in those cheap decorative blankets you could buy from guys who parked their vans in vacant lots and hung their wares on poles. Phoenix didn't get a lot of rain, but these blankets had seen a monsoon season or two; Annie had to work to make out the Diamondbacks logo, an American flag, the familiar silhouette of a mud-flap girl.

On the other side of the drive, two barefoot toddlers stopped dragging a doll carriage across a patch of dusty artificial turf to gaze solemnly at them. Annie tried on a smile, which drew no reaction at all.

She gave up and stopped beside the blanketed trailer. The squad car braked behind her. She got out and the other four cops met her by the Crown Vic's hood. They all wore dark blue windbreakers with gold letters spelling out POLICE on the backs and the badge of the Phoenix PD printed over the breast. Annie counted out the remaining trailers, pointing to each one. "That's the one," she said. "Shit-brown stripe along the side, dry birdbath in front."

The others indicated that they saw it.

"We have a warrant. We'll go in hard. You guys bring the battering ram?"

One of the unis, a patrol officer named Ruiz, nodded, returned to the squad car's trunk, and brought back a tactical entry ram. It was about twenty inches long and would knock in most doors—looking at the trailer in space fifty-seven again, Annie hoped they didn't knock it into space sixty.

"I don't know if he's home, but the cable TV people say his set's on, so let's assume he's there. Ryan and Perry," she said, reading the name on the other uni's nameplate, "you two go around to the back. Ruiz, you get to knock on the door. Matson and I will back you."

They all drew their weapons and approached the hideous box cautiously, keeping other mobile homes between it and them as long as possible. When they were close enough, Ryan and Perry circled around back. Annie gave them ninety seconds, then nodded to the other two and pointed toward the house.

"Let's do this," she said.

The December sky was pale blue, cloudless, as flat as if it had been painted on a ceiling. From somewhere, Annie heard "Silver Bells." That and a scraggly aluminum tree mounted on top of the trailer in space fifty-five were the only reminders that Christmas was nigh.

She swallowed hard as they approached the three peeling wooden steps propped outside the trailer's front door. Something buzzed in her gut, as if she had swallowed a pump motor. She summoned the images of Kelly Montero and Beth Schreib, the murdered high school girls—Kelly with her throat slashed open by a big knife, Beth with dozens of stab wounds all across her chest and neck—to harden herself against whatever was to come.

At Annie's signal, Ruiz drove the battering ram through the trailer's shoddy door, ripping it from its hinges. Matson followed Ruiz in, his weapon extended in front of him. Annie moved in next, feeling the steps sag under her weight.

Inside, Trey Fairhaven stood, unshaven and shirtless, jeans hanging loose around his gaunt hips. He stared toward the doorway, blinking fast, as if they had woken him up. He had two wires in his hands, leading to a mound of something on a table.

"Down!" Annie screamed. She threw herself down the stairs, rolling and tucking as much as she could underneath the bottom one, fully anticipating that she would never rise again. At the same time Fairhaven's bomb—because that's what it was; she had known he had construction experience and should have anticipated this—exploded with a flash as bright as the sun, leaving afterimages burned into her retinas even after she closed her eyes. The booming sound wave hit her at the same time as the concussive wave, while she was falling, parallel to the ground. Heat singed her hair, her flesh.

The trailer flew apart. Weeks later, a piece of flashing from an air duct on the roof was found lodged in the V of two tree branches in Falcon Park, more than a mile away.

ANNIE woke up in a critical care bed at Good Samaritan Medical Center.

After a few moments of disorientation, she figured out that she was in a hospital. There were tubes in her arm and one of those ID bracelets encircling her wrist. One of those tubes must have been delivering morphine or something like it, because she felt like she was lying in a bed of cotton candy. She couldn't quite feel anything except the dull throbbing of her arm, where the tubes went into it. She remembered the bomb, and was surprised to be alive at all. She wondered what had happened to Ryan and the others, and if she had missed Christmas.

And she wondered why it was so quiet. Shouldn't there be beeping noises, the chuff of an air circulation system, something? All she could hear was the ringing in her ears, as if she had gone to a heavy metal concert and sat in front of the amps—something she had done in tenth grade, and largely regretted.

The lights were low, but there had to be a call button somewhere to summon help. After pawing about, she found it, attached to a cord that ran into the wall behind her bed. She pushed it.

A minute passed. The door opened and a shaft of light fell into the room. Annie blinked. A nurse passed through the light, entered, moved her mouth. She was Hispanic, solidly built, with a sympathetic face.

She carried a pad of paper and a marker.

Annie began to weep.

2

THE nurse summoned a doctor, who brought a laptop computer with her. She set it on the swiveling tray Annie's meals would sit on, so she could type and then move it to where Annie was able to read the screen. The nurse stood by the door with her pad, "I'll be right back" still scrawled on the top sheet.

After a few basic questions to determine Annie's physical and mental states—both, Annie thought, should be considered suspect at the moment—Dr. Ganz went into the specifics. "Your left tympanic membrane is ruptured," she typed. "The right one is also damaged, but less severely."

"Will my hearing come back?" Annie asked. Her voice sounded strange, as if it had been recorded and played back at the wrong speed. She was desperately thirsty and had been sipping water from a pitcher by her bed since the nurse had poured some while waiting for the doctor.

Dr. Ganz looked about fifty. Her blond hair, showing traces of gray, was pulled back and tied behind her head. A few strands had escaped her scrunchy and framed her lean face. She wore glasses with black plastic frames, and a gold chain linked their temple pieces so they would hang on her chest when she wasn't using them. She wore little makeup, if any—maybe a touch of lip gloss—and the only jewelry Annie could see was a pair of simple gold stud earrings. She smelled clean, but wore no perfume to undercut the antiseptic odor of the hospital. Annie had the impression that she was a no-nonsense woman, with an undercurrent of melancholy about her. "We can't know that yet," Dr. Ganz typed. "Surgery can repair the membrane. Sorry, eardrum, to real people. But there could be residual scarring on both eardrums, and until we know how extensive that will be we don't know the extent of your hearing loss. I wish I had better news for you."

As Annie read, Dr. Ganz touched her hand. Annie understood it was meant to express sympathy, since the laptop didn't provide tone of voice. And if she had filled the screen with smilies, Annie would have thrown her computer across the room.

"What about the others?" Annie asked. She could tell that her voice quaked, and she had held off asking the question this long because she was afraid of the answer. "Ryan and Matson and the rest, when can I see them?"

Dr. Ganz shook her head as she typed, those gray blond wings wagging as she did. "I'm so sorry, Annicka. You're the only one who pulled through. The EMT said the stairs might have saved you by blocking some of the concussive wave and the brunt of the debris. You were unconscious for thirty-seven hours. You have a concussion and a compression fracture of your left clavicle. Collarbone. Some minor lacerations, a lot of bruising. Basically, considering what you went through, you're in remarkable shape."

Annie felt tears welling in her eyes again. Not for herself, this time. She wasn't ordinarily so emotional—in fact, she took great pride in her ability to shove her feelings into a big black metaphorical garbage bag and leave them at the curb, unless, like the anger that had spurred her investigation of Trey Fairhaven, she could use them to her advantage—but she figured after what she'd been through, she was entitled to a little lapse. She glanced over at the nurse, who had turned her head away but dabbed at her nose with a tissue. "So I'm in great shape, but I'm deaf," Annie said.

Dr. Ganz swiveled the tray again, tapped the keys. "For now," she wrote. "That's not at all uncommon with any loud noise. In most cases the hearing returns, although it's sometimes reduced. Do you hear a ringing or buzzing now?"

"Yes," Annie said. "Like there's a chain saw in my head. Or a combination chain saw/kitchen timer."

"I'm not surprised," Dr. Ganz wrote. "That may or may not go away."

Annie swallowed hard, her stomach suddenly churning, afraid she might vomit right on the doctor's computer. Two days ago she had been a reasonably happy, healthy cop. Now she was deaf and broken, her lover dead. Did she have a job anymore? She didn't see how. She had insurance, but how much would that cover? She had about four months' salary in a savings account, which she had a feeling would disappear in a hurry if she couldn't work.

"Do you have any more questions for me right now?" Dr. Ganz typed. "Or would you like to rest?"

Annie had a million questions, but most of them Dr. Ganz couldn't answer. She tried to narrow down the most important of them. "Have I had any visitors?"

"Several," Dr. Ganz wrote. "In fact there's been an officer out in the waiting area the whole time. If you think you're ready to see people, I can let him know you're awake."

"But . . . I can't hear."

Dr. Ganz pointed at the nurse. "She has a lot of pads," she wrote. "We'll need to do some testing later on, later today or tomorrow, but for now I want you to rest. You can see a few visitors, but Helen will make sure nobody stays too long."

"Helen?"

Dr. Ganz smiled and gestured toward the nurse again.

"Helen," she mouthed. Or said out loud. Annie couldn't tell which.

And that was the crux of her problem.

A patrol officer Annie didn't know had been stationed at the hospital to keep an eye on her. Presumably he was one of several, given the length of time she'd been out. After Dr. Ganz and Helen left, Helen reappeared with the officer, who looked in at her, gave a wan smile, and left again.

Thirty-five minutes later Lt. Dale Carson and detective Errol Hathaway were in her room with her. Each had a pad and a black marker. Carson, lean and dark as 70 percent chocolate, was a heavy smoker who brought the stink of a burning tobacco plantation with him everywhere, and Annie had never been so glad to smell it. It meant she was alive, a condition she didn't associate with hospital rooms.

The last time she had been in a hospital for any extended duration had been when her dad had died, gut shot by a skell on the northeast side of town. Dying had been certain almost from the start, but he had managed to hang on for three days. She had hardly left the building that whole time. Her last conversation with him had been in a hospital room—not this hospital, not this room, but there was a sameness to them all that made the differences pale.

As usual, it had started with one of his war stories. He had come out of sleep and seen her dozing in a visitor's chair, a book spread open on her lap. He had started laughing, and the laugh turned into a hacking cough, and that startled her awake. She blinked and closed the book, disturbed by his red, blotchy complexion. "Are you okay, Dad?" she asked.

He wiped his mouth on the back of his hand. "Right as rain," he said weakly. "Don't I look it?"

"You look like hell."

"Honesty isn't always the best policy, Annie. Anyway, reason I was laughing is I saw you snoozing there and I thought, I hope she doesn't do that on stakeouts. Buddy of mine fell asleep on a stakeout once, sitting in his unmarked outside an apartment complex. He was supposed to watch the exit, make sure the suspect, who was inside, stayed inside."

"But he dozed off?"

"That's right. I guess the suspect came out, saw him there, figured out what was up. Bernie was a hell of a sleeper, once he got going—his snoring was probably shaking the whole car. So he didn't wake up when the suspect started spray-painting his car windows. By the time he did come around, the car was completely blacked out, and Bernie said he thought he was going blind at first." He laughed again, this time managing to do it without coughing or popping any stitches. "Son of a bitch sat there for five minutes, sweating bullets, before he tried to get out of the car and figured out what had happened. Good thing for him the suspect wasn't a violent type, or Bernie would've probably never woke up."

"Good thing," Annie agreed.

Her father's expression changed, the smile flickering away. He wiped his mouth again, as if making sure his smile was gone. "Annie, you got to make me a promise."

She could tell, by his demeanor and tone, that he was going to start talking about dying again. She didn't want to hear it. He had brought the subject up several times since he'd been in the hospital, but the doctors still said he had a slender chance and he was a fighter, goddammit, and she wasn't interested in listening to him talk about giving up.

"I already promised you, Dad. Virgin until married, that's me."

He chuckled, but wouldn't be so easily dissuaded this time. "I never gave a shit about that, Annie. Not since you were out of high school. Long as you're careful."

"Well, if you'd told me that ten years ago, it would have saved me a lot of sneaking around."

"You never could listen for crap," he said. "But I want you to listen now."

"Sorry, Dad," Annie said. Her cell phone went off before she could say any more, and she flipped it open. "O'Brien."

The call was from her lieutenant, telling her about a possible break in a string of check-cashing store robberies she'd been working. She listened, hung up, and turned to her father. "Listen, Dad, I have to run. I'll be back in a couple of hours, three or four at the most, and we'll talk about whatever you want to talk about. Okay?"

He started to say something, but the words caught in his throat and he started coughing again, his eyes tearing up, mucus spraying from his nose. She grabbed a tissue, wiped his face, tossed it in the trash. She dropped a glancing kiss on his cheek. "Love you, Dad," she said before she left his room. "See you later."

Before she made it back to the hospital, he was gone.

She hadn't much liked hospitals before that. Ever since, she had hated them with a passion reserved for few things in life. Traffic jams, skells and creeps—especially those who targeted kids—infomercials, and *American Idol* all had made her list at one time or another, and hospitals became the latest entry.

Now here she was, in a room of her own. At least Carson brought some of the outside world in with him, even if it was in the form of stale smoke.

"You saved me," Annie said. She couldn't tell if she was talking too loud, like people listening to music through headphones or earbuds often did, but she felt she probably was. "I was watching daytime TV with closed-captioning on. That's worse punishment than being deaf."

"Why do you think I never take vacations?" Hathaway scribbled.

"U doing ok?" Carson wrote. His handwriting was neat but he wrote slowly, and he took shortcuts whenever he could. "N E thing u need?"

"That's a notepad, not a cell phone," Annie said.

Carson shrugged and wrote something else. When he turned the pad toward her, it read, "I M LA-Z." Then he flipped back to the previous page, tapped it.

"I don't know what I need yet," she said. "I guess my cell phone would be a good idea, so I can get text messages—if they'll let me use one in here when I'm not on the job. It was in the unmarked. And a laptop, if they have wireless service here, so I can do e-mail. Mostly I need to get out of here. I need my ears back. I doubt they'll let me drink in here but I could use one or two of those too."

"They won't," Hathaway wrote. "Their assholes about it."

"They're," Annie said, pointing to his pad.

Hathaway was a thick guy with the whitest skin Annie had ever seen on a man who had lived in Arizona for more than twenty minutes and fair hair, short and curly. He stared at her and said what she believed was "What?" She pointed again, but he looked at his pad and didn't get it.

"Maybe send Keller over to my place," she said. Nanci Keller was another female homicide detective and had bunked at Annie's for a couple of weeks when pipes had burst in the kitchen of her 1950s ranch house. "Have her bring some underwear, some clothes, pajamas, my robe, and my slippers. There's a Laura Lippman novel beside my bed. And a toothbrush, you know, toiletries. She knows what I need."

Carson was writing furiously on his pad. In a minute, he turned it over. He had written down the things she had asked for, followed by, "Seriously, O'B. If there's anything else you need, just ask. Don't worry about the job. You guys got that scum Fairhaven. I no u were close to Ellis. I'll let u no when the funeral is, ok?"

Annie's chest tightened. Her heart started racing—she could hear it in her ears, altering the buzz with each pulse of blood. She recognized the symptoms of fear—not the heart-thumping, adrenaline-soaked fear she'd felt outside Fairhaven's trailer that had made beads of sweat gather at her hairline on a cool December day, but something more deep-seated. Closer to her core. She just didn't know where they had come from. Now that she tried to isolate it, she realized she had been a little afraid since she woke up, but that had been tamped down, like everything else, by the drugs they had her on. It got worse when Carson and the others came in, but now, when the topic of Ryan's funeral was broached, it reached a level she could no longer ignore.

Was she afraid that Carson knew about them? That might

have mattered once, but it didn't anymore. There were no departmental regs, that she knew of, against having had sex with a guy who had since died.

Whatever had caused it, now it gripped her, keeping her on edge through the rest of the brief, awkward conversation. Finally, the men gave her gentle hugs and left her alone.

Almost immediately, the tension bled from her, as if a spigot had been opened and drained it off.

What the hell? she thought. If she had more mood swings like that one, she might have to see a shrink. And she hated the thought of that even more than she hated hospitals.

Annie bit back a yawn, then gave in to the next one. The doctor had told her to rest, anyway. And the daytime TV really was god-awful.

She nestled back into her pillow and closed her eyes.

3

THE next day Annie was allowed out of bed. The IVs were removed, because she could eat for herself. Everything that hurt—everything the painkillers had blocked—hurt more. Her arm ached and itched where the IVs had been. Her ears rang like mad, like a cymbal crash that never ended, but when she shook her head, instead of clearing them, it just made the racket seem to bounce around inside, and that made an ache rise up just behind her temples. Dr. Ganz had called the buzzing "tinnitus," and said it was caused by damaged hair cells, which Annie thought should be cells that grew hair but were, in fact, the tiny sensory cells in the inner ear that converted sound energy into electrical signals that the brain could interpret.

She shrugged on a blue terry robe over her hospital gown and the clavicle splint she wore—basically two bands that looped under her armpits and behind her neck, all buckling together in the back, to keep her from moving her collarbone wrong (as a fringe benefit, it gave her incredibly straight posture)—and stuck her feet into the softest leather slippers she had ever found. She needed to move, to try to work out some of the kinks that had settled in from lying in bed for so long, exacerbating the aches from the bomb.

The walls of the hospital had generic, nondenominational holiday decorations hanging on them: paper snowmen, snow-flakes, sleighs, and carolers, Mylar tinsel streamers and stars. Walking past a nurse's station in her corridor, Annie saw a couple of nurses working on computers. Lights glowed on the front of a mini-stereo and she wondered if they were listening to holiday music. Would "Silver Bells" be the last Christmas song she would ever hear? It had never been a favorite, so she hoped not. These past few years, she had been partial to the Leon Redbone/Dr. John version of "Frosty the Snowman" and hated the idea that she might die without enjoying it again. One of the nurses, a tall, skinny guy with a shaved head and a lightning bolt tattooed on his forearm, looked up at her and said something. She had no idea what, so she just smiled and kept going. She figured non-English speakers probably acted the same way, pretending they understood, nodding, smiling, and making themselves scarce.

Her room was on the fourth floor of the patient tower. She pressed a down button for the elevator and looked at the framed notices on the wall, counting on the elevator's soft bong and the shush of the doors opening to let her know when it came. She heard neither—*of course, you idiot!*—and it was only a changing of the light on the wall that told her an elevator had opened and was closing again. Annie spun around, making herself dizzy, shoved an arm between the doors, and they opened again. She stepped inside and leaned against a wall until the dizziness passed.

When the doors opened on the second floor, a middle-aged couple stepped in. Stealing a surreptitious glance, Annie could see that they were grieving, their loss fresh and raw. Tears tracked down the woman's face, carving rivers through her light foundation. The man's Adam's apple bobbed and his eyes and nose were as red as if he'd just stared down a hurricane.

Annie didn't recognize them, had never seen either of them in her life, but their sorrow swallowed her whole, as if she had fallen into an unexpectedly deep pool. She caught the doors again and stepped quickly off the elevator. She didn't have a particular destination, just wanted to walk around a bit, learn the layout of the hospital and stretch her muscles, but suddenly she knew she couldn't bear another instant in their presence. When the doors closed, the feeling passed, leaving only a residue of grief, like an oily film.

The second floor held the emergency/trauma unit, where she had been taken after the bomb at Fairhaven's trailer, according to nurse Helen, and surgery and cardiology. The grieving couple could have come from any of those. Annie glanced at the directory on the wall and decided to go up one floor. She pushed the elevator's up button, this time watching for the glow to disappear. The third floor was where women went to have babies, and although Annie had never really thought of herself as mommy material, she thought looking at other people's babies might cheer her up after that horrific moment in the elevator.

What she wasn't prepared for was the intensity of the joy she felt, standing outside a nursery with a handful of parents and friends, looking in at a bunch of strangers' newborns. The emotion swept her up, lifted her off the floor, until she thought her heart would burst from love for people she didn't know, babies she would never hold, fathers and sisters and grandmothers gazing at their offspring, nieces, nephews, and grandkids.

Tears welled in her eyes. Someone spoke to her but she looked away, pretended she didn't know she had been addressed. Quickly, while tears of happiness glistened on her smiling cheeks, she hurried back to the elevator, back to the safety of her room.

What the hell is going on? she wondered. *This isn't me. This isn't me at all.*

4

"IT'S not at all unusual for the victim of a trauma like yours to find herself unexpectedly emotional," Dr. Ellerbee wrote. They were sitting across from each other in the psychiatrist's office, there in the hospital, each with a laptop, IMing so they didn't have to speak. He wanted Annie to speak, so he could try to read Annie's mental state from her voice, but Annie was beginning to feel uncomfortable with trying. She couldn't modulate her volume, her intonation. She feared that she was forgetting how to express herself verbally.

And then there was that other thing. "Not me," she said out loud, then typed the same words into the instant message box. "I don't even like my own emotions. I've spent my adult life chasing them away with work, booze, meaningless sex, TV, all that good stuff. This is just completely alien to me."

"The emotions, or the intensity with which you feel them?"

Annie regarded the psychiatrist, planted behind his desk, his face blank except for eyes that bored into her like drills trying to plumb her innermost secrets. His eyes were brown, his brow animated, each eyebrow seemingly able to arch independently of anything else, his forehead creasing or smoothing or collapsing into a series of wrinkles right in the center. He didn't need to speak to be understood, not with that talent.

"Both," she spoke and typed. As before, though, she kept typing after she stopped speaking. "I mean, I'm not a robot or anything. I have emotions. I just prefer to block them whenever possible. To feel them as . . . I don't know, as superficial distractions rather than anything I really have to deal with. Maybe that's unhealthy or something, I don't know, but I don't think I'd be able to function professionally if I really internalized all the pain and sorrow and terror that a cop runs across. But the feelings I've had since being here in the hospital are totally different, on every level. Strong doesn't come close. Overwhelming. Crying in front of strangers? Never. If I did that, I wouldn't last three days on the job."

Dr. Ellerbee read her message, tapped his knife-edged chin with his right index finger. His suit fit well, but was not stylish or expensive. Annie thought that was an intentional choice—not that he couldn't afford better, but he wanted to create the impression that clothing wasn't important to him. Most people would get the intended impression without going the step deeper to examine what lay behind it. Most people weren't cops.

After he considered for a few moments, he wrote something out. "Are you worried about that? That it might affect your ability to do the job?"

She laughed. Out loud, probably, not that you could prove it by her. "I think deafness has that pretty much settled," she wrote.

"It's temporary," he wrote back.

"Maybe," she said.

He nodded, typed. "Probably. Or so I'm led to believe."

"Probably is what they say. But it doesn't seem to be getting any better."

"You've only been here four days," he wrote.

"I'm a cop, you think I can afford to stay much longer?"

"You have insurance."

"Right. And every day I'm here, I can't work. My savings . . . Never mind, you don't need to hear my financial worries. I'm scheduled for surgery tomorrow, then I have a feeling I'll be booted out of here pretty quick, ears or no ears."

"You're optimistic, though. About the surgery."

She felt optimistic. At least in here, ridiculously sending instant messages to a man ten feet away, she felt like tomorrow would be fine and the day after that would be better. She couldn't bring herself to worry about money, or health, just knew that everything would be fine.

And something else, a stirring that took her by surprise. Sexual attraction? That wasn't an unfamiliar emotion for Annie, but the psychiatrist wasn't her type at all.

But am I his? Is that what's going on?

He stared at her. At her body, athletic, slim-hipped, flat waisted with compact breasts. Her red hair attracted its share of attention, her green eyes and full lips drew stares now and again. She knew the look of someone who wanted her, and he was wearing it.

And she was reciprocating. Against her will. There was something else too, an undercurrent that gnawed at her insides, as if she had swallowed a tiny wolverine.

"Is there something wrong?" he wrote. "You're distracted."

"I think I have to leave," she said. "Right now."

"We're not done."

"Yes, we are." She closed her laptop. He came out of his seat, coming toward her, saying something he knew full well she couldn't hear. She avoided his gaze and his grasp and headed for the door.

"I feel like I'm losing my mind," Annie wrote in an e-mail to Nanci Keller, not only a friend but also one of the most intuitive people she knew. Nanci was a casual friend, the only kind Annie seemed able to make. Casual friends and casual lovers. Nanci knew her way around people, though, and seemed able to connect with them easily, in more intimate ways than Annie had ever mastered. In an interview or an interrogation, Nanci was the one she wanted on her side. "But not in a way the shrinks can deal with. I'm constantly deluged with emotions that aren't mine, but feel like mine while I'm in them. I know I'm not making any sense, but it's like whatever someone else feels strongly becomes my own feeling too. At least while I'm close to that person. Do you think this can really be the result of my injuries?"

Annie sent the e-mail, then signed off the computer. She picked up the thriller she was reading and tried to focus on it, but the words kept coming unstuck from the page, swimming in the air before her, and she set the bookmark back in it and closed her eyes.

5

IN the solitude of her private room—which reflected the hospital's willingness to let cops recover in peace, when there were enough beds to allow it, rather than Annie's financial status—she was blessedly emotionless. The bomb and her injuries had left her even closer to numb than usual, she thought, and the painkillers helped too. She would miss Ryan, although in some sense she was relieved not to have to worry about breaking up with him. She hadn't known Matson or the uniformed cops that well—if she hadn't been in the hospital, she would have gone to their funerals out of a sense of duty, not loss. And while she was worried about her hearing, dwelling on it didn't seem productive. When she was alone she was *herself*, that was the important thing. She spent her time e-mailing her fellow detectives about her cases, all being worked by other people now, reading about deafness online, dipping into the Laura Lippman novel, and sleeping.

A lot of that.

She woke up when nurse Helen came to check up on her. Annie woke up feeling like her blanket had turned to lead, crushing her, and she shoved it off. Helen offered a half-hearted smile. "What's wrong, Helen?" Annie asked.

Helen shook her head. The smile grew broader, but it didn't reach her eyes. "Something's wrong," Annie said. "Don't tell me it's not."

Helen picked up one of the notepads Annie was sur-rounded with these days. "I'm fine," she said.

"No, you're not." Helen flinched, and Annie hoped she wasn't coming across as angry. Tone of voice meant so much, and she had lost all control of hers.

Helen fixed her with a solemn gaze, all pretense of smil-ing gone now. She started to open her mouth, then shut it again. A muscle in her jaw twitched. Annie had interrogated enough people to know when someone wanted to open up but was holding back. She would say a couple of words, but mostly at this stage she would listen. Even the creeps of the world wanted someone to hear them out, sometimes more than they wanted anything else, including drugs, cash, or sex.

That was the one thing Annie couldn't do.

"What, Helen?" she said. *Spill.* It wasn't that she was concerned with Helen's personal problems, but she wanted to know why she felt so mournful every time Helen came around. The first time the nurse had come to her room, after she had awakened in the hospital, she had thought it was her own experience getting to her, the certainty that the others had died, and her own injuries. Since then, however, the sensation returned each time Helen did, no matter how An-nie felt before or after. Even if Dr. Ganz or someone else was in the room, Helen's sorrows overwhelmed the others' emotions.

Annie had been developing a theory. Now she needed to test it.

Helen rested the pad on the end of Annie's bed and wrote for a minute. When she showed the page to Annie, her face was clenched into an emotionless mask, her brown eyes liq-uid, her movements brusque. She was angry that Annie had "made" her write, but write she had.

"My son is 17 and getting mixed up with meth," she had

written. "I'm worried he'll be arrested or die, but he won't listen to me or anybody. So I carry that around with me all the time, and it makes me sad. OK?"

As Annie read, Helen's hand started to shake. Her mask fell away and the grief she had tucked behind it burst out as tears and sobs that Annie could see if not hear. She was caught up in it, her own tears flowing, and she said, "I'm sorry, Helen, I'm so sorry," barking the words and extending her arms. Helen came into them, cautious of her clavicle, and the two women held each other, both crying for Helen's son and for Helen but not at all for Annie.

ANNIE didn't expect to ever be a mother, and she was glad, because as role models went, hers was about as shitty as it got. She remembered telling Matson her usual fiction, on the way to the trailer park where he had died. Mother in France, enjoying herself. It was a convenient story because it was hard to check. Not too hard to find out the truth, if one went to the effort of searching online for old news stories about Annie or her father, but she would usually tell the real story to the people who were likely to go to that much effort. The rest of them, the casual acquaintances, didn't need to hear about the way Claire Jourdan O'Brien had dashed down a gin and tonic and then, with shaking hands, pressed her husband's duty weapon against her right temple and thumbed the trigger. No one wanted to hear about the fourteen-year-old girl who had watched it happen, horrified but unable to stop it.

Before the suicide, Annie and her mother had spoken in a rapid Franglais that her father couldn't begin to keep up with. After, Annie never spoke French again, and for a long time she hardly spoke at all. When her father talked to her at all, it was in cop, that half-secret language rich with skells and suspects, evidence and accusations. They had continued to live together but their lives were increasingly separate, unlinked except by occasional physical proximity, until Annie announced her intention to become a cop.

Her father had been pleased, and that was half of it right there—since they could barely communicate, to tell him something that prompted a smile and a big hug felt like a coup. The rest of it was less clear—she felt that she was carrying on a family tradition of some sort, and she had always been impressed with her dad's social status, but when she really tried to reach inside herself for explanations, she thought some of it was a desire to figure people out, to solve the puzzles that human behavior presented to her. Why would someone rob a convenience store for thirty bucks when they could work at the store and make more than that every day, without worrying about going to jail? Why did people murder their loved ones instead of divorcing them? Why would a woman put a gun to her own head? If police work would answer those questions, it was worth pursuing. And until those questions could be answered, the idea of being a parent was terrifying.

So she wasn't sure how she would handle a situation like Helen's. Probably with violence, she guessed, because that was her typical response to drug dealers who preyed on kids. And seventeen was a kid, as far as she was concerned.

AFTER Helen left, Annie checked her e-mail again. There was a response from Nanci Keller in her inbox.

"I was at that trailer park canvassing for witnesses today," Nanci had written. "Some whack job had coated the entire insides of his trailer with foil, to block alien death rays. Windows too. How did crazy people protect themselves before there was tin foil?

"Anyway, it sounds to me like your empathy meter has gone off the scale. You're feeling everybody else's pain, or happiness, whatever, stronger than you feel your own. Must be strange for you, since you're not exactly Miss Emotional. It'll probably go away, but until then it wouldn't be a bad idea to avoid people with strong emotions, just in case. It's lucky you'll be in surgery tomorrow and won't be at the funerals for Ellis and Matson."

Luck had nothing to do with it. Suspecting something was off-kilter with her "empathy meter," as Nanci put it, Annie had made sure to schedule the surgery in conflict with the funerals. The last thing she wanted was to be someplace where a lot of people were in mourning.

The e-mail contained more about the Trey Fairhaven case—no one doubted that Fairhaven himself had detonated the bomb, but Annie was the only living witness and the department was hoping to back up her account independently, since there was talk of civil actions seeking compensation for damage done to nearby trailers by the explosion. Annie skimmed over that part. She already felt removed from the job, as if the gulf between the hearing world and her new, silent one was too vast to bridge.

But maybe there was something to that empathy business. Annie worried that she was losing her mind, as if her psychological condition had somehow prompted the unprecedented emotional upheaval. She did an online search on the word "empathy" and spent some time reading various definitions and descriptions, scientific and otherwise. She found articles on the difference between empathy and sympathy. She read about people with no empathy, or little—people who couldn't put themselves in anyone else's shoes, who couldn't bring themselves to understand, or care, how anyone else felt. Some of the criminals she had dealt with seemed to have that problem—she had thought of them as sociopaths, but maybe it was more specifically a malfunction in the empathy department. Maybe she had somehow been granted their unused portions.

She kept reading, following link after link.

One of those links took her to a derivation that seemed to have come from comic books, but she wasn't entirely clear on the word's origin: "empath." An empath was someone who was supernaturally empathic. Reading further brought her to the word clairsentience, derived from the same root as clairvoyance. This one expanded on the supernatural aspect. A clairsentient was someone who could know things about other people, psychically, by feeling their emotions.

Annie was not a believer in the supernatural. She didn't go to church, didn't read her horoscope, didn't think the lines in her palm meant anything more than that people needed friction ridges if they were going to hold on to anything. And they came in handy in making identifications in criminal cases. Everyone in Phoenix had heard of the psychic Allison DuBois, the subject of the TV show *Medium*, but the show gave the impression that DuBois worked with the Phoenix Police Department, which wasn't precisely true. Annie had never met DuBois and had always doubted her claims.

But the shock of recognition, as she read about empaths and clairsentience, reached down to her marrow. Someone else had experienced what she was going through and had put names to it. Not only wasn't she alone, she wasn't even unique. It wasn't like there was a club she could join, but the simple fact that others had lived through it made her more genuinely happy than anything had since the explosion.

Best of all, she knew the happiness was *hers*. She was alone in her private room, with no one else near enough to force their emotions onto her. She wanted to clutch her joy to her breast like a beloved teddy bear, but settled for smiling so widely that it hurt her face.

6

ON Annie's last day in the hospital, Dr. Ganz reverted to her communication method of the first day. She typed on a laptop and swiveled it around for Annie to read. Annie was glad for the reversion, which meant the two had to sit close together. She liked Dr. Ganz, and she knew—because there was no fooling Annie these days; not about emotions—that the feeling was mutual.

"Keep the arm in a sling," Dr. Ganz wrote. "See me or your own doctor once a week for the next month, then at least once a month for the following two months. We'll let you know when the sling can come off, but at a guess you'll be able to do without it in another two or three weeks. As long as you're very careful—no strenuous activity, no heavy lifting. Got it?"

"I got it," Annie said. Over the past ten days, she had been working with nurse Helen, Nanci Keller, and some others and thought she had a fairly good handle on her voice's volume now. Tone was still questionable, but she tried.

Dr. Ganz erased the last note and wrote more. When she turned the screen to Annie, the document read, "As for your hearing, the surgery went fine, as you know. There's no repairing or replacing damaged hair cells, so I wish I could promise you that your hearing would return completely, but I can't. I think it'll come back at least partially, when the ruptured membrane heals more. Let's give it a little more time, but if it doesn't come back to your satisfaction, there are lots of alternatives you can explore."

"Like lip reading?"

"Like implants," Dr. Ganz wrote, "or other hearing-assistance devices. Hearing aids. Lip reading wouldn't be a bad skill to master as well. Your hearing will never be what it was, Annie. Even if it comes back, I expect you will continue to have trouble telling direction from sound, for instance. In a noisy restaurant, you may have a hard time picking out your date's conversation from the background noise."

"Like anyone's going to want to date the deaf chick," Annie said.

Dr. Ganz wagged her finger at Annie. Annie laughed. She'd been celibate for more than two weeks and fine with it. Her hair was growing longer than she had ever allowed it to when she'd been on the job, and she had decided to let that continue. She had gained a couple of pounds, eating hospital food and getting virtually no exercise. As long as her clavicle was healing, that would continue as well, like it or not. But physically, except for the collarbone and the ears, the continued ringing and frequent headaches, she was mostly happy with herself. It shouldn't be long before men were hitting on her again.

And if they approached her from in front, she might even know it was happening.

"You're a good patient, Annie. Strong and motivated. Even with partial hearing, you'll be fine."

"Thanks for all your help, Dr. Ganz."

"You're welcome," Dr. Ganz said, speaking the words with studied deliberation. Watching the doctor's lips, Annie knew what she had said.

She had kept the clairsentience to herself, once she had identified it as such. She tested it by intentionally spending time in the ER or oncology or obstetrics, picking up on the powerful emotions roiling through all those places. She couldn't avoid testing it further whenever anyone came to visit her. Annie may have been a self-identified empath, but the supernatural still had negative connotations for her, so she chose not to share that identification with other people. Instead, she did her best to pretend she was herself, even when she had to fight back someone else's emotions and playact what they expected to see from her.

She wondered how that would go outside the hospital's confines. Out in the real world. She couldn't go back to work—not only did the collarbone and the deafness argue against that but the emotional upheavals a cop had to deal with on a daily basis would drive her over the edge. The first homicidal person she encountered would wind up dead, and her career would be over anyway. Better to end it herself, before it was ended by a prison term.

"You have friends waiting," Dr. Ganz wrote. "You ready?"

"I think so," Annie said.

"I'll get you a wheelchair," Dr. Ganz might have said. At any rate, she accompanied the words with pantomime, and Annie got the idea. She didn't want to use a wheelchair, was perfectly able to walk under her own steam. But like junk mail and telemarketers' calls at dinnertime, there was no avoiding it, so she settled on the edge of the bed and waited.

An orderly wheeled the chair in. Annie sat down in it and he wheeled her out of the room to the sitting area where Dale Carson and Nanci Keller waited. Both hugged her gingerly, cautious of her left arm in its sling. After some brief discussion with the orderly, Carson took over the chair duties.

Nanci walked beside the chair, carrying Annie's suitcase. Tall and slender, with thick black hair that refused all attempts to tame it, she wore a red western-style shirt with gold and green accents, blue jeans, and boots. Low-key, for Nanci, since the shirt was snapped all the way up. As they went down the elevator and toward the front door, she kept a smile pasted on her face. But the smile was phony, Annie knew—Nanci was terrified that Annie would want to hang out with her outside the hospital, and she didn't have the slightest idea how to socialize with a deaf person. Annie was tempted to tell her not to worry about it, but Carson didn't know about the clairsentience, and she wanted to keep it that way.

Outside, free of the wheelchair and the smell of the hospital, Annie delighted in a fresh breeze blowing through her hair. She walked to Carson's car and sat in the front seat. On the way to her condo in South Phoenix, just across the line from Tempe, Carson and Nanci chatted. Every now and then Carson tossed her a smile or Nanci rubbed her shoulders (gently on the left side, of course). At her place, they came in and brought her suitcase from the car, but before long Annie feigned exhaustion and sent them on their way, just to be rid of them.

The condo felt stale. Annie opened windows and let the cool January air wash in. Her place was on the second floor, with a garage underneath in which someone from the department had stowed her Ford Taurus (white, like many cars in Phoenix, the better to deflect summer sun) after it had sat in the PD parking lot for a few days. A big front bay window looked out over the bare branches of a mesquite tree; the condo complex's grounds, like most of the Valley of the Sun these days, were xeriscaped to favor the desert's low-rainfall conditions.

Nanci had watered the few houseplants Annie had managed to keep alive, Annie's lack of maternal instinct extending to plants and pets. The place looked like she just had left it that morning—neat, organized, barely inhabited. Annie had never mastered the art of making a home her own. The condo might have been a rental unit, except for a handful of personal objects: some books, a couple of framed photos of her father in uniform, knickknacks she had picked up on various vacation trips in Mexico, Hawaii, California, and New York. She had bought all the furniture at once, telling the salesperson how many rooms she had to fill (two bedrooms, living room, dining room, kitchen, two baths), and two days later a truck had delivered it all. It was vaguely southwestern, mostly blond wood with fabric that reminded her of Arizona sunsets, and if it wasn't what she would have chosen for herself if she had picked out each item separately, it was good enough. For Annie, a chair was something she sat on, not something that declared her personality to the world.

Which, she supposed, said something about her personality right there.

Maybe later she could get in touch with them and put them at ease about spending time with her. She shouldn't have reacted so strongly in the first place, sending them away like that. Nobody loved everything about their friends all the time. She should have been willing to accept that they were uncomfortable and tried to relax them. But she had been so tired, and the tinnitus had been giving her a headache, and she had just run out of patience.

Besides, she had known they wanted to get out of there. The thing about being an empath, she was learning, was that she always sensed what other people were feeling, good or bad. She would have to learn to deal with that if the condition didn't go away.

On the other hand, although she couldn't remain a cop, she believed she'd make one hell of a poker player.

ALONE in the apartment, Annie went into the bathroom and regarded herself in her familiar mirror, with familiar surroundings reflected around her. Everything, in fact, was familiar—her hair, only a little darker than an orange peel; her face with its high, prominent cheekbones and straight nose, full lips, and even teeth; her large, curious green eyes—but that familiarity didn't disguise the fact that a stranger stared back at her from the glass. That person had an ability that the Annie O'Brien she had grown up as, lived her whole life as, could never have imagined. Every time she thought she was getting used to it, she brushed up against someone and caught a thrill of fear or lust or anxiety or contentment or something else. Each time she was snatched out of herself and thrown into that other person's secret heart.

While it was happening, of course, she was caught up in it, but once it faded and she came into herself again, all she knew was terror.

Would this be her life from now on? And if it was, how could she go on? Why had this happened to her? What perverse mechanism made a person have to live inside the emotions of others?

Questions without answers annoyed the hell out of her, which was one of the reasons she had wanted to move up to detective. Answers, facts, solid information, those were the things she liked. This was squishy, uncertain.

She looked at the stranger in the mirror until she couldn't stand it anymore, and then she walked out of the bathroom and shut the door.

7

THREE weeks after Annie got out of the hospital, an approaching storm threw dark clouds into the skies over Phoenix. Strong winds and spotty rain smacked against her windows, shaking them in their frames. She realized it because a dull rattling sound interrupted her reading, and it wasn't until she looked up from the book at the wet glass that she understood that she had *heard* the noise.

She set the book carefully on her coffee table and listened. Mostly, she heard the tinnitus crashing around inside her head. But she could faintly make out the patter of raindrops on the window, the rush of wind, the steady hum of her forced-air heater.

Running down her stairs, Annie threw the front door open and ran into the street. A car pulled out of a garage, and she was certain she could hear its engine and the low rumble of the garage door closing. The wind was louder here, howling between the condo buildings, and even though the sound was as muffled as if she had a couple of pillows lashed around her head, it was real.

I can hear!

She stood outside listening until she was soaked through, then went back in (stomping on the stairs as she climbed, her footsteps coming to her as dull thumps), opened her kitchen cabinet, and with both hands, scooped all her pots and pans onto the floor. Their clanging was like the tiny cymbals of a wind-up monkey, but it was audible. Next she turned on the big TV in her living room, punching the button on the remote and watching the volume bar slide across the screen until she could make out the gentle murmur of voices.

I can hear! The certainty delighted her. *I'm getting better!*

She booted up her laptop and sent cheerful e-mails to Dr. Ganz, to Nanci, and to Dale Carson. Only after the messages were gone did it occur to her that her progress might be a fluke, temporary, that any second the silence might wrap around her again.

She decided she wouldn't accept that possibility. Why should she? This was her first real sign of recovery, it was good news, and sharing it wouldn't cancel it out.

Annie had been living like a hermit, leaving her home only when absolutely necessary. The city's emotional noise was far worse than the aural kind. Everyplace she went there were *people*, people who were glad or afraid, depressed or aroused, suicidal or nervous or high. Pushing a cart through a supermarket was a journey through dozens of emotional states, and the briefest shopping trip left her exhausted. Annie was a fiend for chocolate chip cookies, so not only did she need real food at home but she also had to keep flour, sugar, chocolate, eggs, and baking soda on hand at all times. That necessitated the occasional trip out into the world, like it or not.

When the rain slackened a bit, she went out on purpose. She had been nervous about driving since she got out of the hospital, because of the deafness and the sling on her left arm. But this time she left the sling off and drove to a nearby mall with a big chain bookstore in it. There were always people in the store, and she suspected that the range of topics covered by the books would provoke a variety of emotional responses. She had always been a careful driver, with only one minor parking-lot fender bender fouling her record, and she made it over the wet streets without incident.

At the bookstore, she roamed the aisles slowly, moving in close to people as they browsed the shelves or read in the overstuffed fake leather chairs. The improvement in her hearing hadn't changed—everything was still far away, voices coming to her as if carried by two cans and a piece of string. But it hadn't disappeared either. Something was better than nothing.

It didn't take Annie long to discover that the clairsentience hadn't gone away either, although it seemed a little less pronounced. In the past, when she was in a place with a lot of people, she picked up on the emotions of those to whom she was physically nearest. The same rule seemed to apply now, but she had to be closer than ever to get any emotional input. She bumped up against a woman skimming a *Peanuts* book in the Humor section. The woman was laughing softly, but even before they made physical contact, Annie felt sorrow flowing off her like rain off the roof of her car. She was mourning someone and had picked up *Peanuts* hoping to ease her pain. But Charlie Brown and Snoopy could only dissipate her sadness briefly. Annie had to hurry away before she broke into tears.

In the Business section, a young couple looking at books on real estate were easier to approach. They were about to start shopping for their first home, and their eager anticipation helped ease the pain of the *Peanuts* lady. A gay man flipping the pages of a sailing magazine had just had a lunch date that he believed could turn out to be a long-term relationship. Three tween girls in the Young Adult section were crushing on the skinny sales clerk with long dark hair and a tattooed neck.

Annie couldn't "see" details, but some people's emotions were so strong, so directed, that she might as well have been inside their heads. The idea that she had a supernatural ability embarrassed her, and she felt like a thief, slipping up to people and snatching traces of their emotions.

She stayed less than twenty minutes, just long enough to

determine that the improvement in her hearing seemed to have come with an associated decrease in empathy, but not a complete loss of it.

Her mood soured by the discovery, she went back outside, where the rain had returned, a fierce wind stinging her with it. She felt that the lash of wind and water was somehow deserved, and she stood in it for a long time before getting into her car.

8

THE city was too loud.

Not aurally; weeks had passed, and although Annie's hearing continued to improve, that improvement came at a measured pace. She heard only the loudest noises with absolute clarity. Everything else was muffled, a world swathed in cotton.

Her collarbone was healing nicely, according to her latest X-rays. The surgery on her ruptured eardrum should have been a success too—if she still couldn't hear well, it was because there had been too much damage to the hair cells, and they couldn't be repaired. She couldn't work, so she had tendered her resignation from the police force, much to her regret, and her friends there had thrown a party she could barely stand to attend, so thick was the air with regret and sorrow and anxiety about being near a deaf woman. As if it were contagious.

But she was having a harder time staying in her condo. The days had started crawling by, and she found herself staying in bed later each morning. Sometimes at night she sat up with the TV on loud, until the neighbor on that side banged on the wall hard enough to rattle a framed print. She had bought a telephone with a light on it so she knew when a call was coming in, and with the help of the phone company's TTY device she could communicate that way, but she still preferred text message, e-mail, or instant message. She longed for the day she wouldn't have to use the TTY at all anymore.

Sometimes she just had to get out. She found herself going for walks in the desert. Phoenix's South Mountain Park was the biggest city park in the United States, and there she could wander for an hour at a time without encountering another person. She loved that, because when she was around people they might as well have been screaming at her. The city was loud with emotion, fraught with feeling, and it wore her down. Her overabundant empathy had begun to fade somewhat, but not entirely—it seemed to exist in a delicate balance with her hearing, and only if the latter came back entirely would the former go away.

She hiked in the desert hills until she was soaked with sweat in spite of the winter chill, as if she could force the deafness out of her body, and with it the empathy, as if by replacing every drop of moisture she contained with new, fresh water, she would be born again. Born the way she used to be.

It didn't work. She lost the couple of pounds she had put on in the hospital, and more, and she kept the weight off even though she wasn't working an active job anymore. But it didn't *fix* her.

When Morgan Julliard, an old friend of her father's, e-mailed her and asked for a meeting, she was hesitant. Morgan was a nice guy who had sent flowers and a card while she was in the hospital and had been in touch several times since. But he had been a cop, back in her dad's day, and then a very successful lawyer, and now he ran a nonprofit organization that used DNA analysis to try to free innocent people from prison. If he wanted to get together for a "meeting"— his word—she feared there would be some emotional component to his agenda that she didn't want to deal with.

Finally they settled on coffee, which they would buy at Bean-Anza, an independent coffee shop on Mill, near ASU, but consume while walking by the shore of Tempe Town Lake. There it would be quiet enough for her to hear, private enough for Morgan to speak loudly if necessary, and she could stay away from other people and their messy feelings. After a little more e-mail nudging, Morgan agreed to buy both coffees and meet by the lake.

It was the end of February. Phoenix's winter had been surprisingly wet, but it looked like it was mostly gone, with only another storm or two likely to drop any rain at all before the long, dry spring took hold. Annie met Morgan on a Thursday morning when sunshine glinted off the water in shards as sharp as razor blades. He was a few inches taller than her five-seven, sturdy but not overweight, and ruddy, with a brick-red tint to his skin that had been the same as long as she had known him, lines around his eyes and mouth, a crinkled forehead, and tightly curled black hair that had picked up some silver over the decades, but not much. She had known him since she was six, and he seemed to have been stuck in time, frozen looking just like he always had.

When he saw her, he increased his pace. Holding the twin paper coffee cups carefully around her sides, he gave her a squeeze. "How ya doing, slugger?" he asked. He had called her that since she had kicked a particularly impressive goal in a soccer game when she was eight. "Everything okay?"

Morgan spoke just loud enough for her to hear, as if he knew the precise volume she needed. But then, he had always been great with her, and with her parents. If her father had ever had a best friend, it was Morgan Julliard.

"Been better," Annie said. "But a lot worse too."

"Well, I'm glad you're on the better side." He studied the coffee cups, then handed her one. "Cream and sugar," he said.

"Thanks, Morgan."

As she had hoped, the walkways around the lake were sparsely populated—a couple of skaters, a family with two little blond boys on bicycles, a trio of hard-core walking women in shorts, floppy-brimmed hats, and pedometers. She and Morgan started their stroll. He touched his own right ear. "How they doing?" he asked.

"A little better every week. I can hear you, anyway, as long as you're at that volume."

"That's good." He frowned a little. "What about the other thing?"

During a down moment, she had confessed her clairsentience to him in an e-mail, then immediately regretted sending it. Instead of mocking her, he had been surprisingly supportive. "I think everybody has gifts they don't use," he had written. "Abilities most people never even learn about. Maybe it just took a trauma to bring yours to the fore, but I hope you come to see it as a blessing."

"A little less dramatic than it was. Less obtrusive. Still distracting as all hell, though. That's why I wanted to meet here, where it would be quiet. Emotionally quiet."

"Maybe you're getting used to it, controlling it better."

"I'm not sure controlling is the right word," she said. "But yeah, maybe I'm adjusting to it." From Morgan, she picked up faint sensations of ease and pleasure. He was truly glad to see her and perfectly comfortable in her presence. She would have taken comfort from that even if she wasn't an empath.

They walked in silence for a few minutes, Annie wishing she could hear the lap of water against the bank and the happy sounds of families and the calls of the birds flying overhead. Finally they reached a bench, and Morgan nodded an inquiry. "Sure," she said, and sat down.

"I wanted to see how you're doing, slugger," he said as he sat behind her. He took a sip from his coffee cup. "Because I worry about you. Always have, since your dad passed."

"I know," Annie said. "I appreciate it."

"Miss the job?"

"Like you wouldn't believe."

"Oh, I know what that's like."

"I know, Morgan," she said. She felt almost liberated, having a conversation that was no doubt oddly loud to anyone else but seemed normal to her. It was the first real conversation she'd managed to have since before Christmas. "I just keep feeling like I should be strapping on a weapon, carrying a badge—it's like going out naked."

"You'll get used to it. It'll take time, that's all."

"That seems to be the cure for everything."

"In some ways, yes." He was quiet for another minute, drinking his coffee, watching the lake. "Money holding out?"

"For now. Maybe not for too long. If my hearing keeps getting better, I might—"

"I have an offer for you, Annie."

"A what?" She might have misheard him.

"A job offer."

"I don't do windows, Morgan."

"I'm serious, Annicka. Maybe not a long-term thing, but Operation Delayed Justice has a case going that I think you'd be perfect for."

She held her gaze on him for a long moment, trying to determine if he was joking. It didn't *feel* like he was. His emotions seemed superficial, barely there, but she had the sense that he was being sincere. A faint smile played about his lips, but that was typical for him. "I'm a cop," she said after a while. "Not one of your liberal do-gooders. Or a lawyer."

"We're not all liberals or lawyers. You're a skilled detective, slugger, and that's what I need on this."

"What kind of scumbag would I be trying to set free?"

"He's been accused of the double murder of a pair of teenagers," Morgan said.

"Eeew, the worst kind. A kid killer."

"Did you miss the part where we think he's innocent?"

Every killer claimed innocence, of course. Ninety-nine percent of them, anyway. They were all framed, railroaded, and if they did do it, if they were caught with blood dripping off their hands and the murder weapon clutched in their teeth, well, then it was society's fault, or Mother's. Never their own. "Why do you think that?" *Because he says so.*

"He says he is."

"Uh-huh."

"He's maintained his innocence since the minute he was

picked up, according to the records. I know, that's hardly definitive. But the details of the case seem to support his version of things. You'll understand when you see the file."

"And why am I the perfect person for the job? Why not one of your regular investigators?"

He held his coffee cup between his hands, rolling it back and forth. "That's the best part," he said. "It's in the middle of nowhere, New Mexico. Population is something like negative ten. If you've been having trouble because of all the people in Phoenix, then you'll love Hidalgo County. Wide-open spaces and nobody around for miles."

"Sounds good," she said. It really did. South Mountain Park was fine, but she couldn't live there, and it wasn't possible to avoid people the rest of the time except by hiding out in her condo. Even then, people came to the door sometimes. Getting out into the country for a while, even if just for long enough to continue healing, sounded heavenly. "How long do you think I'd have to be there?"

"That's hard to say. A month, six months. However long it takes. We've had a couple of cases take a year or two. Others, with lots of handy DNA evidence, can be closed quickly."

"Let me think about it," Annie said. "How soon do you need to know?"

"A couple of weeks would be good. Poor guy's been sitting in prison for four years. If he's genuinely innocent, I'd hate to leave him there a whole lot longer."

"I understand, Morgan. And I do appreciate the offer. I just need to see if I feel comfortable doing it. Given . . . you know, my present circumstances."

"Of course. Think it over, slugger, and let me know."

"I'll do that, Morgan."

He kissed her on the top of the head and left, and she sat on the bench a while longer. She hadn't even discussed money with him. Operation Delayed Justice was a nonprofit group, which to her implied low wages. Maybe that was wrong—and maybe, compared to a Phoenix detective's salary, it would be at least comparable. It had to be better than she was earning now, which was less than nothing since her bills continued even when her salary didn't. Disability payments didn't go far.

More important than the money, however, was the chance to get out of Phoenix. When she was a little girl it had seemed like a sleepy desert backwater, but as she grew up, so did the city. Now it was the fifth largest in the United States—no place for someone who wanted solitude. If she waited a couple of weeks to let Morgan know her answer, maybe her hearing would continue to improve to the point that she'd be okay with trying to conduct interviews and investigate a case. She doubted if the PD would hire her back anytime soon, but that didn't mean she couldn't do police work.

Or something like it. As a cop, she was conditioned to assume that if people were arrested and convicted, they were probably guilty. She loved Morgan Julliard, but his organization had always rubbed her the wrong way. She understood that innocent people were sometimes wrongfully convicted, and any investigation that resulted in those convictions being overturned was probably a good thing. But her instinctive response was that if those people had been arrested, they must have been guilty of *something*, so society was no doubt better off with them locked away.

Even the name bugged her. *Delayed Justice.* Justice was an abstract concept, not something that happened in the real world. Police work had never been about justice for her. She had followed her father's example, joining the force to put bad guys away and keep the streets safe for everybody else. Her dad had always seemed powerful and glamorous— friends with the mayor, respected by mobsters, loved by cops and civilians alike. She had wanted to have those things too. Justice had nothing to do with it.

She decided not to make any snap decisions, but to give it a few days, see if her hearing kept getting better. See if she could stand to stay in Phoenix.

For now, that decision was good enough.

9

NANCI Keller wanted to go out.

Annie hadn't seen much of her friend lately—or any friends, really. Although Annie had grown up in Phoenix, she had left most of her girlhood friends behind when she became a cop. Since then her friendships had mostly been sex partners, a few semi-serious boyfriends, and cop friends. The cop friends had, for the most part, vanished after the explosion, when no one could face her without remembering not only that she was deaf but that she had lived while three other cops had died.

But Nanci's discomfort had been fading as Annie's hearing improved. She had called and said she wanted to go out and get wild, "like we used to." Annie had some doubts about it—to Nanci, going out meant going to bars, where the background noise would be loud. Dr. Ganz had been right about that; no matter how much better her ears got, picking sounds out of loud backgrounds remained difficult. So they would go to bars, and Nanci would want to talk, and Annie wouldn't be able to hear a thing she said. Annie would rather go out to dinner, but Nanci would consider a quiet restaurant some sort of heinous punishment.

Annie picked Nanci up at her little house in Glendale—she would be the designated driver, since she was still anxious about driving with impaired hearing and she didn't intend to compound that by drinking. Anyway, she hadn't been drinking much since the explosion. Her pain medicine kept her numb enough most of the time, and when she wasn't numb it was because she was in proximity to someone whose mood overwhelmed hers. Mixing booze with it could have turned a bad situation worse, and she wasn't interested in winding up in the hospital again.

Annie parked on the street and walked up to Nanci's pink aluminum-sided ranch house. The yard was grass, mostly green but with brown patches. If it was skin, it would have itched. The pink paint was sun bleached, more a memory of color than true color, and there were rust spots on it where the gutters and downspouts had corroded in the rain. People thought it never rained in Phoenix, but that wasn't true—it just didn't rain for months at a time, then in summer and winter it all came down at once.

Nanci opened the door before Annie knocked. She wore a glittery gold top that clung to her prominent curves, tight black pants, and black strappy heels, all of it augmented by multiple bracelets, necklaces, and droopy gold chain earrings. Early in her cop career she had complained about always pulling undercover hooker duty, until someone had pointed out that it was typecasting. She never complained again. For Nanci, that was a kind of validation that her success in a traditionally male occupation had not robbed her of her essential, sexually charged femininity. As if anything could.

Tonight she looked like she was going out to get laid, not to spend time with a girlfriend, but that was not at all unusual for Nanci. Or for Annie, for that matter—it had been kind of a specialty of theirs—but that was another thing Annie wasn't ready for. Annie had dressed conservatively for the evening, wearing a bulky cable-knit sweater, jeans, and a denim jacket.

Nanci enveloped her in a jasmine-scented hug, squeezing until Annie flinched. "I'm sorry," Nanci said. She knew to speak up. "Did I hurt you?"

"I still have to be careful about the collarbone," Annie said. "Don't want to re-fracture it."

"I'll keep that in mind."

"You ready?"

Nanci performed an ungainly pirouette. "Don't I look ready?"

"You look ready for a lot of things."

"Be prepared, that's my motto."

"You and the Boy Scouts."

"Oooh, do you think we'll run into them tonight? Maybe not Boy Scouts. But a bunch of broad-shouldered Eagle Scouts would do nicely."

"Nanci, you're thirty-six years old."

"Cougars are the 'in' thing," Nanci said. "I may not be a MILF, but I can dream." She reached inside, grabbed a purse and a light jacket, then came back out and locked her front door. "Haven't you been reading the magazines during your recuperation?"

"Not a lot, no." Mostly she had been reading novels, mysteries and thrillers, her usual genres of choice, but even more so since she'd been sidelined from the real-life action. She opened her Taurus and slid in behind the wheel, fearing the night would go downhill from here.

IT did.

Annie's every horrible expectation was met. They hit three different bars, each louder and more crowded than the last. Nanci drank and laughed and flirted, while Annie nursed club sodas and became increasingly isolated. The more she had to drink, the less solicitous Nanci became about Annie's condition. At the last spot, the Library in Tempe, barely two blocks from where Morgan Julliard had picked up coffee for their "meeting" by the lake, Arizona State college girls in plaid microskirts and tiny white tops fetched the drinks, books lined the walls, and Nanci turned her attention almost entirely to a college man—professor, not student, but years her junior just the same.

Annie could have flirted professionally. She knew that glancing quickly at a man's eyes, then looking away, then looking back again and holding his gaze could say more than twenty minutes of conversation. She had mastered drawing her arms slightly forward as she shrugged, squeezing her breasts together and bobbing them along with her shoulders. She could run a fingertip across the back of a man's hand or around his arm and send a chill through his body.

All of it led to meaningless affairs, but then, that was the point. She wasn't after meaning. She had enough of that in her professional life. She had closed a case in which a young couple had wrapped their colicky baby up in plastic bags and duct tape because his crying was interfering with their crack cocaine buzz. Upon realizing they'd killed the four-month-old, the girl had put him in a canvas bag and taken him to the Wendy's where she worked, storing him in the walk-in freezer for a few days, until another employee wondered what was in the bag. Another case involved two teenagers who had kept their grandmother, the woman who had raised them, a virtual prisoner in her own home for more than three months, torturing her, loaning her out to friends for whatever purposes struck their fancies, and living off her Social Security and pension. A few cases like that were all it took to make Annie think that human connection wasn't all that special—that people could be decent but could just as easily be scumbags, and the best way to get through life was not to rely on them for anything.

On this night, a few men tried to pay attention to her, even hit on her, but she had such a hard time distinguishing their conversation from the background noise that they gave up and moved on to women who could hear them. In her current mood, flirting just for the sake of flirting held no appeal, and neither did making the effort of moving from the wordless kind of flirting to the conversational.

By ten thirty, Annie had had more than enough. She was

tired of being ignored, tired of trying to smile and laugh, tired of the press of emotion, tired of straining to hear. Her muscles ached. Her soft, silent bed called to her.

Dragging Nanci out would be a struggle, but Annie needed air and silence. She tapped Nanci on the shoulder and pointed toward the restroom. Nanci gave her a quick nod, then turned back to her professor, whose hand, Annie noticed, was already resting on Nanci's knee.

It was a dodge. Instead of forcing her way through the crowd to the restroom, Annie went outside. Sun Devil Stadium was just up the street, but she went the other way, out onto Mill, where there were shops and restaurants and a few people about. She passed a couple gazing into a store window full of T-shirts, and a pair of young women who had just emerged from a restaurant hand in hand, each one holding leftovers wrapped in foil shaped like swans.

The quiet was a blessing after the raucous energy of the bar.

Halfway up the block, she saw a man coming her way with his hands jammed into the pockets of a frayed denim jacket. As he passed in and out of the colored lights glowing from shop windows she could make out a fierce expression on his face, his lips clenched, his unshaven jaw as tight as a drumhead, his brow knotted. There was an angry, coiled tension in his step. He looked like trouble, like a human pressure cooker, a guy who needed a fight to blow out the steam gathered inside. He weaved this way and that across the sidewalk, and although Annie tried to get out of his way, his elbow bumped into her as he passed.

"Sorry," she said.

He cranked his neck around, fixed her with a ferocious glare, but kept going.

In his wake, Annie was gripped by the impulse to grab him and snap his neck. She pictured the cracking sound, the rush of blood from his nose and mouth, the life fading from his eyes as death overtook him. Her hands shaped themselves into claws.

The impulse passed immediately. By the time he reached

the corner, Annie recognized that it wasn't her impulse at all, but his, transferred to her by his proximity, by their casual glancing connection.

She had thought he was looking for a fight. But was it worse than that? Was he looking for a victim?

Her first thought was to catch up to him, question him, make sure he wasn't fingering a weapon in one of those jacket pockets. But she wasn't a cop anymore. She had no authority to do so, no badge to back her up.

Nanci, on the other hand, had a badge and gun in her purse. She was intoxicated, but she could probably pull it together long enough to shake the guy down a little.

Annie ran back into the bar, worked her way through the crush of bodies and the almost physical wave of noise, and reached Nanci. "Nanci, you've got to come outside."

Nanci mumbled something. "What?" Annie said, cupping a hand to her ear.

Nanci gave her an exasperated look and repeated it with more volume. "Why do I have to go outside?"

"I'll tell you out there," Annie said, not wanting to shout it in the bar.

Nanci leaned into her professor friend, said something into his ear, and backed it up with a kiss. Then she slipped off her stool and followed Annie into the quiet outside.

"What's going on, Annie?"

Annie pointed toward the quickly receding figure of the tense man, who had turned right on Fifth and was headed toward the dark, empty stadium. "That guy just bumped into me."

Nanci snorted a laugh and steadied herself with a hand on Annie's shoulder. She was sexually aroused, and annoyed by Annie's interruption. "Did you get his number?"

"Nanci, when he ran into me, I wanted to *kill* him. I mean, *really* kill him. But that wasn't me, it was him. He's a time bomb, and I think he's looking for a victim."

"And I'm supposed to do what, exactly? Has he committed a crime? Done anything wrong that you know of?"

"Well, no . . . but what if he does?"

"I can't bust a guy for having bad thoughts, Annie. You know that. I'm not doubting your, whatever, ability. But there's nothing I can do."

"Can't you just stop him? See if he's carrying a weapon? Get his name, in case something does happen?"

Nanci looked down the street. The guy was already gone, the sidewalk empty. She shrugged. "Thought crimes, Annie. Can't prosecute thought crimes."

"I know." Annie couldn't argue, but she couldn't shake the vicious rage that had overcome her when the guy touched her. He had killed, or he would soon, or he would act out in some other violent way. She had no doubt of that. But Nanci was right. There was nothing they could do about it, short of putting him under perpetual surveillance, and even that would be a violation of his rights. The world was full of angry people, violent people. Some of them kept their rage in check for a lifetime. Others climbed into towers or stepped into schoolrooms or offices and opened up with automatic weapons. You couldn't tell ahead of time—not even with supernatural help, apparently—which kind any given individual would turn out to be.

Could she spend the rest of her life fearing the most casual human contact? Avoiding strangers because of what she might sense about them? What kind of life would that be? Annie had been a cop, daughter of a cop and a suicide, never the most trusting person on the planet. But she hadn't been actively afraid of strangers, and she didn't want to become a person who was.

"We've got to go, Nanci," she said. "I need to get home."

"But . . . it's early!"

"Not for me."

"Annie, sweetie, come on. Have a drink with me. Just one."

"No, Nanci." Suborning a crime—the hallmark of the drinker. "I'm done."

Nanci looked at her, then back at the bar. "I guess I can get a ride home," she said.

"You sure?"

Nanci laughed again, and gave Annie a quick squeeze. "Pretty sure," she said. "Don't worry about me."

"You be careful, Nanci."

"Always, girlfriend. Always."

By the time Annie reached the corner, Nanci was back inside. On her way back to her professor, no doubt. Annie wished her well and headed back to her car.

The next morning, she made an appointment with Morgan Julliard.

10

"SEND me away."

"I was hoping you'd say that." Morgan came out from behind his desk and offered Annie his hand. She took it and he drew her into a gentle hug, dipping her in shallow feelings of warmth and welcome. "You sure?"

"I have to get out of the city," she said. "I can't take it here any longer."

"Is there anything specific? A problem?"

"No," she said. "Not really. More just a combination of things." His office was in an old adobe house on Washington Street, downtown, where light rail construction had tied up traffic for more than a year now. She had maneuvered the Taurus off the street into one of the half dozen parking spaces in front of the building. A carved wooden sign next to the house announced the presence of Operation Delayed Justice.

Inside, a young assistant greeted her, filing cabinets and boxes overflowing with papers crowding his desk almost out of the room. From him Annie got a sense of barely controlled chaos, as if he lived in a perpetually harried state that probably extended to his home life. He directed her to an inner office that had probably once been a dining room. It was furnished with antiques, mostly the sorts of things that would have been in a home office rather than a corporate one, with artwork on two walls and massive, crowded bookshelves lining the others. "I guess I've never been here before," she said.

"I don't think so, no."

"It's nice."

"Thanks," Morgan said. He came across just as comfortable as he had before. If everyone was as even as Morgan was, Annie might not mind the empathy so much. It was almost like there was a layer missing in him that overly emotional people had, extra depths to their feelings that made them hard to be around. He might have been superficial, but at this point she appreciated that. "Why don't you have a seat, Annie, and let's talk about the job."

He had a couple of old Mexican chairs flanking his desk. He led Annie to one of them and she sat down. The wood was cool and rigid against her back, smooth under her hands where hundreds of other people had probably rubbed the same spot. "You mind telling me what made up your mind?" he asked, perching on the corner of his oak desk.

"Like I said, a combination of things. I've always lived in Phoenix, but I think I'm ready for a change. The city is so big now, so crowded, and the noise—the emotional noise—is getting to me in a way it never did before. Plus without the job, I don't really have that much to tie me here. No more family, no boyfriend." She swallowed once and continued. "It's hard to admit it, but I guess I don't have a lot of really close friends, period. So why stay here if I have a chance to go someplace that's a little easier to take?"

"I hoped you'd feel that way, slugger, and I hope it's a good move for you. And like I said, it doesn't have to be permanent. The job will be done before too long, and then you can stay there, look for someplace else to move, or come back here. Entirely up to you."

"Thanks, Morgan."

"I've taken the liberty of arranging a place for you to

live," he said. "It's nothing fancy, but it's comfortable, and it's not too far from the prison."

Annie smiled. "You were pretty sure I'd take the job?"

"I hoped so. But even if you didn't, someone has to go out there, and whoever does will need a place to live."

"That's true, I guess."

"Utilities are being billed here. And I've had a phone put in, since cell phone reception is kind of sketchy out there." He smiled and handed her a sheaf of papers. "I also took the liberty of writing you letters of introduction to the local sheriff's office and the prison staff. And Johnny Ortega's file is in here, court transcripts, the whole boat."

"That's the guy in prison?"

"That's right. Everything you'll need before you talk to him is in there. When you do talk to him, I'm sure you'll be as convinced as I am."

"We'll see. If I'm not, what then?"

He moved around behind the desk, pulled open his top drawer, and took out a checkbook. "Then we'll pay you for whatever time you spent on the case, and you can move on to something else. Or we can see if there's another case open for which you'd be a better fit."

He wrote out a check, ripped it from the book, and handed it over. "This'll get you started," he said. "I've got a few papers for you to fill out, and then you'll be on the payroll."

"I want you to know how much I appreciate this, Morgan," Annie said. "All of it." Since running into the scary guy on Mill Avenue, she had thought about almost nothing except getting out of the city. She was empty inside, unless someone else's emotions filled her up, and she couldn't live like that. Maybe in solitude, out in the country, she could rediscover herself.

She had to try, anyway. She had to do something before she encountered another homicidal person in the street and snapped.

THE worst year of Annie's life had been her thirtieth. It had begun the morning after her twenty-ninth birthday party, when she had awakened with a hangover and the sensation that she had dragged her tongue along the street all the way home from the bar. Through the pounding headache and occasional dashes into the bathroom, she realized that the reason she had allowed herself to get so stinking drunk was that she was terrified of reaching thirty, and it was downhill from here to there, and then beyond. She was still a uniformed patrol cop and desperately worried that she would never make detective. And she was policing a city that had ballooned in size over the past decade; growth that showed signs of speeding up, not slowing down. With that expansion came big-city problems—gangs, drugs, jumps in domestic violence, gun violence, vehicle theft, rape, child abuse. Everything bad about cities was coming to Phoenix while everything she had loved about the city was being squeezed out. And in uniform, all she could do was try to stay on top of it, not dig in and try to deal with the root causes of it. She felt like a stranger in her native city, and it frustrated the hell out of her.

Her year got worse from there. The man Annie was supposed to marry, a pilot for America West, got feet so cold he must have frozen the twenty-three-year-old nymphette she hooked up with three months before the wedding. Ongoing car repairs set her back several thousand dollars, most of her savings—so much that if it had happened all at once she would have just bought a new one. She went out one morning and found her neighbor's cat, who visited her so often that they practically shared custody, dead in the gutter, hit by a truck. A few weeks before her thirtieth, her dad was wounded on the job and died three days later. Nothing went right that year, it seemed, not professionally or personally. She had known cops who ate their guns when they hit stretches not half as prolonged or painful. By the time the dreaded birthday hit, she welcomed it, because nothing on the other side of it could be worse than what she had survived on the approach.

This year, since the day of the explosion, seemed on course to dwarf it.

Annie recognized that by accepting Morgan's job offer, she was running away from her problems instead of facing them. She didn't care. How did you face partial deafness? How did you face being battered by the emotions of strangers you ran into on the street? Answer: You didn't. You turned tail and ran, you went someplace where the population density was something like one person per square mile, and if anyone was going to talk to you, it was because you had sought that person out.

Sometimes running away was the only rational response. And Annie was a big believer in rational responses. She would run as far as it took.

IT was the fourteenth of March before Annie was able to get on the road. She got her condo closed up, and Nanci agreed to come around twice a week to check on it. Torn between feelings of abandonment and relief, Nanci promised to collect her mail and send anything important over to the house Morgan had arranged in New Mexico. Her utilities would be left on, and she had a couple of lamps and a radio set with times to go on and off occasionally, in order to make outsiders think the condo was occupied.

She packed three suitcases with clothes for spring and summer, made a shopping trip to Poisoned Pen for enough thrillers to last her a few months, loaded a DVD player, a stereo, and a box full of DVDs and CDs into the trunk. Her ears still buzzed constantly but she could enjoy music again, even watch TV without captions. In the backseat she put a box of food and utensils, and a cooler for perishables. She took two handguns, a Glock 17 and a Beretta Px4 Storm, both automatics. She didn't wear a badge anymore, but she had been on the job long enough that she still needed a firearm close at hand. She packed several flashlights—since being deafened, she had discovered that she hated the darkness. When she couldn't hear what was inside it, she wanted to be able to see, and she had bought flashlights of every size and description, stationing them throughout her condo. Although her hearing was better, the flashlights had become habit and she took most of them along.

Under a bright sun, she headed down Interstate 10, leaving behind the city's crime and noise, traffic and smog, every friend she had in the world, most of her possessions, and the entirety of her past. Her future waited a little more than two hundred miles away, in another town, another state.

It might as well have been another world.

11

HE browsed the tables of the yard sale. He was in San Jose, California, in a neighborhood called Willow Glen, and the house was a California bungalow with pale green stucco walls and thick growth in the back and side yards. The front was grass, healthy and lush, and on top of the grass the homeowner had set up card tables and a couple of pieces of painted wooden furniture, all bedecked with bits and pieces of his life. And of hers, his late wife's.

He felt the gentle Bay Area sun on the back of his neck as he perused the offerings, paying special attention to the things that looked like they had belonged to a woman. A handheld mirror with a plastic back and handle in a tortoise-shell finish. A red cotton bathrobe. A cookbook stained with cooking grease. A cheap plastic earring rack. "Look at that, Mother," he said under his breath, giving her fingers a squeeze. "How tacky can you get?"

Then he put her fingers back in his pocket and kept browsing.

The homeowner sat in a folding lawn chair under an umbrella, wearing a polo shirt, khaki pants, and deck shoes with no socks. He greeted each new arrival in a friendly manner, then sat back and let them shop, answering any questions presented to him. The homeowner didn't know that the man had seen him before, many times. He had no idea that the man had been inside his house—had, in fact, seen some of these items in their original setting.

The man liked to think that if they knew of him at all, the media would have called him the Impressionist. Of course, he was too good for that, too careful. He had practiced his art for years, and there had never been any speculation that his projects had been the work of any single person.

The name had two meanings, each equally applicable, and that fact brought him a great deal of pleasure. First, he was an impressionist in the sense of a copycat, a mimic. He studied the work of those he admired, and he created his own masterpieces in their styles. That contributed to his anonymity—the police assumed that his creations belonged to the original artists, so never widened their nets enough to include him. Since the authorities didn't know about him, the press never caught on either, and so he remained an elusive, unknown master.

The other meaning had to do with the Impressionist school of art. The Impressionists broke every rule. They didn't paint what they saw or try to tell religious stories with their paintings—they painted what they felt. They told real stories about human emotion. They moved out of the studio and sent back dispatches from the real world. In a similar manner, he traveled around the country, creating his canvases and leaving them for others to find and interpret.

But he was an artist, of that there was no doubt. An artist and a scholar, a student of death. He was already more expert than most, because he had made it his life's pursuit, but there was always more to learn. He studied the works of other craftsmen, learned their secrets, and copied them, because only by copying could he truly understand them from the inside. Some of those he copied had been arrested and imprisoned. Copying their work had the additional benefit of confounding the authorities, and making the public doubt them when the word inevitably got out. Others were still working, still painting their own pictures upon the land. The fringe benefits that sometimes accrued here were also pointed—the authorities would find a scene that they wanted to pin on a particular individual, but although the style would be the same as that person's other works, the physical evidence wouldn't match. So did they go to court with that evidence, or try to bury it? The Impressionist enjoyed watching the confusion his efforts created.

He picked up a board game. *Twister*. It took several people to have a good game of *Twister*, two at the minimum. He knew only one person lived in this house now, and from the looks of him, he didn't throw a lot of parties. "Are all the parts in here?" he asked.

The man looked back at him with eyes that sorrow had sunken and creased. "Not many parts to it," he said. His voice caught. He was no doubt remembering playing the game with his pretty wife, their limbs intertwined, bodies pressed against each other. That was what the Impressionist had been trying for. He wanted to see the hurt creep across the man's face as he thought about his loss. "The mat and the spinner, I think is all there is."

"And you want a dollar for it? That's what the label says, one dollar."

"Yeah. I could go down to seventy-five cents if you think that's too much."

"I'll think about it," the Impressionist said. He set it down again. He remembered where the board games had been, in the family room on a couple of shelves beneath a big television set. It had been a comfortable room, friendly, with colorful abstract prints on the walls and thick carpeting. The young couple had no doubt hoped to raise a family in that room. Maybe the homeowner would marry again, have another chance. Maybe he was selling off his dead wife's belongings to make room for a new woman, now that a little more than a year had passed.

Learning the way the survivors reacted was a big part of studying death. After a certain point, the dead were no longer available to watch, but those who stayed behind still had much to teach. The Impressionist watched the homeowner interact with a pair of shoppers who bought a ceramic lamp and some women's dresses. The wife had been, the Impressionist remembered, a size five. The homeowner clutched the dresses a moment too long, as if unwilling to release them now that he had put them on the market and stuck masking tape price tags to them.

Finally, he'd had enough. If he stayed too long, the homeowner might start to wonder about him, would take a closer look and would remember him if he saw him again. That wouldn't do.

He settled on a small painted figurine of the Virgin Mary. It looked like something that might rest on a dashboard, but he remembered having seen it on her side of the bed the last time he was in the house. At the end, she had been praying furiously, so he thought that the thing had some special meaning to her—perhaps even more than her young husband knew about. The masking tape tag on the bottom only valued it at fifty cents, a bargain for her spiritual signpost.

He was often struck by how many people cried out to God—or maybe to a lowercase god, it was hard to tell—at the end of their lives. Failing that, they cried out "Fuck! Fuck!" Was it the divine aspect of sexual activity they were appealing to? Was there so little daylight between the two? Which was sacred, which profane, and when one was looking squarely at certain death, did it matter anymore? For all he had learned about that final darkness, there was still plenty of uncharted territory to explore.

He fished two quarters out of his pocket and approached the homeowner. "I'll take this," he said. He put the quarters down on the table in front of the man's cash box. That way the man would have to pick them up with his fingers, helping to obscure any prints he had left on them—not that anyone would have reason to inspect the quarters anyway.

The woman's death had been blamed on a man who had died during a high-speed police pursuit, when his car had flipped off an embankment on Highway 17, heading toward Santa Cruz. He had killed seven other young women in Santa Clara County, all of them about this woman's age, all physically similar to her. He had killed them the same way the Impressionist had, breaking into their houses when they were home alone, tying their wrists and ankles with nylon rope, then completely swathing their heads in garbage bags and duct tape. He sat with them until they suffocated, then cut away the plastic and left them in lewd poses, partially clothed, on their marriage beds. In each case, the woman's husband had been the first to find her.

The Impressionist knew it was virtually impossible not to leave some trace evidence at a crime scene. A hair, a fiber, a little dirt from the bottom of a shoe, a partial fingerprint on a surface somewhere. He didn't worry too much about it. Trace evidence only did any good if there was someone to match it with, and nobody was looking for him. The fact that any evidence he had left in this little bungalow didn't resemble anything left at the others had ceased to be a concern when the police department's number one suspect had died in a fiery crash. No court appearance, no expert witnesses, no problem.

"Thanks," the young homeowner said.

"Don't mention it," the Impressionist said. "It's a lovely piece." He dropped it into his right hip pocket and sauntered back to his rented car. He would never return to this house, never see the young man again.

As he drove away, he tooted the horn twice and waved his hand. Not at the young homeowner, but at his memory of the wife. *His* creation, one of his masterpieces. He would always remember her, especially with her Virgin Mary to remind him.

12

THE first thing Annie did after she hauled all the stuff from her car into the tiny house, eight miles outside the New Mexico town of Drummond, was to whip up some cookie dough and get a batch going. That way, as she unpacked and found places to stow her things, the house filled with the comforting aroma of baking cookies.

Her condo in the city was much larger than this place, which had only one small bedroom, a cramped kitchen with ancient appliances, a combination living/dining area, and a bathroom in which the toilet and bathtub could very nearly be used simultaneously. Foot-thick adobe walls ate up more of the space.

But if she wanted wide-open spaces, all she had to do was step outside. A small assortment of trees surrounded the house. Beyond those, golden grasslands stretched as far almost as she could see in every direction, until jumbled rocky outcroppings or taller brown ridges blocked her view. Sparsely populated Hidalgo County formed the boot heel of New Mexico, and the Mexican border was just ten miles south. Morgan had told her there was a quiet border crossing at Antelope Wells, which she would never have a reason to visit. The air smelled fresh and clean, the sky was a deep and brilliant blue. Birds hopped around on the trees or took to the air without warning, and their songs penetrated through the buzzing in her ears, although just barely.

Still, after the claustrophobia of Phoenix, it should have felt like paradise. And it almost did.

It was only an uncertain sense of unease itching at Annie that kept it from perfection. She couldn't pin it down, didn't know if it had to do with the solitude Morgan had promised that had seemed so desirable in the abstract but maybe a little scary in practice, with the quiet, or with something else altogether. Every now and then she felt a tickle at the back of her neck. As she walked through the house, the rooms seemed oddly cool or warm, but not in any consistent way—one minute, the kitchen might be toasty from the heat of the oven, the next almost frigid, the next hot again. Was it because of the thickness of the walls, the shade cast by the trees around the house? She didn't know.

Once she was moved in and her cookies were done, she still had daylight left to spare. She took the Johnny Ortega file outside with a glass of iced tea and a plate of cookies, and set them all on a small metal table next to a metal-and-plastic outdoor chair. She watched the birds for a while, wondering what they were. A breeze picked up and set the branches of the trees trembling. That uneasy sensation poked at her once again and vanished. Annie smoothed down the fine hairs on her arms and went to work.

ALMOST exactly four years ago, Johnny Ortega had been picked up fifty-some miles away from Drummond, in the Kranberry's Family Restaurant in Lordsburg—Hidalgo's county seat, perched along the interstate near the county's north end. He had checked into a motel called the Western Skies Motel, across the parking lot from the restaurant. Earlier that afternoon, just outside of Drummond, teenagers Kevin Munson and Carylyn Phelps had been stopped along a small county road changing a flat. According to the state's case, Johnny Ortega was a wanderer who had seen the pair, pretended that he wanted to help, tied up Kevin, and beat Carylyn to death with a jack handle. When he did, he probably hadn't known she was pregnant—authorities weren't even certain if she knew it. Then he changed the tire, used their car to haul Kevin a few miles away, carried him into a fallow field, and slit his throat. Having casually slaughtered the two local kids, he returned to his own car and drove up to Lordsburg.

Those were the bare bones of the case. Much of it didn't make sense to Annie. If he had killed the teens, why stay so close by? Why not put in another couple of hours behind the wheel and head for Tucson or El Paso? What was Ortega doing on that little country road in the first place? It was close to the border, but he was an American citizen, born in East Los Angeles, so presumably he hadn't just crossed illegally. Had he been in Mexico at all? There was no evidence suggesting he had. Plus he was driving his own car, paid for, insured, and registered in California. Why kill Carylyn by the road but then take Kevin so far away—and in Kevin's car, having changed his tire for him—meanwhile apparently leaving his own car parked near Carylyn's brutalized body? Ordinarily if a young male and female victim were separated, it was the male who was killed first, then the female taken someplace where the perp could spend time assaulting her. Not that it couldn't go the other way, but that was much less common. And in this case neither showed signs of sexual assault.

Ortega's court-appointed public defender had brought up some of those questions, but had been easily distracted by the theorizing and guesswork of the sheriff's officers who had built the case. On a couple of occasions it appeared the judge would intervene, forcing the public defender to take more interest in his own case, but ultimately there was only so much he could do. The jury came back with a guilty verdict in less than six hours. Three weeks later, Johnny Ortega was sentenced to death.

Annie flipped through the photographs in the file. Yearbook pictures of Kevin and Carylyn showed seemingly typical rural high school kids, white, cleaned up for picture day, smiling for the camera. Carylyn's smile was less forced than Kevin's, and she came across as outgoing. He had small eyes and a thick neck, and she wouldn't have been surprised to find that he played football for the school team. Crime scene photos were less appealing. Crime scene photographers didn't shy away from gore, but this one had seemed a bit reluctant to really zoom in on the damage that the jack handle had done to Carylyn's pretty head. Kevin's murder was somewhat neater, a quick slice across the throat that had nearly severed his head.

Annie closed the file with a sigh and sipped her tea. The sun had almost dropped behind the ridgeline to the west, its last rays throwing bright spears of light above the hilltops. The shadows under the trees had become darker, denser, on the way to impenetrable.

Morgan was right. Half right, at least. Johnny Ortega had been railroaded. Judging by his testimony and the investigators' notes, he was not blessed with an overabundance of intelligence or mental acuity. His English was only so-so, and he may not have understood everything going on around him. He had a record of committing violent crimes in California, and he'd spent much of his life in foster care, juvenile detention, or prison. He probably wasn't a nice man, and he might well have belonged someplace where he couldn't hurt polite society.

But from the files she had read, she wasn't convinced that he had killed these particular people. Far from it—she wouldn't even have gone to the state's attorney with such a weak case. Lieutenant Carson would have thrown her out of his office and told her to start over.

Unfortunately, Annie's lack of confidence in the Hidalgo County Sheriff's Office would get her exactly nowhere in court. Ortega could have filed an appeal, but had elected not to. The time to raise reasonable doubt had passed. To get his conviction overturned, she would have to find new and convincing evidence of his innocence—four years after the fact.

She would start by interviewing him at the prison, but that would have to wait until tomorrow. For now, the evening had turned cool, and she didn't remember having seen any source of heat except an old potbellied stove in a corner of the living room. The time had come to stop worrying about Johnny Ortega and start figuring out how she would live in this strange new place.

13

A deep, bone-shaking rumble passed through the house. *Earthquake!* Annie thought, snapping awake. Her bed heaved from side to side as if caught in the grip of a giant, palsied hand. A lamp hanging from the ceiling swayed precariously, and the walls spat bits of plaster onto the floor. The bedroom door swung on its hinges.

But through that door, a red orange light flickered, and panic coursed through Annie's veins. Not an earthquake after all, she feared, but an explosion of some kind, resulting in a fire. She sniffed the air and found it hot and pungent, stinking of sulfur.

She pushed off the covers and made for the open door. It was like walking into a furnace. Should she go out the bedroom window instead? She couldn't even call for help unless she could get to the phone in the living room—the other alternative was driving several miles into cell phone range.

While she stood by the doorway, frozen with indecision, the realization dawned that the shaking, jolting motion had stopped, and although the uneven reddish glow continued, there were no sounds of fire. She listened for the muffled crackle of flames, but the house had gone quiet since that initial deep growl. The sweltering waves of heat and the flickering light still said "fire," but the silence said otherwise.

Her insides roiling, Annie went through the open door and down the short stub of a hallway. At its end, the glow painted the wall in roses and oranges.

With sweat rolling off her body, Annie turned the corner into the living room.

And stopped, hands out to brace herself against the entryway.

The living room floor was gone.

In its place was an impossible hole. The room's walls remained intact, but the floor had been gutted, and sheer, rocky cliffs plummeted down into—well, she couldn't tell what. She leaned over the edge to look down and an attack of vertigo swept over her. The cliff walls seemed to tilt and she clutched at the real walls, the entryway that grounded her and let her know that the world had not lost all its moorings, and only that kept her from sailing over the edge and into the abyss.

She couldn't see any bottom to the hole.

She lowered herself carefully to her knees, then pressed herself flat against the hot floorboards so she wouldn't fall, and moved up so that just her head was over the side. From below came a rush of dry heat and that flickering light and the smell that burned her nostrils as if she had pumped acid into them, but the cliff walls faded into the glow and there was no end point, no solidity, nothing but the flaming emptiness that might have been the center of the Earth or the gates of Hell.

A Hell in which Annie had never believed.

Like her unnatural gift—or curse—of empathy, though, did she have to believe in it now that it had been forced onto her?

The glow of distant fire was hypnotic, and Annie felt her eyelids growing heavier, threatening to close. Inside her head, voices sounded—her father, Ryan Ellis, a wife-beating, check-kiting thug named Wil Mortenson she had shot to death once when he aimed a weapon at her—calling to her to join them, and her fingertips scrabbled at the floor to keep her from sliding over the edge. Finally, she could hold her eyes open no longer.

She awoke in the same spot, lying on the floor in the entryway with her head on the knotty planks of the living room floor. The wood was cool, intact. Light streamed in through the windows, the cheerful cries of birds drifting in with it. The sulfur smell—if it had ever been there at all—was gone.

A dream, then? Annie pushed herself to her feet, her muscles stiff and aching from the hours spent flat on the floor of her new house. A dream, but not like any she'd ever had before, and accompanied by sleepwalking.

Was it a vestige of the empathy—something about this house affecting her in a new and profound way? She hoped not. She was hardly in a position to move again so soon.

She went into the cramped bathroom, with trembling hands ran water into a cup, and swallowed three ibuprofen tablets. A couple of shots of something stronger might help, but she didn't want to begin her first full day in a new place, on a new job, by drinking herself into oblivion, however tempting it might be.

Besides, if she had been drinking the night before, she might have been unsteady on her feet, dizzy, and she could well have fallen into that hole.

Because no matter how impossible it seemed, despite the fact that the hole had left behind absolutely no evidence of its reality, she couldn't quite believe it hadn't been there. The fact that she was still here meant only that she had been lucky. One more step and she might still be dropping, falling through the flames and into forever.

14

JOHNNY Ortega was scary.

He was huge, to begin with. Six-seven, and at least three hundred pounds, Annie guessed. He wore a prison-orange jumpsuit, long-sleeved but with the sleeves rolled back to expose forearms bigger around than her calves. Nearly every inch of skin Annie could see was inked. Most of the tattoos had been done in prison; the only colors black, dark blue, and a little red, inks easily available in ballpoint pens. Between his eyes was a tattooed eye, about the same size as her real ones but more symmetrical, wide open and staring. Lightning bolts flared out above his brows, leading away from the center of his forehead. When he blinked, Annie saw that even his eyelids had been tattooed with more open eyes. Tattooed tears ran from the outer corners of both eyes. A life-size rattlesnake head threatened to bite his right eye from its position on his cheek; its body extended down his neck, wrapped around it a couple of times, and its rattles rested on his left cheek. Beneath the snake's coils on his neck were voluptuous women, struggling against the serpent's bulk.

Letters crept from beneath his very short black hair, but if they spelled anything, Annie couldn't make it out.

He was sitting behind a cigarette-scarred wood laminate table. Chains encircled his ankles and waist. His enormous hands were cuffed together, resting on the tabletop. He didn't look up when she was buzzed into the interview room, and the expression on his face, as blank as if he were comatose, didn't change. The stink of sour sweat and stale smoke seemed to have sunk into the little room's atomic structure. She wasn't sure that burning the place would help—those smells would probably permeate this spot until the planet was lost in the sun's supernova.

"Hello, Johnny," she said. "My name is Annie O'Brien."

His lips moved a little. If he said anything, Annie didn't hear it. "You'll have to speak up for me, Johnny. I had an accident and my hearing isn't so great." She drew back the chair across from him, pulling it a couple of feet away from the table. She'd left her gun in the car, knowing she wouldn't be allowed to carry it in here, and she didn't feel safe anywhere within his reach. Now that she looked at him, she was not at all surprised the jury found him guilty so quickly.

"I said, you don't look like no lawyer."

"I'm not a lawyer. I'm—I was—a cop. In Arizona."

"What you want here then?"

"I'm working with an organization called Operation Delayed Justice. Have you heard of them?"

He might have shrugged. Then again, he might have been shaking off an invisible fly. It was hard to tell—a tiny movement around his shoulders. His chains clinked together.

"They think you're innocent. Or that you might be."

"I am."

"That's what I'm here to look into. But I'll need your help."

"Why?"

"Why will I need your help?"

"Why bother?"

The tattoos on the backs of his hands were so close together it was hard to determine form or design. They looked like lines and blocks of ink. But now she saw that on the four metacarpals of his right hand, not counting the thumb that faced away from her, the letters F-U-C-K had been tattooed, beginning at the little finger. On his left hand, in the valleys between the metacarpals beginning between index finger and middle finger, were the letters Y-O-U.

Why bother, indeed?

"Because if you're innocent, you shouldn't be in here."

"Here. Somewhere else." Another shoulder wiggle that could have been a shrug.

She couldn't argue with him. He looked like a guy who belonged in the system, not on the street. He was probably more comfortable behind bars anyway. Holding down a steady job in the straight world would be a challenge, to say the least. Unless the freak show was hiring.

"How are they treating you in here?" She had never been in the position of trying to get someone out of prison, only putting them in. She wanted to hear something that would make the process easier for her.

"It's okay I guess. There's fights sometimes. But there's a blond lady bull gives some of the cons blow jobs sometimes, says she likes inmates and wants to make our time easier. So it, like, balances out, I guess."

"A guard?" she asked. If she could get a name, she could get the guard fired, at least. But that would take away what was probably one of the only pleasures these men had in life, and any guard who regularly performed oral sex on the inmates was riding an out-of-control train that would take her over a cliff pretty fast. She decided she would let it go.

"Yeah. Kind of heavy, you know, but she does it good."

"Did you kill those teenagers?" Annie asked, desperate to change the subject. "The ones they say you did?"

"Not me."

She hadn't picked up a trace of emotion from him since she walked into the room. His blank expression really did reflect his inner self. At least, as far as she could tell from here, but the better her hearing grew, the more she needed to touch anyone to pick up impressions from them. She scooted her chair closer to the table. "Johnny," she said. "I'm not supposed to touch you."

"Okay."

"Do you mind if I do? Just on the hand?"

"Why?"

"I can't tell you that. It doesn't mean anything, not really. It's just I get a better sense of people if I can touch them once." She meant it more literally than he could ever know— as her hearing improved and her empathy faded, it was only through touch that she could pick up any but the most power-ful emotional impressions.

He obviously wasn't afraid of her, so the fear that gripped her as she reached forward was all hers. She looked through the reinforced windows, but the guard outside was picking at his fingernails, not paying attention. "Is it okay?"

"Okay."

She brushed trembling fingers against his knuckles, close to the C and K on his right hand. A quick, tentative contact, and then she pulled her hand back, scooted the chair away again. Now the guard looked up, probably wondering what all the chair noise was about.

"Did you kill them, Johnny?"

"I told you."

"Tell me again, please."

"No."

Nothing had changed. His face was the same. Even with the glancing touch, she could read nothing of his inner state.

"What were you doing that day? The day they said the kids were killed?"

"I don't know. Driving, maybe."

"You don't know?"

"Was a long time ago, right?"

"Yes, four years ago. In a week or so it'll be four years exactly."

"I don't know, then."

"But maybe driving."

"Maybe."

"Okay, Johnny. That doesn't give me much to go on, but I'll look around. If you're innocent, I'll do my best to get you out of here. All right?"

"Okay. Whatever."

Whatever. Life and death didn't seem to make any difference to him. The idea that he might die here didn't worry him. The idea that he might get out didn't please him.

Could any human being really be so vacant inside? Like an abandoned house, his body was just a shell that might once have contained life, but didn't anymore.

"I'll keep you posted, Johnny."

He didn't answer. Annie waved for the guard. The door buzzed, and she left Johnny Ortega where he was.

Where he no doubt belonged.

15

HIDALGO County was basin and range country. Mountainous spines running north and south with high desert valleys between them, so that the land seemed to undulate like waves coming in toward shore, their crests and troughs constantly replacing each other. The average elevation would have been considered almost alpine in the East, but a few hundred miles away, the terminus of the Great Plains fed into the steep-sided, snowcapped Rocky Mountains, so four- and five-thousand-foot elevations were considered tame. Vast ranch lands filled the valleys, with only a few small towns scattered around: Drummond, Animas, Playa, Antelope Wells, Lordsburg ruling over it all from near the northern edge. At the southern extreme, seventy miles from Lordsburg, it dead-ended at the Mexican border.

The prison stood in the county's southern third, about twenty miles from the border, its tall barbed-wire fences surrounded by open fields of buff-colored grasses dotted with gnarled mesquites. Annie wasn't surprised that barbed wire had played such a prominent role in the settling of the West—any region with so much cactus and mesquite was already choked with thorns, some of them inches long. Compared to those, barbed wire seemed almost merciful, an understated version of the native flora.

From the parking lot, Annie looked across the valley at the hills to the west. They were accordion-folded near the top, and she suspected they were thick with trees, although she couldn't make them out from here. Everywhere she turned, she was presented with new vistas of natural beauty so pure and different from her past experience they tore at her heart. She headed for her car, almost reluctant to close herself away from the sights and smells of this crisply lovely almost-spring day.

"Hey!" someone called. A woman in the tans and browns of the Hidalgo County Sheriff's Office was walking toward her. She was slightly built and fair, with a light brown ponytail bobbing beneath her Smokey Bear hat, deep-set blue eyes, and cheeks as round and pink as peaches. Annie guessed she was in her mid-twenties, but she could have been ten years older, with a complexion that didn't show the years.

"Hi," Annie said, still not sure there wasn't someone behind her that the woman was really heading for.

"I'm Johanna," the woman said as she approached. She extended her right hand. "I heard there was a new kid in town."

"You did?"

"Hey, not much happens around a little town like Drummond. We hear about everything." She gave Annie's hand a brisk shake. "Johanna Raines. I'm out of the Drummond substation."

"Annie O'Brien. I checked in at the office in Lordsburg. I'm former law enforcement—"

"Out of Phoenix, yeah, we got all that. And you're down here to bust old Johnny Ortega out of jail."

"Well, not precisely. I'm working for Operation Delayed Justice, and—"

"I'm just teasing you, silly," Johanna Raines said, laughing. "Someone's got to. Especially with where you're living, you're gonna need friends."

"What do you mean?"

"Way out in the middle of nowhere like that. I'd go stir-crazy in about a day."

"I kind of like the solitude."

"You say that now."

Annie shrugged. "Okay, I am kind of new at it. But I like it so far. It's peaceful."

"Peaceful, boring, same thing. Listen, if you need any help with country living, you call me, okay? Your septic tank backs up, your well goes dry, you find a mountain lion in your underwear, whatever. Or if you just want someone to talk to. I could use a friend who isn't from around here, or currently in law enforcement. My father runs the Drummond station and my brother works there too, so I'm kind of surrounded." She handed Annie a business card.

"I'll do that," Annie said. The only vibe she got from Johanna Raines was one of sunny welcome and open friendliness. "Thanks. I can write my number down for—"

"Already got it," Johanna said. "Look, I gotta get inside, but it's good to meet you."

"You too," Annie said. Johanna gave her a smile and turned away, heading toward the prison gate at a brisk pace.

THE spot where Kevin Munson had stopped his car to change a tire was about fourteen miles from the prison, not far as the proverbial crow flew from the house Morgan had rented for Annie, but by road it was twelve miles away. State Road 336 was the major north-south artery in this far southwestern corner, which didn't mean that it was heavily traveled. Since Kevin Munson and Carylyn Phelps, both high school seniors, had been dating and living in their respective family homes, Annie's best guess as to why they were out in this lonely spot in Kevin's car was that they were looking for some privacy so they could repeat the activity that had gotten Carylyn pregnant in the first place.

Annie pulled off at the mileage noted in the court transcript. A rail fence that Abe Lincoln might have split wood for, had he been in New Mexico during his splittin' days, stood about a dozen feet back from the road. The shoulder was grassy but trampled down in spots, by cars or cows Annie wasn't sure. Most likely both. She consulted the crime scene photos to make sure she had the right spot.

She would no longer find physical evidence, of course. Even though the sheriff's department had run the world's crappiest investigation, the passage of four years—not to mention those cows and cars—would have obliterated anything they had missed.

But Annie wanted to see the spot for herself. More than that, she wanted to test her new—albeit somewhat faded from its peak, during her days of total deafness—ability. She knew she could still read people's emotional states. What she wanted to find out was if she could do so long after the people were gone. Maybe it was crazy, but if an emotional state could be transferred from one person to another, like a cold, then mightn't a brutal clubbing with a jack handle generate feelings extreme enough to survive over the years?

She had spent months wishing she'd never had this power, and now that she had a job, a case, she longed to bring it back at its strongest level, in the hopes that it could articulate what had happened here better than the dry, seemingly fact-free sheriff's reports or the semi-humanoid grunts of Johnny Ortega. Kneeling in the dry, scratchy grass, her hand against the ground where Carylyn's body had fallen, she tried to summon that day but couldn't. She had heard ghosts explained as energy left behind by traumatic events. There was no energy here beyond that of the sun warming the earth and some of that heat radiating back. No ghost haunted this road shoulder.

After trying for a few minutes, she got back in the car, checked a map, and drove to where the killer had taken Kevin Munson, more than two miles away, the last part of it down a narrow dirt track that barely qualified as a road. That part still made no sense, not that the rest of it was exactly crystal clear. Why take him so far away, then park and haul him cross-country?

Between the notes in her file, a reduced copy of a diagram made for trial, crime scene photos, and her map, she was able to find where the killer (she refused to think of Johnny Ortega as the killer—if she did that, she would never be able to convince herself that he wasn't) had stopped Kevin's car. From here he had continued on foot. Annie took a deep breath, clutching the documents to keep from losing them in the steady afternoon breeze. The first step was to get through a three-strand barbed-wire fence. If she hadn't started the day by going to the prison, she'd be wearing jeans and could just climb over it, but as it was she wore a conservative gray skirt, a blouse, a suede jacket, and black shoes with quarter-inch heels. Not exactly wilderness-appropriate apparel.

She pushed up on the middle strand with her right hand and down on the lower strand with her left hand, using the papers to shield it from the barbs. She put her right leg through the space, then bent double and squeezed through. Her skirt caught and tore. "Damn," she said, freeing it. When she stood up on the other side she realized she had torn the back of her blouse as well. Could she expense new clothes? Morgan hadn't mentioned that. Worth a try, though.

The field where Kevin's body had been found was half a mile from the road. The pictures showed rocky hills in the background, mostly a pale dun color, with a few especially persistent trees spiking out of them. She walked through dry and brittle knee-high grass in which cholla and prickly pear cacti, mesquite trees, and creosote bushes made up a minefield of thorns. Most were familiar from the landscape around Phoenix, but in a different mix, and here there were none of the tall saguaros so common in her native Sonoran desert city. All of it clawed at her legs. Her expense report would have to include pantyhose too.

The landscape changed abruptly, the grass petering out, the taller shrubs and cacti all but vanishing. She had reached the field in the photos. Bare dirt sloped away from her, then flattened again, creating a wide bowl a few feet lower than its surroundings. In the bowl, the grass was stunted, widely spaced dry tufts poking up here and there. There was nothing even as high as Annie's knee (scratched on the barbed wire, she noticed now, a thin trail of blood across it like an unpaved road on a map). It was as if nothing could grow in this rocky light brown earth, so didn't bother trying. The constant racket of birds penetrated her consciousness, and she saw a few flying around or picking at the earth looking for bugs.

As Annie made her way toward the spot where Kevin had been killed, she noticed something that had been indistinct in the crime scene photos and not mentioned in the reports or trial transcript. Slabs of pale stone, the same color as the nearby hill, lay flat against the ground. There was no discernible pattern to them but they didn't look random either, if only because she had never seen such a thing in nature. The individual slabs were anywhere from three to five feet in length, up to three in width, and a few inches tall. Sometimes they seemed to be arranged in rows, but then the pattern fell apart and they curled around each other or just lay there with no evident relationship to anything else. She got the sense of a graveyard in which a powerful wind had knocked over every headstone, and the image made her shiver.

"What the hell?" Annie asked out loud. There was no one to answer her. She had only seen a handful of vehicles, mostly rancher's trucks, since leaving the prison, and not a soul between Carylyn's murder scene and this place. Late afternoon sunlight slanted, airborne gold, limning the slabs with sharp-edged shadows.

Annie found the approximate location where Kevin's body had been found. She held up the photo, compared its background to her own view of the ground and the hills behind it. Without using the same lens the photographer had, she couldn't be certain she was in the precise spot, since there were no visible landmarks in the photo. But now that she stood among the strange flat stones, she saw that there was one beneath Kevin's body in the photos—at the angle they'd been taken, looking down at him, there was no depth to it and it just looked like discolored earth. The corner was distinct, however, and viewing it with this new knowledge, she could make out a little shadow at its edge.

So without certainty as to which stone he had been killed on, she was sure it had been one of them.

Why didn't this come up in court? Didn't Ortega's lawyer come out here and look at the scene? Didn't the public defender's office have an investigator who could look at this? She didn't know what any of it signified, but it was strange enough to have raised doubts in her mind and presumably would have done the same in the minds of the jurors.

Annie tore her gaze away from the stones and made a slow revolution, looking into the distance. If the defense had done such a miserable job, might they have missed a ranch house, a possible eyewitness who could testify that Johnny Ortega had never been here? How would a stranger in the area have even found this place, without knowing it existed? No testimony indicated that he had ever been to Hidalgo County before, except passing through on the interstate.

To the south, left of the pale, rocky hills, the mesquites and creosote bushes grew tall and thick, and some other trees rose up above them, live oaks, she thought, their branches thick with mistletoe or some similar parasite, dried out and yellowed. Oaks seemed out of place at this elevation, but she saw more ranked up the hills, and decided they must have just moved down from there. Through the brush and trees, Annie thought she saw something man-made. A house? No, there wasn't enough to it for that. She started toward it, checking her footing with every couple of steps so she didn't trip over any of the slabs or anything else. The ground here was littered with stones, two or three inches in diameter, and it would be easy to fall.

As she got closer to where she thought she had seen a wall, some sort of structure, the brush got thicker. *Hell with it,* she thought, *I've already ruined these clothes.* Wishing she had boots and gloves and maybe a suit of armor, she shoved through the thorny branches, snagging flesh and fabric at every step.

Finally, however, she knew her first glance had been correct. There was a wall, or part of one, about six feet tall, made of adobe that had melted in the elements until its edges were as rounded and softened as brown sugar. She pushed her way to it, taking a few more cuts on her arms and legs in the process. It was more than a wall, it was a corner, and there was a bare space within it. She had found the remains of a building that must have been deserted here decades ago, if not centuries.

Not just a single building, she realized after a few moments spent looking around. Another wall poked up through the brush, and still another. Annie spent twenty minutes picking her way through the dense thickets, and she knew she was in a town or village, long since left behind by its residents. It contained at least thirty buildings, mostly small houses. Some of the structures were bigger, though, maybe churches or public gathering places.

It didn't show on her map, which included places like Shakespeare and Cloverdale and Steins that she had heard were old ghost towns. Did that mean this place was even older than those? Or was it completely unknown? And what was its relationship, if any, to the valley of stone slabs?

There were no old-timers about to provide answers, no tourist brochures or handy trail guides. And the light was fading fast. Annie wanted to get back to her car before full dark enveloped her, while she could still see what few landmarks existed. Retracing her steps, shredding skin and clothes even more, she worked her way back to the little valley and from there back to where she had parked at the edge of the dirt road.

And as she approached the white Taurus through the gathering gloom, she distinctly saw a male form leaning against its right front fender.

16

HE wore a sheriff's uniform and the smile of someone holding back a laugh. His black, curly hair was long for a cop's—which didn't make it long, but it brushed his ears and his collar. His SUV was parked about twenty yards down the road from her car. "I was afraid I'd have to go looking for you," he said as Annie approached. When she hesitated at the barbed-wire fence, wondering if she had enough skin left on her body to risk slashing more of it off, he jogged over. "Hang on," he said. He put one booted foot down on the lower strand and lifted the middle one with two hands, creating a space large enough that she was able to maneuver through with only some of her already destroyed clothing getting snagged.

"Thanks," Annie said, unkinking her back.

"Saw your vehicle sitting here," he explained. "Engine was still warm, so I left it alone. Then I came back by a little later and it was still sitting there. I thought I'd wait a few more minutes to see if you showed up before I decided to get concerned."

"Why concerned?" Annie asked.

"Some rough country around here," he said. He was tall, a little on the thin side, but with broad shoulders and a deep chest that filled out his uniform shirt nicely. "It's not hard for a tourist—not that we get a lot of them, but a few come around, from time to time—to get lost or hurt. Plus sometimes vehicles are left for illegals, and if I thought that's what this was, I'd have to call Border Patrol. Anyway, I'm glad I waited, because I'd have hated to make a big fuss if you were just . . . I don't know, birdwatching or something."

"Something," she said. "I'm Annie O'Brien."

"Oh, you're her? I'm Leo Baca."

"Seems like everyone I meet works for the sheriff's."

"There aren't a lot of big employers around here," Leo said. "Sheriff's office, Border Patrol, state prison. Guess you just got lucky. Who else did you meet?"

"Johanna. Raines?"

"Right, Sheriff Raines's little girl. She's good."

He was standing between Annie and her car. She started around him. He came across as nice enough, and the sensation she had picked up when he lifted the fence for her was one of amiable curiosity, but he was a guy with a gun between her and her means of escape, and that made her nervous. "Sounds like you've heard of me too."

"We've all heard about you. Not a lot new and different happens in southern Hidalgo County, so we pay attention when something pops up."

"So that's it? I'm an oddity?"

"More or less." He smiled when he said it, which she found a little reassuring. "At least, it got people talking around the house when we heard you were coming. Honestly, I've only been here for about a year, so everything's still odd to me."

Annie made it to her car, leaned against the same fender he had been leaning on, and took off her shoes, one at a time, shaking out all the debris that had gathered inside them and tried to grind her feet into hamburger.

"Do you know anything about an old town back there?" She indicated direction with a shake of her head. "It's abandoned now, but there are a bunch of ruins. Old houses and some larger buildings too."

Leo craned his head over his shoulder and looked, as if it could be seen from here. "I don't know much," he said. "But like I said, I haven't been here all that long. You know how it is in a new place—people who have always known about something don't bother mentioning it to newcomers, because they just assume everyone knows what they do. Unless there was a resident there who had a complaint or some criminal tried to hide out there, I wouldn't have had a reason to go there. About all I've heard is that there used to be a community out this way called New Dominion, but that it's long gone."

"I don't think there are any residents, except maybe lizards, snakes, and spiders," Annie said. "And last I checked they didn't tend to have phone service, so calling nine-one-one is probably out." She actually didn't know what it was like to be in a new place, having never lived anywhere but Phoenix—if you didn't count one night in rural New Mexico—but she was willing to take Leo's word for it.

He smiled. It was a good smile. His teeth were a little uneven—no braces in his past—but it was pure and friendly. She hadn't touched him yet, hadn't even shaken his hand, but the sense she got was that he was a plain, old-fashioned nice guy. Maybe too nice to make a career of law enforcement. Then again, as he'd said, there weren't a lot of other employment options around.

"How'd you wind up here, Leo Baca?" she asked, slipping her right shoe back on.

"Answered an ad. I was in Albuquerque, working for the PD there, but I kind of felt like I wasn't making a lot of progress professionally. Hidalgo County ran an ad in the local paper and I sent in my résumé. Next thing you know, I'm driving out for an interview, and then I'm moving."

"You like it?"

"It's sure different." He chuckled. "Yeah, I like it. It's beautiful country. Peaceful compared to the city. Not a lot of gangs and such, you know?"

"I do," she said. "I used to be on the job in Phoenix."

"So you know what I mean. At first I was afraid it would get boring out here, but it hasn't. It's just . . . it's a bit more laid back is all."

"What about the people? Has it been a big adjustment getting used to rural types?"

"They're good folks. Ranching families, most of them. Took a little getting used to, at first—we don't think of Albuquerque as the big city, but compared to this it is. I don't know how much you know about Hidalgo County . . ."

"Not a lot."

He settled next to her, leaning against the Taurus's passenger door. The vehicle shifted under his added weight. The light was almost gone; stars had begun to wink into view overhead. "Okay, Arizona, here's a quick local history lesson for you. Most of the state's original population—back when it was a territory—was Native Americans, Mexicans, Spaniards, and some Basques, which is what my background is. But after a while, a large group of emigrants came from Great Britain. These people settled here in Hidalgo County and kept pretty much to their own kind, without a lot of intermarrying with those who were already here. They settled this far-flung corner of the territory, brought in cattle, and started ranching. Their roots reach back into ancient British history. There's a family in the area, the Wells family, and old John Wells told me once that he can trace his genealogy back to Celts who fought the Roman occupiers at Hadrian's Wall, in the second century after the birth of Christ. These people are a little on the obsessive side about it—some of them call themselves the last true Celts, and to hear them talk you'd think they were still warriors who painted themselves blue and went into battle naked."

Annie laughed.

"I know," Leo said, "but I'm not exaggerating. All the people still living in Great Britain have their bloodlines all messed up, that's what John Wells told me. But here, they've stayed pure. They're also kind of combative, antigovernment. John Wells told me all this as he was ordering me off his property, where I had gone to investigate an illegal immigrant's complaint that he'd been pistol-whipped. Well, I can believe it. Even if someone's here illegally, you're still not supposed to hit them with a gun. They say they're anti-government because they're still pissed over the Roman Empire's occupation of Britain, but that seems like a stretch to me."

"Sounds like it," Annie said. "I've heard of holding grudges, but that's ridiculous."

Leo chuckled. "Another one, Jeremy Stone, called me a 'jackbooted thug' once."

"Nice that they're supporters of law enforcement."

"They like Sheriff Raines. He's one of them. He's not even the real sheriff; he's a lieutenant. There's only the one sheriff, up in Lordsburg. But the sheriff pretty much lets Martin rule southern Hidalgo County like his own fiefdom, because he can get cooperation from the locals down here that the rest can't. They stay in touch on important issues, like when an ex-cop from Phoenix is moving into the area, but otherwise the Raines family—with a little help from outsiders like me—runs the show down here, and has for generations."

"Wow," Annie said. "I had no idea."

"Basically, if most of New Mexico seceded from the Union, it would be to reunite with Mexico. But if southern Hidalgo seceded, it would be to reunite with a Great Britain that hasn't existed for a thousand years. Of course, if New Mexico seceded, a lot of Americans wouldn't notice because they already think it's just a part of Mexico. If you drive around and look at some of the houses, especially in Drummond proper, you can see the British influence in the architecture. A lot of the houses around here are Mexican-style adobe, like yours, but lots of others look like they'd be right at home in England or Wales. Ancient England, even, with lots of Celtic ornamentation on them."

"Interesting," Annie said, already glad she had run into this guy. Talking to him was comfortable, which she guessed meant he was at ease with her. His voice was loud enough naturally to be heard over the bird cries and the small rushes of wind. "I never would have guessed that."

"It's one of our little secrets, I guess. Hidalgo County, homeland of the last true Celts. I don't know who settled New Dominion, but if that was really its original name, I'd guess it wasn't Spaniards or Mexicans."

"Makes sense."

"Anyway, it's been generations since anyone has lived there. That I'm sure someone told me."

"Well, all you have to do is look around at the ruins and you can see that," Annie said. "There are hardly any intact walls. Some stone foundations, some bits of eroded adobe, that's about it."

"Funny that you found it so soon after moving here, Annie."

"I was looking at the Kevin Munson murder scene. It's right near there. Do you know anything about a field full of flat stone slabs?"

He was silent for a moment, looking out toward the field through the thickening dusk. "No," he said finally. "Sounds odd."

"That's where Munson was killed." She knew she had just said this, but felt the need to reiterate it. She still couldn't wrap her head around the why of it, or the weird appearance of the stones themselves.

"That was way before I moved here. I've heard some talk about the case, but the killer was locked up by the time I came."

"Johnny Ortega may not be the killer," Annie said.

"That's right, that's why you're here, isn't it? You really think he's innocent?"

"I don't know yet. That's what I intend to find out, though."

"How are you going to do that?"

"Well, Leo, I don't know that yet either. I guess I should get home, make myself some dinner, and figure it out."

"Okay." He handed her a business card. "If there's anything I can do, call me."

"You guys sure are helpful," she said. "I don't have a card to return. But you have the number, right?"

"I believe I can put my fingers on it if I need it."

"What I thought."

"It's been a pleasure meeting you, Annie."

"Likewise."

He started toward his SUV, then stopped. "You know, your place isn't far from here. From where it sounds like New Dominion is, anyway. There's some hills behind it?"

"Right."

"Just go over the hills behind it, and there you are."

She'd had a sense of that, from her map, but it didn't show all the natural formations so she wasn't sure how close it really was. "I didn't know that."

"Yeah. You can't drive that way, but when you were at the old town site you were probably closer to the house than to your car."

"I'll keep that in mind if I want to make friends with those snakes and lizards."

He smiled again. This time, he did shake her hand, and his touch was warm, easy, safe. "You drive safe, now."

"I'll do that."

She got into the Taurus and watched him in her rearview mirror. He climbed up into the SUV's cab, started the engine, flashed his lights at her a couple of times, and drove away.

Annie followed, already thinking about a long, hot bath. But images of naked warriors carrying long swords and massive shields, their faces painted blue, kept intruding on those thoughts, and she hoped she could shake them before bedtime.

17

THEY walked with flashlights in their hands, beams spreading ahead of them to illuminate the uneven ground, the rocks and cacti and other menaces that might wait in their paths. It was early in the year for rattlesnakes, but the most likely time to step on one was when you weren't watching out for them.

Anyway, they needed the lights to follow the man's trail.

Sheriff Martin Raines knew it was a man because every now and then he had walked across soft enough earth to hold his footprints. He hadn't been taking any pains to hide his tracks, as illegals would have. Anyway, illegals would have been walking toward the vehicle, not away from it.

It wasn't often that two abandoned vehicles turned up in southern Hidalgo County in the same twenty-four-hour period. Leo Baca had spotted one, still warm when he called it in, and said he'd check it out. But Gary, Martin's son, had seen this one, a Lexus SUV, of all things, early this morning, its hood already cold. It hadn't budged since. It was parked on the side of a seldom-traveled dirt track and could have been sitting there for days.

Now they followed a trail of broken branches, occasional

footprints, snags of fabric, and most disturbing of all, a couple of empty plastic water bottles, clean but completely dried out. They'd been dumped sometime in the last few days. Which meant whoever had wandered away from that expensive vehicle was going through water—a good thing, it wasn't a particularly hot day but it was dry—and there was no way to tell how much he had carried with him.

Maybe they'd find a nature photographer or a backpacker comfortable in his tent. But it didn't have that feeling to Martin. It felt more like someone who had chased off after a bird or something and hadn't made it back to his vehicle for whatever reason.

"How far you suppose he walked?" Gary asked. He was about twenty feet ahead; his young eyes were better at picking up faint trail than Martin's were these days. Martin had taught both his kids everything he knew about tracking when they were young. He really wished they had Johanna along— that girl had night vision like a barn owl—but some things a man should do, and this was one of them.

"No telling. He had a good head start."

"Guess he did," Gary said. "Prints don't look like hiking boots, though."

"No, they sure don't. Look like city shoes to me."

"What I was thinking."

"It'd be nice to find him soon though," Gary said. "I'm workin' up a powerful hunger. Plus he's heading kind of south-southeast, but if he winds up in Mexico, he won't do us no good."

"We'll find him. I don't think he's trying to hide, and if he's not, then it's just a matter of staying with it."

"That's what I'm afraid of. Staying with it through dinner and maybe breakfast tomorrow."

Martin didn't answer. They had brought along some candy bars and a couple of those energy bars that Johanna liked, which Martin thought were sort of like eating crunchy soil. But those wouldn't last too long—another hour or so and he'd be eating granola and liking it. Gary was twenty-seven but he still ate like the horse he had been at seventeen.

Gary was a big fellow too, a couple of inches taller than Martin's six feet, and heavy, thick through the middle and broad in the shoulders. If it came to wrestling for that last Hershey's with almonds, Martin was afraid the boy would whip him.

"Give me a good-sized rock," he said, digging through the pouches on his duty belt. "About the size of a fist."

Gary did as he was told—he had always been a good boy that way—scouring the ground for the right stone. By the time he found it, Martin had come up with the nail he always carried. Gary handed over the rock, and Martin knelt beside one of the missing man's footprints. He positioned the nail at the indentation made by the heel of his right foot and pounded it in with the stone. He could easily have pushed it in, but he wasn't sure if the pounding was part of the magic or not. "He won't get away now," he said when the nail was driven in to its head. "That'll slow him down."

"Good thinking," Gary said. "Guess I should carry some nails too."

"Never hurts to be prepared," Martin said.

He hoped they found the man soon. And alive. Especially that. If it took all night but the guy was alive, that would be fine with him.

IT didn't take all night.

They had indeed gone through the last Hershey's bar, and the energy bars were starting to sound appealing. It was 10:39 by Martin's Timex.

The man had climbed most of the way up a rocky slope before he slipped and broke his leg.

Gary found the skid mark first, a stretch about seven feet long where the rocks had been scraped away. At the bottom, a splash of blood painted a thicket of stiff grass, black in the flashlight beams. From there it was only a couple dozen feet, following the footstep-scrape pattern the man had left as he dragged his broken right leg in search of shelter. What he had found was an overhang that gave him about two feet of shelter from the sun. But it did nothing for the fact that a shard of bone jutted out through his flesh and khaki pants about four inches below the knee and nothing for the blood that had spilled all down the slope beneath him in spite of the half-assed tourniquet he had made from his camera strap, the words Canon, Digital, and EOS printed in bloody white letters on a black background.

When they reached him his head was tipped back against the rocks, mouth open (a fly crawled out of it as Martin played his flashlight beam across the man's face), eyes closed as if he was taking a short nap. A useless cell phone—did he really think he'd get a signal way out here?—lay on the ground near his right hand. An expensive digital camera, strapless, was tucked up next to him. One more plastic water bottle, empty, was a couple of feet away, as if he had tossed it after most of the strength had left him.

"You think we did that?" Gary asked. "His leg?"

"Can't really say. Hope not." Martin touched the man's neck. "He's not too cold," he said. "Probably just died a few hours ago."

"Our rotten luck," Gary said.

"Yeah." Rotten luck was right—it was a waste, an opportunity snatched from them, and Martin resented it. He fished around for the guy's wallet. In spite of the fact that the man had climbed almost to a six-thousand-foot elevation, he only wore a light windbreaker over an expensive T-shirt, the khakis his bone shard had cut through, and street shoes. His cheeks were prickly with a couple of days' stubble, but his face was soft and pale, his hair white and neatly trimmed. He was no outdoorsman.

He found the wallet in the man's left rear pocket and flipped it open. "Name's Mark Beaudry," he said. "From Las Cruces."

"Came a ways to die, didn't he?"

"There a good place for it?"

"Some better than others, I expect."

"Might be at that," Martin said.

"We gonna haul Mr. Mark Beaudry out of here, Pop?"

"Tonight? By ourselves?"

"You want to make this hike again tomorrow?"

"If it means bringing extra hands to help carry, yes. Not to mention being able to see the ground without a flashlight. I'd as soon not duplicate his mistake, if it's all the same to you. And I don't know how far you've ever had to team-carry a two-hundred-pound man, but in about a half mile he's going to feel more like four hundred. We'll come back in the morning with about four more guys so we can trade off. And we'll drive in as close as we can get. Any luck, we won't have to haul him more than a mile or two."

"You going to write up the report, Pop?" Gary asked. "Or you want me to?"

"You can do it tomorrow," Martin said.

"Wish we could use him. Make things a lot easier."

"Yeah, well, sometimes you appreciate things more you got to work more for 'em."

"I guess that's so."

"It's so. You can count on it."

Martin didn't have the flashlight on Gary, so he didn't know if his son nodded or shrugged or rolled his eyes. Didn't matter anyway. Some things a father could teach a son and the lessons would stick, while others had to be learned the hard way. This might be one of the latter.

He started back toward the road, hoping Gary knew enough to follow.

18

HER name was Lauren Heller and she claimed a relationship to the author Joseph Heller that the Impressionist believed was entirely imaginary. He didn't understand why she bothered; in the circles she moved in, the phrase *Catch-22* was only vaguely understood, the book and its author entirely unknown. He had heard her mention Joseph Heller within ten minutes of meeting a guy in a bar who had probably struggled to make it through tenth grade and had never read to the end of a book that had more than thirty pages.

Probably she felt like she needed something to set her apart from all the other chunky brunettes in Los Angeles, of which there seemed to be no shortage, in spite of the overabundance of willowy blonds and silicone sisters one tripped over with such regularity there. In the places she frequented on her off-hours, the Hollywood dives and hotel bars and late-night coffee shops, her kind was commonplace.

She wasn't especially pretty, although there was something about her eyes, a kind of heavy-lidded, exotic quality to them, that he thought could be sexy in the right light. Heavy, busty, not too bright or too pretty, Lauren carried herself with a kind of desperation the Impressionist found sad. Instead of waiting to be noticed, she approached men who wanted nothing to do with her, or men who would be happy to have female attention whether or not the female in question had anything to do with a once-famous author. She didn't quite bend over and stick her rear in the air, but she made it clear that she was available for the price of a drink or two and a kind word.

The Impressionist's mother would have called Lauren a tramp, had she known about her. "Tramp" was her most vicious epithet that wasn't racial in nature (although sometimes it was—blacks and Hispanics were more likely to be referred to that way than white women), and she had used it liberally in the days when she had been out of the house a lot.

That didn't happen much anymore. She was eighty-four, and her health wasn't good, and she spent most of her time in a bedroom on the second floor of the Impressionist's house. Her memory was bad. When the Impressionist had returned from his quick trip to San Jose, he had walked into her room (after dismissing the nurse who had stayed with her—he couldn't leave her alone for long, not in her state) and called her name, and she had looked right at him and said, "Philip, where have you been?"

"I'm not Philip," he'd said. "Philip's dead." Philip was a high school sweetheart of hers, but she had married the Impressionist's father, William, not Philip, and Philip's head had been torn off on an oil rig in Wyoming in 1962.

She had waved her hand at him—her right, the one missing the ring finger and little finger that the Impressionist had stitched together and kept in a plastic sleeve in his right front pants pocket, along with a Montblanc pen—as if to say that of course she knew he wasn't Philip. But she couldn't remember his name until he gave it to her. After he went downstairs and came back up she would likely forget again.

She wasn't good for much anymore, old Momma. But for all the people he had killed, for all his scholarly approach to the subject of death, she was the one person on Earth (himself included) he wished he could spare from that final reck-

oning. He kept her fingers with him because he couldn't take
her along everywhere, and because he knew someday, sooner
than later, most likely, they would be all he had left of her.
She wasn't using them, after all, and they made him feel that
she was close by.

But in her prime, she'd had a mouth on her and a caustic
disdain for anyone who didn't meet her particular standards
of propriety. Hence all the tramps she felt surrounded her.

What tramp Lauren didn't know was that she was special
indeed. Word had barely begun to filter out into the population of the Los Angeles basin, but there was a new man
in town, and that man was definitely attracted to her kind.
He had met four of them so far, over the course of seven
weeks—met them in their own homes, where a man like him
could have his way with a woman like her. A day later,
maybe two, these four women had been found, only they had
been decorated—not with precision or an artist's flair, more
like the enthusiastic efforts of a clumsy nine-year-old wrapping his first Christmas present. The decorations consisted of
dozens of stab wounds, cuts, slices, then finally a major inci-
sion through which he withdrew the intestines, wrapping
them around the women like fleshy ribbons.

The killings had made the news, each time. But the first
had been taken as a separate incident. When the authorities
saw the pattern, they had clammed up, hoping to prevent
a general panic and keep the perpetrator from basking in
attention.

They knew what he was, though. A serial killer, probably
working out his sick psychosexual fantasies as he murdered
his victims. Los Angeles Robbery-Homicide had put its best
detectives on the case, called in the FBI, consulted with the
L.A. County sheriff. A task force was working the case
around the clock.

Which made it the perfect time for the Impressionist to
step in. He left Momma with the nurse again and left for L.A.
There, he spent time combing through the case files and
looking at the scenes. He knew exactly what the murderer
looked for and what he did once he found just the right

woman. He knew everything he needed to know. He could practically see through the killer's eyes, dream the killer's dreams.

Lauren couldn't. She didn't seem to know that while she might not have been every man's type, she was definitely his. She didn't alter her habits at all—she went to work in the billing office of a big industrial design firm, and then she went out to drink and meet men, and at some point during the night she went home to get a few hours sleep before starting it all over again.

The killer hadn't found her yet. The Impressionist had. Which made her all the more unique, because she wouldn't end up one of five, or seven, or twelve, or however many would fall before the killer was caught. Everybody would think she was, but in fact, she would be one of one.

She would know it too, right before the end. She would know that even a copy could be a one-of-a-kind work of art. He would make sure of that.

He owed her that much.

19

BACK at the little house she would have to start thinking of as home, Annie changed into jeans and a sweatshirt, poured a glass of iced tea, cooked up a couple of chicken breasts and some brown rice, and tossed a salad. She put on Led Zeppelin's *Physical Graffiti* CD while she cooked, playing it loud enough to feel the driving bass of John Paul Jones and John Bonham's thunderous drumming. During the quietest days, she had missed music most of all, and as her hearing had started to return it was rock with prominent bass and drum lines that she had turned to first.

Her dinner prepared, she sat at the little wooden dining table, scratched and gouged over the years by who knew what, and read one of Robert Parker's Spenser mysteries. Sometimes she needed to set aside a case and engage her mind in some unrelated activity in order to allow fresh insights to come to her. The Spenser novel was engaging enough to distract her from Johnny Ortega's case, and she could use inspiration from any sector at this point.

She was washing dishes when the phone rang. It was the first time she had actually heard it, and she was surprised that it had an old-fashioned ring instead of a modern electronic tone. She dried her hands and went back into the living/dining room, where the phone—the only one in the house, besides her cell—sat on an end table beside a lumpy brown sofa. She turned down the music, sat down, and picked up the handset. "Hello?"

"Annie?"

"Yes?"

"It's Morgan."

She was still having trouble recognizing even the most familiar voices, since everything came filtered through the tinnitus that continued to ring in her ears. "Hi, Morgan," she said.

"How are you finding life in New Mexico?"

"It's . . . interesting, so far. I mean, it's a beautiful place, and you were right about the solitude. There's a lot of that around."

"That's what you wanted, right?"

"Exactly." She sat on the sofa. A spring jabbed at her butt, and she shifted a little to her left, stretching the phone's cord—an old-fashioned coil cord; where did someone even find a phone like this in the modern world?

"Have you met Johnny yet?"

"Today, in fact."

"You never did let grass grow under you, slugger! How'd it go?"

She told Morgan about her conversation with Johnny, her doubts about the state's case, and briefly described her visits to the crime scenes. She held off on giving any details about the strange stones in the ground or discovering the ruins of New Dominion, since neither seemed to have any bearing on the case, and she didn't mention Leo Baca. "So not a lot of definite progress," she said after summarizing. "But it's early yet."

"Early for you, Annie. Not so much for Mr. Ortega."

"I know, Morgan. If he's innocent, I'll work on getting him out of there as soon as I can."

"That's all I need to hear, Annie. If there's anything you need, just let me know."

"I will, Morgan. And thanks again for the opportunity."

"I only offered it to you because I knew you could do the job, slugger."

She had barely finished the last of her dishes when the phone rang again. Had Morgan forgotten something? This time she settled into a more comfortable spot on the sofa before answering.

"Annie, this is Leo Baca. We met earlier today."

"Of course," Annie said, summoning up a mental image of the slender, handsome deputy. "What's up?"

"I just wanted to let you know how much I enjoyed shooting the breeze with you," he said.

"I liked it too."

"I'm glad to hear that. I wonder if you'd be interested in continuing our conversation sometime. Maybe over dinner?"

That took Annie by surprise. Because it was over the phone, perhaps, instead of in person—she believed she still retained enough of her empathic abilities to know when a guy was about to ask her out. She had been able to do that before the explosion, and she hadn't picked up on that vibe earlier in the evening.

"Are there restaurants in Hidalgo County?" she asked, stalling for time.

"Not a lot of fine dining opportunities," Leo said. "For that you have to go over to Bisbee or Tucson, or here in the state, Silver City has some nice places. Las Cruces and El Paso aren't too far. And I can show you the best Basque cuisine in the state—although you have to be willing to put up with my mother."

"Is that hard to do?"

"She's a mother, you know? Other people like her. I love her. Sometimes I can't stand her, but I love her."

"Gotcha," Annie said. A fleeting thought of her own mother came to mind, holding Dad's gun in quaking hands that only settled down when she was pressing on the trigger with her thumb.

"So, what do you think?" he pressed.

Annie wasn't sure how to respond. She had liked Leo

when she was talking to him. But how much of that was her own affection or attraction and how much was his for her, simply reflected back on him by her overabundance of empathy, she couldn't tell. This was the first time since the explosion that she'd been asked on a real date, instead of simply being hit on in a bar. And the fact that she had enjoyed her conversation with Leo complicated things more. So did the fact that he wore a badge—she had dated plenty of cops, but part of the idea of coming to New Mexico was about changing old patterns. That particular old pattern ranked high on her list.

Her silence was stretching on long enough to be as uncomfortable as that sofa spring that had crept over and started jabbing her in the ass cheek. "I think I need a little more time, Leo," she said. "It's not that I didn't enjoy your company, because I did. But everything is so new to me right now, and I've got so much work to do on the Johnny Ortega case that . . . well, I think I just need to get settled in for another week or so before I give any thought to that sort of thing."

"It's just dinner, Annie."

"I understand that. And I don't want you to think I'm shooting you down. I'm just . . . putting you off. For now."

"I guess I'll take what I can get," he said.

"Thanks, Leo. And I'm flattered that you even asked."

"Well, you know, it's not like we get new women moving into the area every day. Especially new single, attractive women. Especially ones who know what it's like on this side of the line."

The thin blue line, he meant. The brotherhood of cops, which included the small but growing sisterhood of which she was a part.

"I'm sure we'll have dinner together sometime soon," Annie said. "And before that, I'll probably run into you on some deserted country road."

"I'm looking forward to it," Leo said.

"Me too," she said, half surprised to realize that she really was.

Later, she turned off the music, stepped outside, and listened to the night noises of the open countryside. A breeze shook the branches of the trees and rasped the dry grasses together. An owl hooted from someplace nearby, although she couldn't pin down its location. Mostly, what she heard was quiet, but not the kind of quiet caused by deafness. The real kind, caused by a lack of people.

She walked around her house. Grass brushed her ankles. Tree limbs waved in the night wind. The quiet was like a cocoon around her, isolating her from the wider world. Soft scratching noises might have been animals—this was cattle country, but she had also seen plenty of rabbits around, and she was sure there were rodents, field mice and the like—or birds or just plants shifting in the breeze. She liked the solitude, but there was an unsettling aspect to it as well, especially when she remembered her dream from the night before. Beyond the rim of light coming from her house the darkness was almost absolute, and the stars—more than she had ever seen at once the night before, but shrouded tonight in wispy clouds—did nothing to penetrate it. Anyone could be out there in the darkness. *Anything.* Annie wasn't much of a dog person, but a dog would at least provide some company and bark at unexpected visitors.

Should I be wearing a gun if I'm out here at night? she wondered. She shook her head. That was foolish. There were hundreds of square miles of barely inhabited rural country around her—the chance that some ax murderer had happened to zero in on the lights of her little house, amidst all this darkness, was virtually nonexistent.

Maybe she was freaked out because she knew now how close the ruins of New Dominion really were—just a couple of miles, behind the house and over the hills, off which the evening's cloud-hidden half-moon barely glanced. *Not that there's anything particularly scary about broken-down walls,* she reminded herself. But at night it seemed more sinister than it had during the day. The fact that people had lived there and then abandoned it seemed to imply that they had died there too, and maybe not in pleasant ways.

She shook her head once again, trying to knock the silliness loose. It was just a town. People stopped living there because there were better places to live, closer to the main roads. This had been Apache country once, and maybe the original settlers of New Dominion had tried to live there during the days when Apache raiders controlled the area. Perhaps they had relied on a creek that dried up or a crop that failed.

Annie went back inside, to where there was light and with the push of a button she could have music or the voices of people from radio or TV around her. She settled for TV, its picture barely distinguishable but the sound working, leaving it on even when she went to sleep. Her dreams were unsettling, full of the flutter of unseen wings, faces that loomed suddenly out of the darkness, and other, less identifiable dangers. She woke up a little after two, sweating and without feeling rested at all, and wondered for the first time since she had arrived if coming here was a bad idea after all. Then she sat up in bed, put on a DVD of *The Maltese Falcon*, lost herself in its black-and-white world, and finally drifted off to sleep again.

20

IN the early mornings and late afternoons, when the sun hovered close to the hills, yellow-tinged light slanted across the valley and brought every leaf, blade of grass, bird wing, and cactus thorn into stark relief. The sheer physical beauty of her surroundings at these times was heartbreaking in its absolute purity, but although Annie felt a clenching in her chest when she admired it, wishing she could hang on to just that view, just that instant, forever, she also knew that in another two or ten or twelve hours another moment would come along that was equally special and stunning. The hills around her changed rapidly as the sun moved, indigo to purple to chocolate to umber, ending up near sienna when the sun was at its zenith, then reversing the process at day's end.

She took her coffee outside. The morning's crisp air and golden light made her wonder how she ever could have been bothered by the lonely darkness of the night before. Birds flitted from tree to power line to the tops of tall yuccas. The yuccas had white stalks erupting from spiny balls and stems of older spines gone brown, and they swayed when even the smallest bird landed on them. The birds' morning songs were everywhere around her, cheeps and chitters and chirrups, coos and caws.

Annie saw more birds here in ten minutes than all day in Phoenix, and although there were doves among them, none of them were the pigeons that seemed to have taken over every city in the world including her native one. She recognized doves and quail, the ungainly dash of roadrunners that they followed with surprisingly graceful short soaring arcs as they cleared fences, the black flapping ravens and the swooping vultures with white fingertips at the ends of broad black wings, the russet tail wedges of red-tailed hawks. The birds she couldn't identify were far more numerous. There were tiny ones and large, birds with round heads, birds with spiky crests or topknots, quick little ones that darted around frantically and bold, patient ones that stared down at her from tree branches or power poles like the intruder she was. She would need to pick up a field guide somewhere if she had any hope of identifying them all. Somehow that seemed important. *A girl has to know her neighbors,* she thought, *and they're all I've got.*

She was making toast when the phone rang yet again. She pushed down the toaster handle and went to answer it.

"Annie, it's Johanna Raines." She sounded as chipper and cheerful as the birds outside.

"Hi, Johanna." She couldn't summon anything close to Johanna's exuberance, after the rough night she'd had.

"Hey, have you had breakfast yet?"

Annie thought about the toast in the kitchen. She missed cordless phones—it hadn't occurred to her that she shouldn't start it, then answer the phone in the living room, because if it burned she wouldn't be there to stop it. "No, not yet."

"Good. Because I was thinking this would be a good time for you to meet some of the locals."

"Okay . . ."

"There's a great little café in Drummond called Greenfield's. It's on the main street, you can't miss it."

"What's the main street called?" Annie asked. In the kitchen, her toast popped.

"Main. We're not terribly imaginative about such things around here, sometimes."

"I need to get in the shower. Can I meet you there in about forty minutes?"

"Sure," Johanna said. "I'll get there and grab us a table. See you soon."

Annie lived only about fifteen minutes from town, but forty would give her time for that shower, and to eat some of her toast. She was too hungry to wait that long before eating anything at all. She buttered one slice, downed that, and broke the other into crumbs that she tossed into the yard for the birds.

After her shower, she put on some quick makeup and drove into Drummond. The town really was tiny. Open fields bumped up against a line of trees at the town's edge, then widely spaced farmhouses gave way to smaller wood-and-stone homes, with a handful of adobes mixed in. The lots were fenced, here at the town's edge, mostly with wire fences, some of which confined dogs, horses, burros, goats, chickens, or all of the above.

After a couple of these vaguely defined "blocks" came the commercial district. Buildings spread out from an intersection and lined both sides of Main Street, some of them prefab ones with corrugated steel walls, Quonset huts on steroids, while others used stone-and-timber construction that, as Leo had mentioned, did remind Annie of pictures she'd seen of Great Britain. There were a few adobes here too, and stucco-sided buildings meant to resemble adobe. She drove past the sheriff's substation, a firehouse, a church, a feed store with bales of hay and stacked watering troughs out front, a gas station, a little grocery store, a place that sold liquor and rented videos, a second gas station, this one with an auto repair shop next door and tires arrayed on a double-decker rack beside one of the bay doors, and a library not much bigger than some closets she'd been in.

People walking between the stores eyed her with a mixture of friendliness and suspicion. Some offered waves, while others turned away, as if she might be contagious even from inside her car. Toward the end of town, past a medical/dental clinic and a hardware store, stood Greenfield's Bakery/Café. It was a stand-alone building with a gravel parking lot on two sides and a paving stone walkway leading to the front door. A wooden sign shaped like a golden crown hung over the door, and the building itself was the same stone-and-timber construction she had seen here in Drummond, but nowhere else in the Southwest.

Annie parked in front and pushed open the multipaned glass-and-wood door, stepping into the smells of baking bread and pastries, rich coffee, and spicy Mexican foods. It was just after eight and the place was crowded, with a dozen tables occupied and people standing at a glass bakery counter. Johanna waved from a table near the back wall.

"I guess it's a good thing you came early," Annie said. "This place is booming."

Johanna shoved a menu at her—a single sheet of colored printer paper, covered in small type. "It's kind of the only game in town," she said. "Well, almost. There's another place a couple of miles out, but that's dinner only. They have the best breakfasts and lunches here, anyway. American, Mexican, pretty much whatever you want."

"Smells great." Annie did a quick scan of the café's other patrons. They were all white; many, like Johanna, pale and fair, with rosy cheeks. This close to the border, she expected to see more Hispanics. Or *some* Hispanics. There were none in sight.

"They do a good job."

"Have you ordered yet?"

Johanna tapped the steaming white mug in front of her. "Just tea," she said. "I waited for you. Had to keep one hand free to grab my gun, in case someone tried to take the table."

Annie perused the menu for a moment and settled on scrambled eggs with biscuits and gravy. The toast had held off hunger pangs until the instant she walked in the door, but now they were back, stronger than ever. A waitress came by, plump, blond, and red-cheeked, and took her order.

While they waited, Annie told Johanna about the explosion and the temporary deafness that followed, mostly to explain why she might ask for many things to be repeated. The café was just noisy enough to make following the thread of a conversation difficult for her. She left out the part about the exaggerated empathy, not wanting to frighten the poor young woman.

Johanna watched her, wide-eyed, as she told what had happened at Trey Fairhaven's trailer. "Wow," she said when Annie finished. Both breakfasts had come (huevos rancheros for Johanna, with rice) and they were eating as they talked. "That must have been crazy."

"That's one word for it. Anyway, that's why I'm here, instead of back in Phoenix—a half-deaf cop doesn't do anyone any good."

"I guess not. But you can hear okay now? Except for the background noise here?"

"Mostly," Annie said. "Places like this, with a lot of background noise, are the worst. I'm still not that good at determining the direction a sound came from. I can't make out really soft sounds, like whispers. But I'm a lot better than I was."

"That's good. That must stink, having to give up your job because of something that happened to you on the job."

"Pretty much. But on the flip side, if I hadn't given it up, I wouldn't be here."

"Yeah, most people don't come to Drummond unless they have a specific reason to. It's not exactly a tourist spot, or even on the way to one."

"It's peaceful, though."

Johanna leaned closer, but kept her voice audible. "When you're growing up, it's boring. There's not much to do except watch TV, drink, and get in trouble."

"You seem to know everyone in town," Annie said. Since she had entered the café, Johanna had greeted every new arrival by name, and introduced her to most of them. Most chatted for a minute about the weather or some mutual acquaintance. As they came to the table and greeted her, Annie picked up bits and pieces from them—most were in good spirits, happy to see Johanna and interested in the newcomer, but some smiles masked anxiety over beef prices and troubled marriages and problem children. One woman was mourning the loss of a cat that had been with her for twelve years, another was tingling over an erotic e-mail exchange she'd had before leaving the house.

"That's not hard to do in a town this size," Johanna said. "You see the tree?"

She pointed at a mural on a white plaster wall behind them, to which Annie hadn't paid much attention. Now that she looked, she saw it was a kind of family tree, with names painted on the branches and leaves. The trunk said "Drummond." On the main branches she read the names Raines, Hadley, Graham, Wells, Howell, Stone, Weaver, Church, Conway, McKeen, Fryar, and Smith. Different names decorated some of the lesser branches, but all the branches intertwined at various points instead of remaining separate and distinct. "That's the town tree," Johanna explained. "The names on the big branches are the town's founders, its original families. Where the branches intersect is where the families married into one another. More recent arrivals are on the smaller branches, and individual names are on the leaves hanging off the branches."

"So there's a Johanna Raines leaf up there somewhere?"

"More like a bud," Johanna said. "This goes back to the town's founding in 1933, so by the time you get to my generation there's not a lot of space left."

"Are a lot of those families still here? You're a Raines, and I think you introduced me to a Conway and a Weaver this morning. Leo Baca said something about Wellses and Stones yesterday."

"Most of us are still around. I don't think there are any Fryars left, except maybe the descendants of some Fryar women who married into other families. The name has died off, anyway."

"That's fascinating," Annie said. The café's décor was otherwise unremarkable—strictly utilitarian tables and chairs,

the glass-fronted bakery display counter, plain white walls.
The only other things she noticed were a stuffed and mounted
bobcat head above the door into the kitchen and a high shelf,
about two feet below the ceiling, on one wall, that held small
figures of animals made with sticks and leaves. She would
have guessed them to be the toys of Native American children, but they looked new. Reproductions, probably, although
that struck her as a little odd in a café without a hint of Native American about it. She turned back to Johanna, still
awed by the effort that had gone into the tree mural. "In
Phoenix, they'd have to have a wall as high as the Empire
State Building to do a town tree. Even that probably wouldn't
do it. Maybe the Great Wall of China, if the tree was painted
on its side."

"Makes my job easy," Johanna said. "In a place where
everybody knows you, your mother, and your grandma,
crime is pretty minimal."

"I'll bet."

"Not that we don't have some. And people passing
through, like your Johnny Ortega, don't have that restriction
on their activities."

"He's not my Johnny."

"He *is* guilty," Johanna said, suddenly serious. "There's
no doubt about that."

"We'll see," Annie said. To change the subject, she
quickly added, "So, how far back has your family been in
law enforcement? My dad was a cop, and my grandfather,
but that's all."

"It's kind of the traditional occupation in our family,"
Johanna said. She took a drink of her tea and poured some
more from a china pot. "As far back as the founding of
Drummond, there's always been a Raines wearing a badge."

"That's cool," Annie said. "A real legacy."

"I'm the first girl who's done it, though." She fingered the
badge on her breast. "I get some crap from my dad and my
brother, Gary. But I couldn't see doing anything else, especially being some ranch wife. Nothing against ranch wives.

They're amazing people and I really admire them, but that's just not me. So here I am."

"Yesterday I came across some ruins, out in the middle of nowhere. Leo said it was a town called New Dominion."

"That's right."

"Do you know anything about it?"

"Not a lot. Just approximately where it was. It was a long time ago."

"Somebody must know," Annie pressed. "Who's the town historian? Every small town has a history buff, right?"

Johanna added cream and sugar to her tea and stirred it rapidly. "I don't really know. If I think of anyone, I'll tell you, though."

Annie wasn't in physical contact with Johanna, but she thought she would have noticed the woman's sudden chill even without enhanced empathy. Since she had brought up New Dominion, Johanna's level of enthusiasm about their conversation had dropped considerably. She decided to give up on it, for now. "I should probably get on with my day," she said. "Looks like you're working today too."

"I am. Shift starts at nine, so I should get going too."

Annie grabbed the check off the table. "I'm on an expense account," she said. "Thanks to Operation Delayed Justice." It wasn't true, but she didn't want to make Johanna pay for a meal that had made her so uncomfortable at the end.

"Well, they're good for something, after all." Johanna said it with a grin, but Annie could tell she wasn't entirely kidding. She'd have been the same way, a couple of months ago. "Anyway, it's good luck for a stranger to part with some coins when arriving in a new place."

"It is? I've never heard that one."

"Oh, it's an old superstition around here. Isolated communities, you know—they pass some pretty strange ideas down from one generation to the next."

"Well, I'm happy to part with these, if a twenty counts. And thanks for inviting me out, Johanna," Annie said, digging for her wallet. "You're right, this place is great, and it's good to meet some of the locals."

"You're practically one of us now," Johanna said. "So this is your place too. They'll treat you like family from now on."

"Will they give me a branch? Or a leaf?"

"You'll have to stay a while to get that," Johanna said. She smiled and put on her Smokey hat. "But in time? Who knows what you'll get."

21

ONE of the hallmarks of a successful detective, Annie believed, was curiosity. Her father had always encouraged her to develop that trait, an effort that had caused conflict with her mother. But her mother had been a timid woman, fearful of everything, particularly everything American. The whole country seemed to her too large and too loud and simply too much, and it had slowly driven her into a hole from which the only escape was oblivion. Annie took after her father in most regards, including that one, so while she knew she should be working on the Johnny Ortega case, New Dominion had captivated her attention and she decided she'd allow herself to investigate it for the rest of the morning.

Back at the house, she unplugged the phone from its wall jack, glad it wasn't so ancient that it was actually hardwired in, and plugged in her laptop's modem cable. She hadn't been online since her move, so first she had to search for a local access number. Any kind of high-speed Internet access short of satellite, Morgan had assured her, was still years, if not decades, away from reaching this isolated place. The TV in the house didn't get real reception either—she could bring in only ghostly pictures and voices on a couple of channels, static on the rest.

Dial-up did the trick, though. In a few minutes, she was online, checking e-mail (nothing of special note, although it took a few minutes to respond to the well wishes of a few friends on the occasion of her change of scenery). Then she opened Google and did a search for "New Dominion"+ "New Mexico."

She learned nothing she didn't already know, which was precious little. Most of the references that came about talked about contemporary New Dominion as a destination for hard-core ghost town aficionados, some accompanied by photographs taken by people who had visited. Annie knew what it looked like now—what she was curious about was what it had looked like in its heyday, and what had happened to it. She found a few glancing references to the town's abandonment in the 1930s, but no helpful details.

Giving up on that route, she got back in the Taurus and dropped in at the Drummond branch library. It took only a couple of minutes to ascertain that the little one-room library didn't have the depth of material that she needed, although it seemed to have a good selection of children's books, a story hour program for kids, and a reasonable range of recent best-sellers for the parents. When Annie described what she was after, the librarian recommended the county's main library in Lordsburg.

Annie made the drive north on New Mexico State High-way 338, an old, cracked, pale gray ribbon of two-lane sliced every few miles by cattle guards as it unspooled through vast ranch holdings, rolling hills of straw-colored grass broken up now and again by craggy outcroppings. She blasted a Dixie Chicks CD and watched the scenery flit by, the raptors standing watch from the tops of power poles, the rabbits and road-runners darting across the road. At one point, about halfway to Lordsburg, she spotted a small herd of pronghorns browsing on a distant grassy bluff.

The Lordsburg-Hidalgo Library was in a beautiful Pueblo-style building at the corner of East Third and Pyramid in downtown Lordsburg. Compared to Phoenix, Lordsburg barely qualified as a city, but after spending the early morning in Drummond it was downright metropolitan. The streets were wide—and paved—with actual sidewalks and stoplights every now and then, and some of the buildings were two and even three stories tall. Fewer than three thousand people lived in Lordsburg. She didn't know the population of Drummond, but so far she had seen about forty people there, and for all she knew that may have been everyone in town.

Two Hispanic women worked quietly, as expected, behind the library counter. One of them looked up and beamed a smile at Annie. Ten minutes after walking in the front door, she was sitting in front of a microfiche reader, paging through issues of the local newspaper, the *Lordsburg Liberal*, from the early 1930s.

In early 1933, there were a lot of front-page stories about aspects of the Depression, which probably didn't hit rural New Mexico as hard as it did some other places. She scrolled past stories about the death of Calvin Coolidge, the inauguration of Franklin Roosevelt, and the rise of Adolf Hitler. Books by authors who were Jewish, or simply not members of the Nazi party, were burned all across Germany. For three days in early March, banks in the United States were closed by order of the president. Even from this side of history, reading headlines about things that had happened long before she was born, she got a chill from the knowledge of the horrors that had been about to descend upon the world.

Johanna had said Drummond was founded in 1933, so that was where she wanted to start looking for information about the end of New Dominion. The two towns were so close together physically that she thought there must have been some overlap. She dug deeper into the papers then, past the national and world headlines and into the reports of ranch foreclosures, high school sports and town meetings.

And then she found it.

The *Liberal*'s prose from March 23, 1933, was breathless,

often crude, but she read through that to find the nuggets of solid information mixed in with the overhyped reporting. It wasn't so different from trying to figure out what was true and what nonsense in an interrogation.

> "Unspeakable tragedy shook the southern Hidalgo County township of New Dominion yesterday," the first article began. "In an incident too horrible for description or even sane understanding, most of the small town's population met their Maker. A handful of survivors of the incident and subsequent conflagration refused to go into detail about the day's terrors except to report that Hell had come to Earth and stricken down their families, friends, and loved ones."

The article continued in the same maddeningly nonspecific vein. She jotted down the date on a piece of scratch paper and continued. A few days later there was another article, slightly more in-depth and less hysterical. It reported that seventy-two people had died during the "incident"—which was still not defined, but the words "unholy" and "inhuman" came into play, along with the return of "unspeakable." Jeremiah Raines, Hidalgo County sheriff, described the scene as one of "unbearable cruelty and the worst sort of perversity imaginable. I shall see that carnage in my nightmares until the day I leave this Earth behind to sit at my Creator's feet." The town had reportedly been founded in the 1890s, but details about its history beyond that simple fact were scant.

Annie scanned a few more articles, but they didn't provide much illumination. *Something* had happened in New Dominion. Seventy-two of the town's residents hadn't survived it. That was, apparently, the bulk of its population. The survivors said they were moving away, that New Dominion was "cursed ground" upon which they would never again set foot.

No one was ever arrested or charged with a crime in connection to the incident, as far as she could determine. Construction on the first homes in Drummond began on the first of May, and New Dominion faded from the news altogether.

She sat back, letting her eyes rest and trying to soak in what little she had learned. It was no wonder the town had been abandoned, allowed to return to the earth, and no wonder that no one seemed anxious to talk about it. If the people who founded Drummond had a connection to those who had survived New Dominion, or even knew about what had happened so close by, their stories had probably been passed down from generation to generation. When Annie had been growing up in Phoenix she was told to avoid certain neighborhoods, but no matter what her father knew about those streets it had to pale beside the devastation that had struck New Dominion.

Annie returned those microfiches to the librarian and asked for a more recent set, from yet another March, four years ago. The librarian shook her head sadly. "Those records were online," she said, "not on microfiche. But the *Lordsburg Liberal* went out of business recently, and their website's gone. I can show you the website for the *Hidalgo County Herald*, though. It's only a few years old, so it wasn't around on the dates you were looking for previously, but anything from four years ago will be there. You might also try the *Douglas Dispatch* from Arizona, and the *El Paso Times* and the *Voice of the Borderlands*, from Texas. I can show you those too."

"That would be a big help," Annie said.

The librarian set her up on another machine. On the *Herald*'s website, she searched the archives for "Johnny Ortega." There was a brief story from the time of his arrest, then another one, more in-depth, from which Annie learned that Kevin Munson had a reputation as a town troublemaker, a fact that hadn't come up in trial, where he'd been painted as a near saint. In fact, he'd been in trouble for bullying smaller kids, for petty theft and vandalism, and for being drunk and stoned in public. The baby Carylyn Phelps had been carrying was his, which was implied at trial but not made explicit. Townspeople interviewed by reporters had tried to say nice things about the teens, but often had difficulty doing so. "She was real pleasant," a woman named Henrietta Hadley said. "Always had a smile on when I saw her, anyhow."

But these stories didn't do much to deepen her understanding of the case, and Annie's stomach was beginning to protest that she had skipped lunch. She left the library and drove around until she found the Grapevine Café, where she ordered a grilled chicken salad and an iced tea, and tried to intuit a connection between New Dominion and Kevin Munson that would explain why he had been taken to that field to be killed. Nothing came to her, however. Too much time had passed between the two events, with only the physical proximity and the March dates, decades apart, connecting them.

After lunch, but before she left the mobile phone reception zone that Lordsburg offered for the wilds of the county's southern reaches, she called Morgan Julliard. "I was curious," she said, after the opening pleasantries. "Have you ever heard of an abandoned town down here called New Dominion?"

He considered for a moment. "Doesn't ring any bells. Is it important?"

That was the question, wasn't it? "I don't know yet. Kevin Munson, the male victim, was killed in a field right outside the old town site. But the town was deserted in 1933, after some sort of catastrophe killed most of its residents. So I don't see how they could be linked."

"Well, I can try to do some research, see if I can find anything out from here," he offered.

"Okay, that'll be good, Morgan. It's probably not at all important. But I like to look at all the possibilities." A train rolled by on the tracks that paralleled Motel Drive, where the restaurant was. It moved slow and easy, as if it didn't really have any special destination in mind. She watched it go, wondering offhandedly where it was heading and what was contained within its steel cars. Too bad there were no trains that carried answers to impossible questions, she mused.

"That's why I hired you," he said. "I'll let you know what turns up, slugger."

She hung up and started the Taurus, bound for home. She had spent most of the day ignoring Johnny Ortega's case, and he was still rotting in a prison she would pass on her way south. The idea that she had wasted a day depressed her, and she hoped Morgan could come up with something that would make all her effort worthwhile.

22

BACK at home that night, Annie ate a simple dinner, listened to some music, read, and went to bed.

While she slept, a wind kicked up, fierce and insistent. She heard it, took momentary pleasure in the fact that she could hear anything well enough to be awakened by it, then rolled over, wrapped a pillow around her head, and went back to sleep.

Not long after that, another noise made itself known even over the wind. It was a persistent but uneven knocking sound. Annie tried to ignore it, but it wouldn't be ignored. She struggled to come up from sleep, like a swimmer trying to reach the surface before her lungs burst. When she was almost there, the thought came to her that it might be someone knocking on the house's front door.

That woke her up. She glanced at the clock and swore quietly. Three twelve. She drew the Glock 17 resting on her nightstand from its holster, took a flashlight, and moved silently toward the door, leaving the light off, watching the windows for any sudden motion. All was dark beyond them.

The knocking continued. It didn't seem to be coming

from the door, though. She waited on the inside, pressing her ear against it, the palm of her left hand. No vibration. She took a few deep breaths, blew them out, steeling herself. She had never considered herself a courageous person—more an unimaginative one, putting herself into the occasional dangerous position because she couldn't think of any better way to deal with a given situation. Now she had stepped back into that boat. She could go out the other door and around, or she could go through this door. The knocking seemed to be against this wall, near the corner. Dull, powerful thuds, high up on the wall. It was no animal, unless perhaps a bear standing on its hind legs, and it didn't sound like the staccato rapping of a woodpecker.

She took one final breath and turned on the flashlight, then threw the dead bolt, spun the doorknob, and went outside, Glock and light pointing toward that corner of the house.

Three human heads hung from the eaves, tied to a hook there by their long hair. The heads were male, large and thick-featured and scarred, with bushy mustaches, strong chins, and bad teeth.

They swayed in the powerful wind, bumping into the side of the house at the end of each arc.

The skin on them, Annie realized as she tried to hold the light steady on them (glad she didn't have to shoot, since her hands were suddenly shaking), had been painted blue.

"Jesus Christ," she said. "Who the fuck would—"

Her question went unasked.

One of the heads, facing her, winked an eye and opened his mouth. "Welcome to New Dominion, Annie," it said.

ANNIE sat up in bed, soaking wet. She grabbed the Glock and the flashlight, both still on her nightstand. She switched on the light and scanned the room, fighting back panic. The room was empty, though. Outside, the wind whistled, but there was no insistent rap at the wall.

Just the same, on unsteady legs she got out of bed and

hurried to the front door. It was closed, the deadbolt still latched. She opened the door, and went out, training her light on the eaves near the corner.

No heads, and no hook.

Another fucking dream, then, that's all. It had been a nightmare, probably brought on by Leo Baca's descriptions of Celtic warriors from the day before, mixing up in her head with the research she had done about New Dominion.

She went back inside, locked the door, peed, and went back to bed.

But she didn't sleep for a long time, almost until dawn began to lighten the sky.

23

IN the morning, feeling more wrung out than rested, Annie made the toast that had largely eluded her yesterday, tore into an orange, and poured herself a cup of strong coffee. When she drained that she poured another. More sleep and less caffeine seemed like a good prescription, but she wasn't sure how to accomplish that if her subconscious mind was intent on harassing her every night.

She took her breakfast outside and sat there watching the morning's bustle of activity, feeling a little like Snow White, except that the birds and rabbits and the tiny brown lizard scampering up the side of the house weren't helping her get dressed or clean house, and they sure weren't helping her get Johnny Ortega out of jail.

She was on her own there.

After eating and showering, brushing her teeth, slapping her cheeks a few times, trying to sting herself into full wakefulness, and applying the minimal amount of makeup she had been wearing since the explosion, Annie drove over to Drummond, to the sheriff's substation there. The *house*, they called it, if they were like most other law enforcement people

she had known. There were a couple of departmental Tahoes
parked in front, white with gold striping on them and the
legend HONOR SERVE DEFEND written around the shape of
Hidalgo County on each door. The building itself looked like
something left over from the old West, the front sidewalk
shadowed by a wooden overhang supported by log posts.
Behind that was a wood-sided, single-story structure with a
central door and a barred window on either side of it. She
caught herself looking for the hitching post, which it had
probably had until recently. She saw people on horseback
every day out here, and some of them no doubt rode into
town instead of driving.

Above the sheltering overhang was a sign that simply read
SHERIFF. The same seal as on the vehicles, in the shape of
Hidalgo County, was painted on both front windows in gold.
Annie walked in the front door and found Leo Baca talking
to a woman who sat at a wooden desk facing the door. The
woman wore civilian clothes: tight jeans and a multicolored,
embroidered western shirt and boots. She looked like she
might be one of those people who did ride into town. Maybe
the hitching post was out back.

"Hey, Annie," Leo said. He offered Annie a friendly smile.

"Morning, Leo, how are you?"

"Can't complain. Or I could, but Rosemary here would rat
me out to the boss."

"I'm Rosemary," the woman at the desk said. She had a
computer, a multiline phone, and one of those old-fashioned
stacking in-and-out trays on the desk.

"Annie O'Brien." She shook Rosemary's hand, getting a
sensation of a woman with no big secrets to hide and only
mild sorrows in her life. "I figured you must be."

"Annie used to be a big-city detective," Leo said. "She's
all about the deducing."

"That right?" Rosemary asked. Her eyes, Annie realized,
were purple. Liz Taylor eyes. They were startling to find in
her deeply tanned, country girl's face. Rosemary had an
earthy scent, as if she had spent time in the stables before
coming to work.

"Could Leo tell a fib?"

"Maybe a little one," Rosemary said.

"Yeah, that's what I thought. I guess she's got your number, Deputy Baca."

"Did you just come here looking for me?" Leo asked. "Because you can always dial nine-one-one if you need me in a hurry. Rosemary doesn't mind."

"Actually, I wanted to see the evidence in the Ortega case," Annie said. "I was hoping it's stored here and not Lordsburg or Santa Fe or someplace like that."

"We have an evidence locker here," Leo said. "I'm sure it's here. Can you look it up, Rosemary? Ortega comma Johnny. It was before my time."

"Four years ago, this month," Annie said.

"There you go," Leo said.

Rosemary tapped on the keyboard for a minute, then jotted something on a Post-it and handed it to Leo. "Thanks, Rose," he said. He turned to Annie and gave a little bow, with one hand out like a maitre d'. "Right this way."

He led Annie down a hallway lined with framed photos of former Hidalgo County sheriffs (the current one hung in the front lobby, next to a picture of the current Lieutenant Raines and one of the governor) to a locked door. He unlocked it, opened it, and let her into a space crammed with cardboard boxes and plastic bins, each carefully labeled and arranged on orderly numbered shelves. Tapping the Post-it he carried, he surveyed the shelves until he found the spot he was looking for. "Here you go," he said. There was one big box in the space, with the case number she had seen dozens of times printed on it. Red tape sealed its edges.

"This could take a while, Leo. Do you need to stay with me while I go through it?"

"Let's see . . . you're not an officer of the court, are you?"

"I'm employed by an attorney, but I'm not a member of the bar. I don't have a PI license, and obviously I'm no longer a cop."

He considered for a few moments before answering. Annie didn't blame him—by rights, she should have had an observer from the department watch everything she did in there, and they could have barred her completely. She actually wanted someone watching, so if she did find something amiss, she couldn't be accused of tampering with evidence. "We're pretty casual around here," he said.

"I want to keep everything on the up-and-up," she reminded him. "As far as I'm concerned this is an open death penalty case."

"I understand, Annie. Tell you what. I can set up a table in front, where Rosemary can keep an eye on you. It'll give you plenty of room to work. That do?"

"That'll be fine," Annie said.

"Let's go, then." He took the box, and she followed him back down the hall, past the photos of serious-looking men, most with thick mustaches and glowering stares. Back in the lobby, she made small talk with Rosemary while Leo fetched a folding six-foot table. He set it up against a wall, where Rosemary would have a clear view of anything Annie did, and then rolled in a desk chair from another office. He was right, they were casual. Annie was about three steps from the front door, and if Rosemary left to go to the bathroom or make a copy, she could be gone with the evidence before the other woman got back.

Annie didn't intend to run off, though. She wanted to do this right.

Leo headed out on patrol. Under Rosemary's watchful eye, Annie broke the box's seal, making a note on an accompanying card indicating who she was and when she had done it. Inside were plastic bags, also sealed, containing various items—the clothing worn by Carylyn and Kevin when they were killed and by Johnny when he had allegedly killed them, the jack handle that Carylyn had been beaten with (the knife that slit Kevin's throat had never been found), copies of some of the photos she had already seen.

What was more notable than what was there was what wasn't. Annie didn't see any hair or fiber or other trace evidence, and none had been introduced at trial. The state was claiming a guy found fifty miles away had killed these two kids, but had never presented any definitive physical evidence putting him in direct contact with them. The state claimed that Johnny's tire tracks were found near where Kevin's car had broken down, but only showed photos of those tracks to back up the claim, instead of a cast of them. A partial fingerprint on the tire iron had been identified as Ortega's, and the tire iron, found beside the car, was the same brand as Kevin Munson's jack. But without further trace evidence, an argument could be made that the tire iron could have been planted.

If she had access to a first-rate crime lab, she could have had the clothing analyzed. If they came up clean, or if hairs or fibers or epithelials on them pointed to someone other than Johnny Ortega, that wouldn't be enough by itself, but it would help. Since she doubted that Hidalgo County had such a lab, she left the clothes in their bags and picked up the tire iron, leaving it sealed in its transparent bag.

Annie had brought her files in with her, and now she opened one up and flipped to the photos of the tire iron as it had been introduced at trial. One of the pictures showed a hairline fracture about an inch down from the bend in the steel. Annie pressed the plastic bag against the tire iron in her hands, but couldn't find that crack. She looked at the photos again, looked at the tire iron, back and forth until she felt like the referee at a tennis match.

No crack.

A definite crack in the photo, but no crack here.

How can that be?

Was this actually the tire iron found at the scene? Or was it the one in the pictures? How could one be shown in the courtroom and photographed for the files, but a different one be sealed into the evidence box? And which one really had Ortega's fingerprint on it, if either?

Something was very wrong here. This was the worst sheriff's department she had ever seen, or the worst district attorney's office, or both.

Or Johnny Ortega had been railroaded.

She was leaning toward the latter.

She took out the pictures of the tire tracks. Johnny Ortega drove a '75 Chevy Nova, and the tracks in the photo purported to match his, in terms of tire wear and size. Separate photos showed the tires on Johnny's car. A cast would have been more convincing, but apparently the photos had been good enough for the New Mexico jury.

Annie put the items back in the box. If she could line up a forensics lab, she might want to come back for the clothes. When she was done, she looked at Rosemary. "Can you seal this up again?"

"You're all done?"

"Not that much to see," Annie said.

"Okay."

"Thanks for your help, Rosemary." Annie gathered up her files. "I'm sure I'll see you around."

"You can count on it," Rosemary said.

When she got outside, she noticed that there was still a chill in the air. It would likely stick around a lot longer at this four-thousand-foot-plus elevation than in Phoenix, where the temperatures had already been edging into the eighties when she left. She got into a car that hadn't turned into an oven and drove back to her little country house.

24

SOMETHING had been nagging at Annie since she looked at the tire-track photos at the substation. At home, she took her copies out again. When she looked more closely at the closest shot of the tire tracks, something seemed off. There was a wooden ruler in the picture, for size reference, but it had been set down parallel to the tire track, not across it, and a few inches away. She brought it closer to her eyes, glad it was her hearing that had been damaged and not her vision. As it was, the photo was blurry and didn't show much tread mark detail.

The tire measurement didn't look a whole lot wrong—but it looked wrong.

She checked the pictures of Ortega's car. One of them, a close-up that showed a nick in the tread purportedly identical to a mark in the tire track photo, also showed the sidewall code on his Nova's tires. They were 205/70-14s. Her cell phone had a calculator function, and since it wasn't good for much else here, she used it to divide the 205 by 25.4, converting millimeters to inches. That came out to just over 8.07 inches. That should have been the width of the tire tracks found beside Kevin's car.

Which was something else that should have come out at trial, had Johnny Ortega been assigned a decent public defender instead of, she was increasingly left to assume, a comatose one.

Annie laid a sheet of blank white paper against the photograph and marked off the inches, as indicated by the ruler. Then she moved her markings right onto the tire track.

It was almost ten and a half inches wide.

The track in the photo had not been made by Johnny Ortega's Nova.

She turned next to the picture showing the position of Kevin Munson's car in relation to the tire tracks. They were almost directly parallel, a few feet apart. It seemed very unlikely that Kevin would have pulled off the road just there, then moved the car, then gone back—especially with a flat. He would have pulled off and stopped until the tire was changed. Which Kevin didn't live long enough to do.

It was possible that he pulled off next to existing tire tracks in the soft dirt of the shoulder. But that wasn't what the DA claimed.

Who else, she wondered, could have made those tracks? They were much wider than a passenger car like Ortega's would have made.

A horrifying thought dawned on her.

She didn't have access to all the fancy databases she'd used when she was a cop, but sometimes Google worked just as well. She checked the standard tire size of a 2003 Chevy Tahoe. She wasn't sure what model year the Hidalgo County Sheriff's Office's Tahoes were, but the ones she had seen over the last few days were several years old, so she picked 2003 at random.

It turned out four-wheel-drive Tahoes from that year had been issued with various standard equipment tires, but the most common were 265/70-16s. It figured that a rural sheriff's office, patrolling an area with more miles of dirt road than paved, would want tires on the large side. Annie discounted the 245, which was the smallest original measurement, and divided 265.

Just under ten and a half inches.

She laughed out loud. One of the sheriff's numbskulls had driven right over the crime scene, then moved the vehicle out of the way and claimed the tire tracks were made by a suspect vehicle. Rather than giving it a moment's thought, Ortega's public defender had simply accepted it.

Until now, Annie had been acting on impulses and hunches. Now she had some solid evidence that the state's case had been rigged from the start. Best case, the sheriff's investigators had been hopelessly incompetent. Worst case, someone had targeted an innocent man and managed to get him sentenced to death.

Well, that's why Morgan hired me, right? she thought. *I guess it's time to earn my pay.*

25

ANNIE headed back to the prison. So far that was her least favorite place in Hidalgo County, and one of the few she'd had occasion to visit twice. There had to be some sort of universal lesson in that, but she was in no mood to look for it.

After the standard humiliating check-in procedure, she was taken to the same interview room she had used before. Johnny Ortega was brought in, wearing his usual fetching orange jumpsuit and chains. When he was settled and the guard had left them alone, she fixed him with her best interrogator's stare. He returned it with his best blank expression. "Johnny," she said, "do you remember me?"

"You want to get me out of here," he said. His voice gave away nothing about how he felt about that, or about Annie. More significantly, neither did anything else about him, even when she touched his hand across the table.

"That's right. Because the more I look into it, the more I think you were set up. You didn't do it, did you?"

"That's what I been saying."

"Well, now someone believes you. But I'm going to need your help. Who would try to railroad you into prison?"

Ortega shrugged.

"You have no idea? No one who hated you enough to do this to you?"

"Plenty of people don't like me," he said. "But no one around here."

"Did you know people in Hidalgo County before all this?"

Another shrug. "Don't think so."

"Think hard, Johnny. Have you ever spent time here?"

"Just passing through. Like last time. On the Ten."

Interstate 10, he meant, where he had been picked up. "What about the south end of the county? Near the border?"

"Never been there."

"You've never been to Drummond? Or Cloverdale, or Antelope Wells?"

"Nope. Just on the Ten. Driving through to L.A. or back east."

There was much about this case that had never made sense to Annie, but this was probably the thing that made the least sense. Had he been chosen entirely at random for this frame job, if that's what it was? Just a guy in the wrong place at the wrong time, a guy who looked scary enough that a jury would happily convict him of anything in order to get him off the streets?

Now that she believed he was probably innocent—at least of this particular crime—she wondered how he was getting along in prison. Prison was a hellish place for anyone, and the compromises he must have made to survive, the concessions to the guards, to those more physically powerful than him, or more prone to sudden violence, must have been terrible. Annie pictured him sitting down to lunch at the Hispanic table, or, this being the southwestern corner of New Mexico, more likely the Hispanic section, separated by invisible racial walls from the blacks and the American Indians and the small handful of whites. She doubted that there were any rich white people in this facility, and probably not many from the middle class. Prison offered a crash course on race and class, on who society valued and who they were willing to lock away like unwanted dogs in the pound.

According to a brochure Morgan had given her when she signed on, more of the per capita American population slept behind bars every night than in any other country, however oppressive those other countries were believed to be. When she had been a cop, she was focused on filling those cots. Now that she was off the job, sitting in the middle of a prison, surrounded by inmates and guards (who, if she had run into them on the street and out of uniform, she wouldn't have been able to tell apart), her point of view was shifting. *Is it because of my increased empathy?* she wondered. *Or did my badge function as some sort of moral blinders, keeping me from seeing what these high fences really were?*

Annie blinked, cleared her throat, remembering what she was doing here. "So you were passing through. You stopped for the night, checked into a motel, had dinner at a restaurant."

"That's right. First I took a nap. I remember that. Then I went for dinner."

"And then the sheriffs came and arrested you."

"I wasn't even finished my fucking peach cobbler."

"I'll buy you all the peach cobbler you want once we get you out of here."

Ortega cracked a smile, showing broken teeth and gold. "I eat a lot of cobbler."

"I bet you do," she said. "The thing is, I can't get you out of here if we can't figure out why you're in here."

"I been puzzling on that four years now and I still don't know shit, ma'am."

"Well, I guess I'm catching up to you, because that's about where I am too." She sat in silence for most of a minute, just looking at him as if she could read the story of his life in the ink on his body. But his tattoos all ran together, losing their meaning until they looked less like individual designs and more like camouflage, like a pattern of light and shadow thrown by sunlight through tightly interlaced branches.

Which reminded her of something else she wanted to ask him. "Johnny, have you ever heard of a town called New Dominion?"

He didn't even think about it. "No. Should I?"

"You're absolutely sure?"

He rubbed the top of his head, his palm sounding like sandpaper against his closely cropped hair. "I been to New York once. And we're in New Mexico, right?"

"Right. New Dominion, Johnny. Think."

"Sorry, ma'am. It don't mean nothing to me."

"That's all right, Johnny. I just had to ask." Her empathy, diminished as it was from its peak, didn't necessarily act as a lie detector, but between that and her years on the job, she thought she knew when someone was being straight with her. If New Dominion rang any bells for him, he was hiding it well. She still wasn't entirely sure there was a connection between the old town and the site of Kevin Munson's murder, but she wasn't convinced there wasn't.

She thanked him for his time—not that he had any shortage of that—and made her exit.

26

LEO called shortly after Annie got home—there was no answering machine or even voice mail on the phone, so for all she knew he could have been calling for hours—ostensibly to ask if she had found whatever she needed in the evidence box. It took a couple of minutes for him to get around to his real reason for calling, but when he did, she agreed to have dinner with him that night at the Apache Trail steak house, a couple of miles from Drummond. She still wasn't sure that dating was a good idea, but she needed something to shove the thought of Johnny Ortega sitting in a prison cell out of her mind.

Since she wasn't ready to have visitors, they agreed to meet at the restaurant at 6:30. Annie got there first and leaned against her car in the gravel lot, arms crossed under her breasts, watching a family of quail working their way across the road. They reminded her of kindergarten students lining up for class—a couple of adults in front, then an unbroken string of smaller ones scooting along behind them, dark plumes bobbing in front of their foreheads like cartoon characters with question marks floating above them. For a mercifully brief period in her early twenties—embarrassing in retrospect—Annie had worn her hair in a similar fashion, banded on top and curling forward. When a car came, the quail scattered, but once it was gone they immediately re-formed the line and kept it together until they had all van-ished underneath a mass of tumbleweeds stacked up against a fence on the far side. The lowering sun caressed the western hills, the sky around it a washed-out yellow, but to the east, it had turned an almost metallic cerulean blue.

Leo pulled up in a red Dodge pickup truck just as the quail disappeared. He'd changed into civilian clothes, a yel-low pearl-buttoned western shirt with smile pockets, snug Wranglers, and square-toed western boots. He had a flat stomach, lean hips, and long legs, and he could have been the guy for whom such clothes had been designed. Annie had changed too, but stayed casual, wearing jeans and a charcoal V-neck T-shirt with a royal blue silk shirt over it, left unbut-toned and untucked. He grinned as he looked at her, and she thought she had done something right.

"Howdy, ma'am," he said with an accentuated cowboy drawl. He smelled like he had come straight from the shower, and his cheeks were shaved smooth. "Been waitin' long?"

"Just a few minutes," she said. "Enjoying the sunset."

"They do 'em up right around here."

The building was a redbrick square with a flat roof and a wooden door, its windows covered by dark wooden shutters. It looked like it had been built to withstand Apache raids and, judging by the age of the bricks, could well have been. But the aromas wafting out had started her mouth watering as soon as she drove up.

"I hope this is okay," Leo said, catching her inspecting the place. "I should have asked if you're a vegetarian or any-thing."

"If it moos, oinks, clucks, or baas, I probably eat it," she said. "This smells amazing."

"They know how to grill a steak. They cook everything over open flame, using mesquite logs. It's all from around here too—they buy grass-fed meat from local ranchers, and even the mesquite's cut locally. I guess the beer comes from someplace else, but that's about it."

"If we stand out here much longer," she said, "I'm going to eat the walls."

Leo laughed and opened the front door. He held it for Annie and she stepped into a dark, wood smoke–scented little piece of heaven that had broken off and fallen to earth. One side of the place was a saloon; glancing in there, Annie saw neon beer signs, pennants, and a crowd of people gathered around the bar, talking and laughing loud enough to be heard over the country music coming from a jukebox. A pool table stood in one corner with no one using it.

A curvy waitress named Devon greeted Leo with a friendly hug and told them to sit anywhere. Leo picked a booth against the wall from which he could see the front door and she could watch the cooks working over a flaming iron barbecue pit that wouldn't have looked out of place on a cattle drive. The table and bench seats were knotty pine, polished to a shine and varnished, and the décor was strictly western, John Deere and Remington rifle posters on the walls, COWBOYS and COWGIRLS painted on the restroom doors.

After they ordered their steaks and sides, they engaged in the casual, getting-to-know-you conversation common to all first-daters. He told her about his large family back in Albuquerque, and she gave him the edited version of her life, including the explosion and temporary deafness but leaving out the apparently supernatural ability that had accompanied it. She almost told him about the nightmares that had haunted her since coming here, too, but held them back, as if they, along with her empath abilities, were some sort of weakness to which she didn't want to admit.

The steaks came, every bit as delicious as promised. "Maybe there really is something to this grass-fed thing," Annie said between mouthfuls.

"Oh, absolutely," he said. "I can't even eat feedlot beef anymore. Makes my stomach hurt just to think about it."

She waved him off. "Don't tell me. I hate hearing about

stuff like that. I'm sure it's terrible, but what if I move back to the city and can't find the grass-fed stuff in my local Albertsons?"

"Then shop someplace else. You know what's funny? Don't get me wrong, I appreciate having another city person here to talk to. The folks around here are about as nice as anybody could be. And everybody sees the same TV shows, has access to the same magazines, city or country, but there's still kind of a gap between rural and urban people that's hard to bridge. I mean, Albuquerque is no Phoenix, thank God, but even so, I didn't grow up the way people here did, with 4-H and raising animals and knowing how to drive a tractor. Anyway, what I'm trying to say is that we city people think of ourselves as so sophisticated and advanced, but out here they've known the benefits of eating grass-fed meat and fresh local vegetables forever, and we're still trying to overcome our fast food and frozen dinner habits."

"Wait," Annie said. "There's something wrong with Phoenix?"

He laughed, and she joined in. "Hey, I grew up there," she said when she could speak again. "It's not the city it used to be. Or it's ten times the city it used to be. I still love it, but I'm liking the rural life too."

Almost in spite of herself, she was having a good time. It still disturbed her that she couldn't honestly distinguish the way she felt about Leo from the way he felt about her, but she was willing to let that slide for the moment and simply enjoy the meal and the company. She hadn't been particularly prone to strong emotions for a long time—she thought she had walled that side of herself off after her mother's death, and then sealed the wall in that horrible year when her engagement fell apart and her father died. What she didn't know now was whether she was really starting to feel again, or if it was just her hyper-empathy sensing feelings directed at her.

The attraction seemed real, and it took her by surprise. Leo Baca was a genuinely nice guy. But Annie had a long history of falling for bad boys, the casual, fun-loving types she believed were like her, even though she knew that from the moment they got together they had joined a race to see who would back away first. Although she was just getting to know Leo, she could already tell he wasn't that kind of man.

Through the meal, she tried not to lose sight of her real goal. As soon as she saw a way into it, she broached the topic of business. "So what do you really know about the murders of Carylyn Phelps and Kevin Munson?" she asked.

"Really?" he asked. He looked a little surprised that she would bring it up over a social dinner, which was a testament to the fact that he didn't know her that well yet either. Annie had never let the niceties of social protocol interfere with an investigation, and she didn't intend to start now. "Not much at all. I know they were local kids, they got killed, and Johnny Ortega took the fall."

"Do you think he did it?"

"He was arrested, tried, and convicted. To me that makes him guilty."

"But you know innocent people go to prison too."

"Once in a while, sure. I think it's most likely pretty rare. I think most criminals are a special breed of person with some sort of moral deficiency, and whether they get busted for the crimes they do or for ones they didn't do, the important thing is that they go away."

"You think putting them in prison does any good? With a recidivism rate of sixty or seventy percent?"

"To me, that just confirms that they should have been in the system in the first place. Why let them out if they'll just do more crimes on the outside?"

She could have quoted statistics from Morgan's literature, but she was still surprised that the man she had grown up knowing as a cop and a no-nonsense attorney had turned into some kind of quasi-liberal do-gooder, and she didn't want to sound the same. Anyway, arguing with Leo would only detract from her real agenda. "Well, I'm not so sure, but I have to find out. I wouldn't ask you to do anything wrong, Leo, but I wonder if you could have a look at your internal files on it. It seems like a weak case, but maybe there's something in there that I haven't seen, something convincing."

"I don't know what you've already seen," he pointed out.

"You tell me what's there and I'll tell you if I have it or not."

"I don't know, Annie. That feels like working for the enemy."

"I'm not the enemy, Leo. I'm just trying to close a case that maybe wasn't closed right the first time. That's what cop work is, right? Closing cases?"

He poked with a fork at the remains of his meal. "I guess so. Becoming a cop was a lifetime dream for me. I didn't have any in the family, but I always saw the uniform and badge as representing some sort of ideal. Truth, justice, and the American way, right? I didn't just want to put bad guys away, I wanted to help people, people in trouble. Then I got into it and found a lot of people more concerned with making stats and stroking their own egos. It was a little disillusioning, I guess."

Life with her father had taught her at an early age that police work sometimes had very little in common with justice. She decided to leave that unsaid, though. She'd heard a lot of cops say the same sorts of things that Leo had just said, and in most cases they didn't mean it—they were more like her dad, but they thought it sounded better—especially to a woman, she supposed—to claim the high moral ground. She brushed her fingers against Leo's hand, however, and her diminished empathy was still strong enough to let her know that he meant what he said. A rare individual, then. She worried that police work would burn him out young, but maybe that was less likely to happen in a rural setting than an urban one. "People in prison can also be in trouble, Leo. Especially if they're innocent. What kind of trouble is worse than that?"

"Okay, I surrender," he said. "I'll have a look, okay? What I can't do is promise to show you anything I find. That'll be my call. You're an outsider and if I see something that shouldn't be shared out of the house, I'll hold it back."

"Deal," she said, knowing it was the best one she would get.

"Okay," Leo said. "You ready to get out of here?"

"I am ready." She didn't know if rural dates were different from city ones, or if the fact that he was a transplanted urbanite would dictate what he expected after dinner. But when they both stood up, he put his hand firmly against her back, between the shoulder blades, and she felt a rush of heat that was both unexpected and somehow very welcome.

They left the restaurant hand in hand.

27

HE kissed her the first time outside the restaurant, under the moon, with her back mashed up against the side of his truck and his arms looped around her back, his hands pressing her into him. His lips were soft but after the first gentle kiss, he crushed them hard against hers, as if that first touch kicked off a testosterone surge that reminded him that he was male, and a cop, and so had to take an aggressive posture, leaning into her. She had been with enough cops that it was a familiar syndrome, but not an unwelcome one. He moved one hand up, his big palm cupping the back of her neck to control the position of her head, and the other down to the bottom of her waist, just above her ass. Annie's breath caught and she dug her fingertips into his muscular back and pushed her tongue between his teeth. He met it with his own, then pulled back. When he spoke, his voice had a raw huskiness to it.

"We can't stay here," he said. "It'd be . . . unseemly."

Annie laughed. "What a great word."

"I mean, a sheriff's deputy caught with his pants down in a public parking lot. Bad for the departmental image."

"Pants down?" she said. "You're awfully confident."

"I know what I want," he said. "And believe me, they don't build these jeans with enough space in them for the way I'm feeling, so whether you're up for it or not, they can't stay on much longer."

"God, you're romantic," she said. "I bet you get a lot of girls with that sweet talk."

"I don't want a lot of girls. At the moment there's only one who interests me at all."

"Devon?"

He blinked, surprised. "Oh. Too late for that. She was the first local lady I got together with after I moved here. She's sweet, but she's not really for me."

"You're a player, is that what you're saying?" She was just teasing him, but an instant's anger flashed behind his eyes. It was frightening and exciting at the same time. Maybe he wasn't an entirely nice guy after all. She wanted him mostly nice, but now it looked as if there might be an edge to him that made her heart skip.

"Not a player. Just a single man looking for a bright spot in a troubled world."

She leaned into him, kissed his cheek, nuzzled his neck, and spoke with her lips against his flesh, tasting salt and sweat. "I'm a single woman, and my world is every bit as troubled. And my jeans are feeling kind of restricting too. Where can we go?"

"My place isn't too far," Leo said.

"Which is why you suggested this restaurant?"

"That, and it's the only decent dinner place for thirty miles."

"Good point. I'll follow you."

"You can ride with me."

"I'll follow you," she repeated. She hated being stuck at someone else's house without her own wheels.

She hurried to her Taurus, and by the time she got it started his truck was already waiting at the parking lot exit, its left blinker flashing. She was glad for the few minutes alone, to try to figure out how much of the heat pulsing through her body was her own and how much his.

Separated from him, she still felt it—the urgency lessening slightly but not going away. She touched herself through her jeans, and a powerful shiver of anticipation ran through her body.

THE first time she had been naked with a man, Annie thought she had encountered a riddle made flesh: What's hard and soft at the same time? Since then there had been many men, but she still found something fascinating, almost magical, about an erection.

Especially when, as with Leo Baca's, it filled her up, moved into and out of her with a steady rhythm. For all the sex she'd had, she had never felt anything like this. Her empathy kicked into high gear again as soon as he was inside her, so she felt not only her own sensations but his, the way he responded to her touch, to her liquid heat. She felt his lips and tongue on her nipples and she tasted nipples on her tongue, sensed them hardening beneath teeth and lips. She felt him thrusting into her moist center and she felt herself surrounding a shaft she didn't have. She was hands and mouths and genitalia, flesh touching flesh, slapping together, sweaty and slick, and the sensations built and built until she was almost overwhelmed, and then he came and she did too, twice, once as her and once as him, muscles contracting around him, around herself, waves of pleasure spreading throughout her body as if she was a pond and he a stone thrown into her.

When they were done she was more spent than she had ever been, used up, wrung out. She dozed in Leo's arms for twenty minutes. Then, awakened by her infallible internal alarm, she woke up, kissed Leo good-bye, silenced his objections, and drove home through the night.

28

THE LAPD's task force hadn't yet figured out how the killer was getting into the homes of the women he murdered. That was because they weren't the Impressionist, with his practiced eye and deep sympathy for those who had the courage and conviction to actually carry out acts that so many others dreamed about, fantasized about, but could never do. The cops on the task force were no doubt focused on trying to find some link between the women, besides the obvious one of their physical type. Did they go to the same gym? Drink at the same bar? Rent videos from the same shop? Had they ever met? Did they have any acquaintances in common? All those questions were standard ones and the police had to ask them. But they wouldn't lead in the right direction, not this time.

Because there were no real, solid connections beyond physical appearance. They had never crossed paths, or if they had, it hadn't made any difference to their lives. He saw them anywhere—at the mall, the supermarket, the movies, the ATM. It didn't matter. He followed them home and learned about them, just as the Impressionist had. But that first en-

counter? That was random, and randomness was hard for
police detectives to cope with. This didn't mean there
weren't similarities between them, just that those similarities
had nothing to do with how they were initially spotted.

For the Impressionist, it had only been a matter of driving
past the murdered women's houses and thinking about their
lives. They were all working women, single, homeowners.
One had kids, the other three didn't. They had all lived in
detached, single-family homes in lower-middle-class suburban neighborhoods. None of them came remotely near being
wealthy.

Driving down their streets, the Impressionist noted the
houses in foreclosure. These were often boarded up, vacant,
with FOR SALE signs littering the yards. One couldn't live on
such a street without a little trepidation about what the future
might bring. A job change, a layoff, a devastating illness, and
your house could be next. All these years after the birth of
the women's movement, women still earned seventy-five
cents to every dollar men did, so single women living alone
or with kids had to be even more anxious about their futures
than families with more than one person working.

He had spotted Lauren Heller at a coffee shop near her
office and noticed that she matched the killer's physical standard. Following her, he had learned that she fit the other
criteria. She lived alone on a block with two foreclosed properties on it. A little digging afterward let him know that she
was a homeowner, not a renter. He knew she drove home
from work north to south, turning off Olympic onto her own
street and following it five blocks to her house, then reversed
that in the mornings—a route that took her past four additional foreclosures. The whole thing had already kept him
away from home for more than a week; he had to call
Momma a couple of times a day, and check in with the hired
caregiver between those calls. He had never kept any souve-
nirs at home, so he didn't worry about anything incriminating
being found.

Momma's fingers were stiff and rubbery in his pocket,
and they reminded him of home.

When he had learned as much about her as he needed to know, he rented a gold sedan, had magnetic signs printed up that identified him as Steven Mertz, a Realtor with Majestic Realty, and had cards printed with the same information on it, along with a fake phone number and address. He stole a pair of license plates and put them onto the sedan. He dug two FOR SALE signs out of lawns in a different suburban neighborhood, far across town, and on Friday evening he put them in the back of the sedan, posts sticking out of his trunk, and parked his car in front of Lauren Heller's house. It was six fifteen. She was always home from work by five thirty, and when she went out drinking she usually didn't leave until after seven. She'd be there, probably having dinner alone in front of the TV. He had seen her several times through the window, sitting at her kitchen table, a small TV on the counter showing *Friends* reruns.

He rang her doorbell. She came to the door still clutching a paper napkin, wiping her mouth. "Yes?" she said.

He looked chagrined. "Oh, man, I'm sorry. I came while you're having dinner. I'm so sorry." He took a half step backward, away from the door. "I'll just come back another time, sorry."

Lauren looked at him, looked at his boring Realtor's car with the sign on the door and the trunk full of lumber, looked at him again. He offered an apologetic smile, spreading his hands and hunching his shoulders. "It's okay," she said, "I was just finishing up. What can I do for you?"

The Impressionist tried hard to blush. He cast his gaze down at the sidewalk, then swung it up to meet hers. Successful Realtors couldn't be shy people. "I was . . ." he began. He stopped himself, leaned in a little closer to her. "One of your neighbors is in foreclosure. It's not looking good, and I was just there checking out the house, for the bank. It'll be going on the market in a couple of weeks. Then I noticed your house, which is just . . . it's charming. Really nice. So I thought I'd drop by and see if you think you're planning to be putting it on the market anytime soon."

"No," Lauren said. "I mean, I hadn't planned to."

"Of course not," he said. He scratched the top of his head. "Can't blame a guy for trying, right? All these foreclosures— it's a tragedy is what it is, an American tragedy. Maybe the worst part is that tragedy for some people is opportunity for others."

"That's true," she said. She squeezed the napkin into a tight ball. "What do you mean, opportunity?"

He lowered his voice again. Now they were coconspirators. "Well, some people are going to get great deals on those foreclosed properties. The housing slump won't last forever, and when prices take off again they'll clean up. But here's the thing—each foreclosure on the block lowers everybody else's property values, in the short term. So when your neighbor that I mentioned, and a couple of others I happen to know are in some trouble with their lenders, are foreclosed on, then even if you did want to sell this lovely home, you'd be in a hole you couldn't dig out of. That's why I stopped by— to suggest that if you were going to want to sell anytime in, say, the next four or five years, that you should really consider doing it right away, before those other homes go on the block. Real estate used to be worth something, but right now you'd be better off putting your money into long-term CDs than counting on this property to appreciate. You have a window, but it's not more than a couple of months long, and after that you're stuck here for at least five years."

He started to step away again. "But you're probably fine here, so I'm sorry to have disturbed you."

"No," Lauren said. She almost reached out for him—he saw her stop her arm. "I mean, do you really think my house is worth much now?"

"This place?" She kept the yard neat—or the gardening service she hired did—but it needed a coat of paint and some basic maintenance. "I've only seen it from the street, but it definitely impressed me. It's loaded with curb appeal. If the back and the interior match, or even come close, then I'd say it's one of the best properties on the block. It's something that can still bring a decent price—for another few months, anyway. After that, all bets are off."

She considered for a couple of seconds, but it was for show—her mind was already made up. "Would you like to come in for a minute, take a look around? I mean, if you're not too busy. Like I said, I hadn't been planning to sell. But five years is a long time to hang on to it if something else happens in my life."

"At least five years," he said. "Could be more."

"Would you mind?"

He looked at his watch. "I do have an appointment at seven."

"I won't keep you," she said. "I'd just like to know what you think I could get for the place."

He looked at his car, as if he wanted nothing more than to drive away. The more he made her think he didn't want to go in, the harder she worked to invite him. "I guess I could. For a few minutes."

"I was just going to make some tea," she said, stepping away from the door so he could get in. "If you'd like some."

"That's not necessary, but thank you." He went into her house, turned in a circle, pretending to admire it. Her décor was as pedestrian as everything else about her. "Nice," he said. "Did you hire a decorator?"

"No," she said proudly. "I guess I just have an eye for things."

Near the end of the circle, he grabbed the doorknob, closing the door slowly, inspecting it for squeaky hinges or other structural issues. "Seems solid," he said. "And a deadbolt, good for you." He shut it, threw the deadbolt, opened it again, and repeated it a few times. When he finished, it was locked.

"It's . . . you've locked it," Lauren said.

"I know."

HE knew the instant she died.

He wasn't sure precisely how the original got into the women's houses, although he was pretty sure his method wasn't far off. But he had read the medical examiner's reports, so he knew precisely what had been done to them after that, and he followed that to the letter.

He duplicated the original's method: dozens of stabs and slices, no single wound severe enough to kill. He watched the delicious agony registering on Lauren's face throughout the four hours he spent with her. She was naked the entire time, bound with thin nylon rope and gagged, lying on her kitchen floor. Twice, she passed out and he had to bring her around with the smelling salts he carried. As he cut, he touched her, explored her body, latex gloves protecting his hands. The original killer no doubt did more, but Lauren Heller wasn't the Impressionist's fetish object, and he only did enough to make investigators believe the same person was responsible for her murder. He was sure they would, because he mimicked the wounds so carefully, matching the ones he'd seen in file photos.

That was what he did. That's why he was the Impressionist, if only to himself.

But the moment of her death—that was *his* moment, his own personal goal. That was where he went to school.

That moment was of special import in this case, because he thought it would be his last lesson before his ultimate transformation. All of this had been in the service of one goal—learning what he could about death so that when he reached the stage at which death would be his to control, to give and take at will, it would no longer be a mystery to him.

One second, Lauren's eyes were wide and bright with fear, red-rimmed and bloodshot from crying and trying to scream around her gag. The next, her eyelids fluttered as her body was wracked by a heaving paroxysm. Her hands and feet batted the floor, like a dreaming dog trying to run. An instant later, she was still, eyes open and staring but somehow vacant, that spark of life having fled at last.

After it was done he washed his gloves off in the kitchen sink. His clothes were covered in her blood, and he left tacky footprints with every step. He roamed around her small, quiet house with its furnishings from IKEA and Target. She bought photographs already in frames, rather than framing anything that had special meaning to her. It was only in her bedroom that he got a taste of the contradictory urges that drove her. Inside her walk-in closet she kept a collection of toys and accessories worthy of a porn producer's props department—vibrators of various descriptions, strap-ons, leather bustiers and miniskirts, clamps, cuffs, rope, a ball gag—if he had known she had all this, he wouldn't have bothered improvising with his own ropes, rags, and duct tape.

But on the dresser facing her bed, she kept candles devoted to various saints, and on the wall behind it hung a crucifix carved from white stone. He stopped and looked at it. It really was nicely sculpted, making Christ's agonies on the cross real and immediate. Particular attention had been paid to a wound in His side, from a Roman soldier's sword. The legend was that water had run from that wound, along with the expected blood, and the sculptor had made an effort to differentiate those fluids by slightly altering the textures.

Ordinarily he would have checked back in, after a year or so had passed, to see if she had anyone who would be selling off her things. He made a point of not buying earlier than that, because he didn't want to arouse any suspicions. He would definitely like to own that crucifix one of these days. It might have had special meaning to her, which was important—but to him, it was far more than that; it was an omen for this specific moment, telling him he was on the right path.

The path to a new self. New, and better than most people could ever conceive of. And because of that transformation, he didn't expect to be coming back here, ever.

He had seen the last of Lauren Heller and her mundane possessions. She would be beneath his attention in the glorious days to come.

29

MARTIN Raines would have been the first to admit that he was not a handsome man. He had narrow, pinched features, a face that was all chin and forehead, skin so thin that red veins showed everywhere. His eyes were tiny slits that hid eyeballs so pale and gray they disconcerted people. His hair was thin, and he wore it slicked back off his forehead. He was an important man, though, from a powerful local family, so he had married above his station, physically speaking, and the good Lord be thanked, his kids had inherited some of his wife's looks instead of just his.

Right at the moment, though, you could hardly tell. Gary ran full out, his jaw hanging slack, tongue tucked at the corner of his lips. His face was flushed with effort, his eyes squinting, maybe even tearing up a little in the wind that had picked up overnight, gusting out of the east. He looked just as homely as his father, and that was no blessing.

The two of them were hot in pursuit, and they couldn't slow down just because exertion brought out an unfortunate family resemblance. Martin tore his gaze away from the face of the son he loved more than any other man on Earth and returned it to the ground, where at least a dozen people's feet had left a trail a Cub Scout could have followed.

"Illegals, you think?" Gary had said when they first came across the tracks. They were less than a mile from the Mexican border, and the back trail would have led directly to it, and across, he was certain.

"I'd say so," Martin said. His son may have been much better-looking than he was, at most times, but had maybe suffered a bit in the smarts department to balance things out.

"Bunch of 'em."

Martin had already started counting the different shoe prints, different sizes, different gaits. "Eleven, twelve, in there."

"How long?"

"An hour, tops. Probably less." The wind was already blowing, and would have started breaking the prints down if they were any older.

"Sweet," Gary said. "We only need one."

"We only need one," Martin agreed. "Let's go."

They had been following the tracks for the better part of an hour, starting in that gray period before sunup. The sun was above the hills now, and running was becoming a sweatier business. But the people making the tracks were walking fast, not running, and Martin and Gary were gaining on them. He thought about trying the nail trick again, but remembering the result last time he had done that, decided against it. They'd catch this group, soon enough. Then they'd pick the one who best suited their needs and either let the rest go, or kill them on the spot.

Once they had theirs, he didn't much care one way or the other about the rest of them.

The more distance the illegals put between themselves and Mexico, the sloppier they became. A trail of candy and chip wrappers, plastic Tampico bottles they had used to carry water, and dirty diapers let Martin and Gary know they were still on the right path. Finally, a little after ten a.m., they heard voices speaking Spanish, and the squalling of the baby who had been filling those diapers, coming from the other side of a low, rock-strewn ridge.

"We got 'em!" Gary said.

"I believe we do," Martin said. He tugged his Colt from its holster. He liked the feel of its crosshatched grip against his palm. "I do believe we do."

As they started up the incline, they heard the growl of a motor, the rasp of rubber on rough road. "Truck!" Gary said. "Someone's pickin' 'em up!"

"Hurry!" Martin shouted. He broke into a run again. Gary followed close behind.

When they cleared the hilltop, Martin looked down the far slope. The illegals were scattering below, crouching low, trying to stay hidden behind thorny bunches of mesquite branches just beginning to get their leaves. A white truck with a familiar green stripe stood with doors open, and two men in olive drab uniforms shouted commands in Spanish.

"Shit!" Gary said. "Border Patrol!"

"That's right." Martin yanked on Gary's arm, pulling him to the ground. "Stay down. If they miss any of them, that's who we go after."

Gary settled on his stomach, watching the border ballet taking place on much-trodden dirt paths beneath them. "You think they saw us?"

"No. They weren't looking up here."

He had his eye on one of the Mexicans, a man wearing a pale blue denim shirt, jeans, and yellow boots. The guy was young, still in his teens, maybe, or early twenties, and wiry. He was working his way far to the east of the rest of the group, some of whom had already surrendered. If anyone got away, it would be that guy, and from his vantage point on the ridge Martin could track his movements better than the Border Patrol agents at ground level could.

It wasn't often that he hoped to see someone elude BP, but in this case, he was rooting for the little guy. *Go, buddy, go, go!* he thought. *Make a break for it!*

But the woman carrying the screaming baby gave up, and

when she did, the guy turned around and came in, hands held high. The kid's dad, Martin guessed. "Damn you," Martin muttered. "Why couldn't you have stayed out there?"

They were all loaded into the back of the Border Patrol truck, probably no more crowded than they would have been had they reached the ride that was probably waiting for them on a side road somewhere. The truck drove away, and Martin stood, scouring the land to make sure no one had escaped capture. But the ground was empty, nothing moving but the birds and the mesquite branches swirling in the breeze.

Hours wasted, another day half gone, and they were still empty-handed.

"Let's go on in," he said. "And hope we catch a speeder on the way."

30

JOCELYN Moreno, district attorney for southwestern New Mexico, was a short, stout woman with an unexpectedly ready grin, a throaty laugh, and a sense of humor expressed in subtle ways. Her office was all business except for a credenza covered in plastic wind-up toys—chattering teeth, walking cartoon characters, bugs, and other beings, including a Godzilla that shot sparks from its mouth when she demonstrated it to Annie.

The drive to and from Lordsburg was beginning to feel like a daily commute. Annie took a few cookies and a steel thermos of ice water with her, turned the tunes up loud and broke the speed limit on the highway, keeping an eye out for law enforcement all the way. Fortunately, although Jocelyn Moreno's territory covered Luna, Grant, and Hidalgo counties, on this Monday she was in the office on De Moss Street in Lordsburg, so Annie was saved having to drive another hour or so out of her way.

She had spent the weekend putting together what little she knew for sure, organizing it all into a cohesive—and, she hoped, convincing—narrative for the district attorney's benefit. There had been some downtime, too, in the evenings, mostly spent with Leo Baca after his duty shift. Fortunately, the nightmares had abated—the truly terrifying ones, anyway. There were still bad dreams, anxiety dreams, from which Annie awoke tense and sweaty, but they weren't like those of her first couple of nights.

On short notice, DA Moreno had carved out twenty minutes by giving up some of her lunch hour. She had Mexican food from Rico's brought into her office and ate in front of Annie, offering her tastes of everything while Annie pitched her case. Annie picked up a sense of impatience from her, a feeling that her attention was scattered in a dozen directions at once, and knew she didn't have much of a window in which to make her pitch.

Annie started with the supposed murder weapon, the tire iron with the magically self-healing crack. From there she went into the lack of proper investigation of the clothing Johnny and the two teens had been wearing. She ended with the tire measurement data she had turned up. "The tire tread that was referenced in court was not from Johnny Ortega's car," she said. "It's impossible to prove at this point, because the tires have probably long since been disposed of, but based on the tread size that track was probably made by one of the sheriff's department's own vehicles."

"Sure you don't want any chips?" Jocelyn asked. "I'm not going to be able to finish them."

"Thanks," Annie said. "I'm fine."

"Ms. O'Brien, you've definitely cast some doubt on the prosecution's case here."

"That's the idea," Annie said.

"However, the prosecutor who tried this case retired eighteen months ago. And we're not in front of a jury now. Reasonable doubt isn't good enough. If you want to overturn a conviction, you're going to have to come up with a lead pipe cinch."

"But—it's been four years. And the investigation was so sloppy—"

"Granted."

"It's just hard to find definitive proof at this late date."

Jocelyn scooped some guacamole off her plate with a chip, tucked it into her mouth, and dabbed at her lips with a napkin. "Nevertheless, if you want Mr. Ortega out of prison, I need clear and convincing evidence. You understand the bar that sets?" She fixed Annie with a steady gaze. From the cock of her head and the set of her jaw, Annie knew that she wasn't willing to budge.

"I understand," Annie said. It had been a long shot, but one she'd had to play, since there wasn't a whole lot to work with. She thanked Jocelyn for her time and left the office. As soon as she got out into the open air, she had a sudden, powerful craving for Mexican food.

On the way back home, before leaving cell phone range, she called Morgan to tell him about the meeting.

"Sorry it didn't go better," Morgan said after she had described it. "She's right on the law, of course. But it's not unreasonable to hope for a little more flexibility."

"Any less flexible and she'd snap right in half," Annie said.

"Here's an idea," Morgan said. "If you can get the sheriff's office to release the clothing to you, you can get it to an independent, licensed lab for analysis. It might not hold up in court, but if a real inspection doesn't turn up any transfer linking Johnny to the victims—or better yet, does turn up evidence of a different killer—maybe Moreno will back down."

"The Phoenix PD's crime lab won't look at evidence from a New Mexico crime," Annie said. "And that's the only place I know people."

"There's an independent lab in Tucson that's done some consulting work for me. I'll call them and set it up, and you see if you can get the sheriffs down there to release the stuff."

"I'll work on it," Annie said. "I'll let you know when I get an answer."

"Good luck, Annie. And good work so far."

She hung up and dropped the phone onto the passenger seat. Good work so far? As far as she was concerned, only the sight of Johnny walking out of prison would mean that she had done good work.

She had a feeling that was still a long way off.

MARTIN Raines eyed her with suspicion that came across like a neon sign when he gave her hand a perfunctory shake. "I'm not currently a law enforcement officer," she reminded him. "But I was for many years, and I'm employed by an attorney licensed to practice in New Mexico, running a legal rights organization that operates in all fifty states. I'm well aware of the importance of maintaining an evidentiary chain of custody."

"Well, that's just fine," Sheriff Raines said. He was sitting behind his desk in a small office crowded with guns, hunting trophies, and filing cabinets. Annie stood, since there were no visitor's chairs to sit in. "I'm not questioning your credentials or your understanding of the process. I can't say I'm thrilled by what I take to be an opinion that our procedures here are in some way lacking, but my daughter likes you. As, I gather, does Deputy Baca."

"We've become friendly," Annie said. Not giving away much, but not lying either. She didn't know how much Leo might have said about their relationship.

"All that aside," Raines went on, "the fact remains—if you take the evidence out of this building, then as far as I'm concerned, the chain of custody is broken. Anything your independent lab might find out would be suspect in my eyes."

The only eyes that count are the DA's, and maybe a judge's, or the governor's, Annie thought. She decided against saying it out loud. Virtually every person she had met in Drummond had been pleasant and friendly, until this one. He seemed to have a chip on his shoulder, or something weighing heavily on him, and it affected his outlook. "Yes, sir. I understand that."

"I wish there was something I could do for you."

"Yes, sir."

He reached across the desk to shake her hand without

standing up. His right eye opened wider than usual, exposing a rheumy gray eyeball that she would have guessed was blind if it didn't seem that he could see just fine. She shook his hand again, quickly, and released it, stifling an urge to step into the bathroom and wash her own hands immediately with very hot water and lots of soap. Whatever weighed on him, it was a crushing load; he felt like he was about to collapse under its weight.

Annie left the office and went back to her car, almost dizzy from the runaround she'd been given. *The evidence was never examined before it was put into storage, but it can't be examined now because it's safely in storage. How does that make sense?*

Inside the town of Drummond, she still had cell phone service. Standing outside the Taurus, she called Morgan back, got his voice mail, left a message. Next she tried Jocelyn Moreno, but the district attorney had already left her office for the day. She left a message there, as well.

She kicked a rock so hard it flew thirty feet and bounced off the side wall of the library, then got into the car, started it, and gunned it through town, almost daring one of the sheriff's officers to stop her. No one did.

31

INSTEAD of going home, Annie returned to the crime scenes. First she drove to the spot along the road where Kevin's tire had gone flat. She parked behind the spot she had identified earlier as the exact location where Kevin's car had been parked, walked up, and looked for the tracks she had made a few days before. Wind and the passage of other vehicles had scoured them clean. She got back into her car, drove across the shoulder, parked on the other side and walked back.

Her tires had made deep, distinct grooves in the soft earth. Since it was unlikely that the dirt had been replaced over the past four years, except through the natural process of weathering that always went on, she had to believe that Kevin's car and some other vehicle had made similarly distinct tracks on the day of his death. She had, in fact, seen the photos. No other car had stopped on the shoulder that day, or its track would have been visible too. It was the same time of year, the dry spring season, so it was highly unlikely that rain would have wiped it clean between the time of the murder and when the sheriffs arrived on the scene. And there had been no mention of rain in the report, in any case.

So only Kevin's and the sheriff's vehicles had stopped there. If Johnny Ortega or anyone else killed Carylyn Phelps on this spot, he or she had come here with Kevin and Carylyn, walked to the scene, or parked on the pavement, or far enough from the site that any tracks were either not seen or were completely obscured by the emergency vehicles that showed up.

Her immediate curiosity about this place satisfied, Annie drove back over winding roads to the dirt track from which she had hiked to the strange field of flat stones and the New Dominion town site. Once again, she had come wearing professional garb, nice pants and flats and an off-white silk blouse, instead of the grubbies and boots that made sense for wilderness hiking. One of these days she'd have to wise up and keep a change of clothes in the car. She shrugged, imagining Morgan's expression when he got the bill for yet another outfit, and eased through the barbed wire.

Ten minutes of hiking brought her to the stone field. A mule deer eyeballed her, twitched its namesake ears, and bounded away. High above, a hawk soared in lazy circles. Annie was starting to understand why people were drawn to this place and to others like it—the ranchers who worked the land, seeing such beauty every day, the hikers, hunters, and campers who sought it out as an escape from city life. Since the explosion, she had sought out solitude, and now she was finding that the brand of solitude that came with wilderness had an advantage over the kind you got simply from sitting inside an apartment with the curtains drawn. Beauty and open spaces and sunshine had healing properties she had never known about. She wasn't sure it was something she would be able to leave behind, now that she had found it.

The field of stones looked just as it had before. This time, she didn't even have the crime scene photos with her. She couldn't begin to guess which stone Kevin had been murdered on. They all looked more or less the same: about the same size, all three or four inches high. They had all been worn at the edges by weather. They had been here a long time—some were split by grasses or other plants that had grown up through them, and corners that had no doubt once been sharp were now smooth. She knelt down on one, touching its surface, fingering its edge, trying to imagine what it might have been for. Graveyard was still the best she could come up with. She had seen a graveyard where the stones were more or less flat instead of upright, but that was at a prison. And they had been considerably smaller than these slabs.

This had been a waste of time. If there were answers here, they'd long since been blown away by the winds that whipped her red hair across her face, fluttering her torn blouse.

Annie heaved a sigh and pushed to her feet. These shoes weren't meant for this kind of abuse, and they were pinching her feet. For that matter, her spirit wasn't meant for this kind of abuse—every step forward seemed to toss her back several. She had only been at it a few days, and certainly she had worked cases in Phoenix that had taken a lot longer. But the frustration that had led her to kick a stone in town bore down even more heavily on her now. She wanted to chase someone down an alley, draw a weapon, slap cuffs on somebody. She wanted to do something more helpful than this metaphorical head-banging.

Her gaze was drawn back to the mesquite and unlikely oak thicket that hid New Dominion from view. Almost without realizing she was doing it, she started walking toward the empty town. Her clothes, already partially trashed, would be completely ruined when she forced her way through there again. And she couldn't imagine it had changed a lot since her last visit. It hadn't changed in the past fifty years, she was sure, except to disintegrate little by little.

The mesquite thorns, some as much as two inches long and nail-hard, jabbed at her. The branches grew so close together she had to push them out of her way and make sure they didn't snap back onto her, and sometimes there were layer upon layer of them to contend with. Her hands were sliced, her legs jabbed. At one point she stopped, convinced that she had taken the wrong route this time. Dozens of branches blocked her path, so dense that they'd be almost impossible to work through. But when she looked back, she saw that she had already worked most of the way through just as treacherous a thicket. She swallowed and kept going.

Finally she emerged amidst the ruins of the town. Something seemed different than before. Was it just that she had come at a slightly earlier hour? The hills on either side of the town blocked direct sunlight for most of the day, and only diffuse light fell on it now. She shook her head. *That's not it. But what, then?*

Annie sniffed the air, realizing that part of what had changed was the odor. On her last visit, all she had smelled was the surrounding foliage, the high desert plants that so determinedly blocked access to the site. Now she caught traces of different things, things utterly familiar in other settings but alien here. She thought she could smell wood smoke, horse manure, running water. Those were the scents of a town, of human habitation, domesticity. They wouldn't have been out of place in New Dominion's heyday, but now? She had to be imagining them.

As she moved between the ruins, though, another impression dawned on her. She could make out more of the buildings than she had last time. Walls seemed taller, more distinctly separate from the growth that had done its best over the decades to tear them down. And as this occurred to her and she looked more closely, she saw that the buildings looked more whole than they had before. Had she just entered the town from a slightly different angle? Was this a side of it she hadn't found before?

She had spent time walking through it, though. She hadn't seen it from every angle, but she believed she had seen all the buildings. Now she looked down; even the path was clearer, the roadways that had once connected the buildings more evident. Surely no one had started a town beautification project in this desolate place, had they?

Finding a building she was certain she had looked at before, Annie examined it more closely. She remembered the way local stones had been laid into mortar, but now there appeared to be more of them, and their sides were jagged, not dulled by the passage of years. The walls were higher than she remembered, taller than she was, where before they had been shoulder height at the most.

Acting on a hunch, she knelt beside the structure and pressed her hands against the wall. The rocky surface was rough and cool beneath them, biting into her palms. She left them there, willing her senses to open.

She detected a kind of pulsing buzz. After several seconds, she realized it was her old enemy tinnitus, back again and stronger than it had been for weeks. It muted all other sounds: the watery rush of wind through leafy branches, the chatter of birds.

And then the world fell away completely.

Annie was still on her knees, but the wall before her was intact, reaching up to a steep, shingled roof. She turned, her attention snagged by movement. The town had been re-created, each building as it had been in its prime, solid, sturdy, and whole, the roads hard-packed, rutted but passable. Dark scatterings of horse manure were everywhere on them.

But the strangest things—not that the rest of it wasn't strange—were the people.

What had been an empty, abandoned set of ruins was now an inhabited village. Annie would not have been willing to swear that it was a village that had ever existed on Earth, though. The men—there were eleven or twelve of them, she guessed, scattered about the town—wore loose black pants or shirts with long tails, sometimes both, but most had their chests on display, sometimes arms and shoulders and legs too. They were uniformly gaunt and hairless, with long chins and noses, prominent cheekbones and sunken eyes. Their skin was a vibrant, aggressive yellow, the color of sunflower petals in the fall. If the people communicated with each other in any way, she couldn't tell.

Moving around the men were women, also hairless with the same yellow skin, but utterly naked, and voluptuous rather than emaciated like the males, with wide hips and pendulous breasts. Tattoos of the deepest black, mostly in

geometric shapes, decorated their breasts, bellies, and geni-
tals, following and accentuating their natural curves. Some of
them carried loads in woven pouches or earthen jugs, while
others just walked silently among the men, as if on parade.
Annie didn't see any of the men taking notice of them, or for
that matter the women paying attention to the men. No one
ran into anyone else, but for all the interaction they had, they
might have been occupying the same general area during
entirely different eras.

The whole thing lasted less than a minute. Annie lost her
balance and fell back onto the ground, and when she did
her hand came away from the wall. That threw her back
into the present, amid the ruins of New Dominion. No yellow people were there, half clothed or completely nude.
Not a single building was intact. Everything she had just
seen had been some sort of hallucination, she supposed.
Empathy for other humans was one thing, but picking up
sensations like that from an old wall of stone and mud? It
wasn't possible.

Not that she had ever had hallucinations before. Or would
have believed her empath power possible before she had
experienced it in the hospital.

First time for everything, right? Even two firsts at once?

Because she couldn't have *seen* all that, not really. It
wasn't something that could have existed. It certainly
wasn't America, even a relatively isolated corner of it, at
any point between the 1890s and the early 1930s.

Whatever it had been, Annie was glad it was over.

She hoped never to see anything like it again.

32

WITH hands still shaking from what she had witnessed, or imagined, Annie fitted the key into the front door lock of her rented home. She was turning it when the phone inside began to ring. She shoved the door open and ran in.

"This is Annie O'Brien," she said.

"Ms. O'Brien," a woman's voice said. Annie couldn't place it at first, but the tinnitus that had struck her at New Dominion had only lessened slightly. "It's Jocelyn Moreno."

"Oh, hi," Annie said. The district attorney.

"I got your message from earlier today. Here's my suggestion. If you can get someone from the sheriff's office to accompany you and the clothing from the property locker in Drummond, I'll authorize it. That person doesn't have to be on duty, and considering how tight everybody's budget is these days, it would probably be better if someone would volunteer to do it on his or her own time. But that way you could get the clothing to a lab and have it checked out. You're absolutely right, we should have done that in the first place."

"I appreciate that," Annie said. "I'm not sure that Sheriff Raines—"

"I'll speak with Lieutenant Raines," Jocelyn said. "He'll understand. He can come across as gruff, but he's not unreasonable."

"I'll see who I can come up with," Annie said. "Can I call you back in a few minutes?"

Jocelyn gave her the number of her Silver City office. "I'll be here for twenty more minutes," she said.

Annie thanked her again and hung up. She found Leo's number and called him on his cell, hoping he was within range. He answered on the third ring. "Annie?"

"Hi, Leo. You in town?"

"Sitting here filling out paperwork," he said.

"I don't miss that, I can tell you."

"I'm sure."

She laid out the DA's offer for him. "I'm off duty tomorrow," he said. Which she had believed to be the case, since he had worked over the weekend.

"That's what I wanted to hear. You want to make a quick trip to Tucson?"

"Does it have to be quick?"

"Let's make it quick getting there. If we want to take our time getting back, that's probably okay, as long as we get an early start tomorrow morning."

"I was thinking we could spend a lot of time on the return trip," he said.

His meaning broke through slowly, like someone chipping away at a thick block of ice. "So, I should pack an overnight bag?"

"That wouldn't be a bad idea."

Annie pondered Leo's suggestion. Spending the night together was a big step, different than dinner and sex. At least in her eyes. She liked sleeping alone, and she had liked it even more since the bomb, when being alone was the only time she could truly know her own mind. But away from Leo, she remained attracted to him—not in love, or even verging on it, but she liked being with him and he made her feel good. She believed she did the same for him.

"Did I throw you?" he asked.

"No, I'm . . . to be honest, I'm thinking it over. But okay, sure. Sounds like fun."

"I'll pick you up in the morning, then? Eight o'clock?"

"I'll pick you up at seven. This is my job, not yours. You're on your day off. And I can expense the mileage. So I'll see you tomorrow."

"Okay, Annie, looking forward to it."

"And, Leo?"

"Yes?"

"Thanks for doing this."

THE wind picked up even harder that night. When Annie woke up, disoriented and still suffering from the tinnitus that had recurred in New Dominion, for just a moment she thought she was near a roaring river. Rubbing her eyes, sitting up, she remembered where she was, far from any river, and knew that the sound must be a steady wind powering through the trees.

She showered and dressed quickly, ate a small breakfast, and went to get Leo. He was waiting when she arrived, out of his door carrying a green nylon backpack before she had even brought the Taurus to a stop in his dirt driveway. She popped the trunk and he put the backpack there, then got in the passenger door. "Hey, Annie."

"Hey back."

A bigger gust came along just after he closed the door, a whirlwind twenty feet across that kicked up dust, leaves, and tumbleweeds into a brown spiral stretching a hundred feet high. They sat in the Taurus watching it, feeling the car shake under its force, and laughing. When it had moved on, Leo said, "Toto, I don't think we're in Kansas anymore."

"Well, let's get going, then. Maybe there's a wizard waiting for us somewhere."

With a working cop in the car, she felt compelled to obey the posted speed limits. The time went fast anyway, as they talked about anything and everything, and by ten in the morning they had dropped the clothing off at a lab in a warehouse district near Tucson's downtown.

The vast expanses of pavement and steel tugged at Annie. She hadn't been in a real city since leaving Phoenix, and while it hadn't been that long, there were moments when it felt like an eternity. She enjoyed rural New Mexico, but she had been raised in a more urban environment, and this brief excursion reminded her that there were aspects of city life she loved too. On the way out of town they passed a tax office with a sign holder in front, an overweight, bearded man dressed as the Statue of Liberty, swilling from a huge mug that she hoped contained water, and they both started laughing again. "Some things you just don't see in Drummond," she said.

"I'm not sure my eyes will ever recover from seeing it here."

"You'd be surprised at what you can get over." A little disingenuous, that—she was a long way from over whatever the bomb blast had done to her. *Mostly* better wasn't the same as *all* better.

"Maybe if I spend some time looking at a beautiful redhead, it'll help."

"We'll see if we can find you one." She turned onto Congress Street, which would take her back to the freeway. "You want to stick around Tucson for lunch?"

"I have a better idea," he said. "Go east, young woman."

A little less than two hours later she eased into a parking spot in the Lowell district of Bisbee, an old Arizona mining town that mostly clung to mountainsides a mile up. Behind the parking lot was a vast hole in the ground that Leo identified as the Lavender Pit Mine, named after a man named Lavender, he said, and not for the color. When they got out of the Taurus he led her to the chain-link fence and they looked down. The pit was terraced all around, with flat stretches that seemed precarious from here but probably provided enough space for giant mining equipment to drive up and down, and far deeper than she had guessed from the car. A pool of something at the bottom looked black and oily. "Wow," she said.

"Yeah." He waved an arm in the air. "Around here you'll see a lot of rusty hills that aren't hills at all—they're tailings. Piles of the dirt taken out of this hole, back when it was a working mine."

A collection of sand-colored buildings clustered around the pit's edge. She could see a couple of trucks among them. "It's not now?"

"Not for years," Leo said. "They keep a skeleton crew here, because if they ever abandoned it they might have to restore it. Plus, if the price of copper goes up enough, it might become financially feasible to start working it again. For now, though, it pretty much just sits here like this." He turned her around, pointed at a row of storefronts across the parking lot. A co-op grocery store stood on the corner, and next to it was something called the Bisbee Breakfast Club. "That's where we're having lunch."

"Not breakfast?"

"It's after one thirty. If you want breakfast, we can see if they serve all day."

They did, and it was delicious. Annie tried not to compare one lover with another—especially when that other had died in a terrible explosion—but she realized, watching Leo eat his lunch, what a relief it was after spending time with Ryan. If Ryan could have used a spade instead of a fork, he would have. When he got his hands on a bag of chips or popcorn or peanuts, he upended it over his mouth and poured; she couldn't imagine how he could chew what fell in, but maybe he didn't bother. Was it a guy thing, or was it unique to him? She wasn't sure. Maybe Prince Charles had to be constantly reminded that he was royalty, or he would go out in public with a feedbag strapped to his head, tilting it back whenever he wanted another mouthful of oats. But Leo seemed to have been trained in the use of all the common utensils, he closed his mouth when he chewed, and he kept the greater proportion of his food inside his body rather than on his clothes. A blessing, she thought.

After lunch, Leo directed them back to old Bisbee, which they had passed by on the way to the restaurant. Here the hills were steep, almost cliffs, and the houses perched on their sides looked as if a strong wind would shake them loose. Downtown, the buildings were mostly brick, from the turn of the last century, she guessed. She saw a lot of antique stores and art galleries. They stopped in a few, then found Atalanta's Music & Books, where Annie bought a western bird guide to help her identify her nearest neighbors. They spent another hour or so browsing in the shops, then got back on the road, headed further southeast.

"Tell me about Martin Raines," she said as she drove down Highway 80, out of the mountains surrounding Bisbee and into a broad, flat valley. "He seems like an odd duck."

"That would be one way to describe him," Leo said. "But you aren't really trying to get me to talk smack about my boss, are you?"

"Only your immediate boss," Annie said. "You were hired by the real sheriff, right? In Lordsburg?"

"True. I think Martin can fire me, though. He could certainly make life hell if he wanted to."

"Someone doesn't even need to be your boss to do that."

"That's true enough."

"So what's his story?"

"I've told you some of it already," he said. "He gets to run things in the southern half of the county because he's related to the founders of Drummond, and it's such a tight community that he can get cooperation from people who would as soon shoot the real sheriff as talk to him."

"The antigovernment types you told me about the day we met."

"That's right. They think the federal government is Satan. They're only marginally more generous about state and local, but they tolerate Martin."

"And his family."

"Yeah, Gary and Johanna are like extensions of Martin, as far as they're concerned."

"What about Basque immigrants from Albuquerque?"

"That's a little more iffy. I've yet to prove myself, I guess. Or maybe it's just that proving myself isn't in the cards—I'm not a family member or born into the community, so I'll always be an outsider."

"I'm surprised Martin let you get hired at all."

"I don't think he was given the choice. Sheriff Teller wanted someone from the outside working down there. They all thought I was a spy, at first, but really I'm just supposed to provide a little different perspective, and some experience from a different environment."

Annie pulled up behind a slow-moving pickup, its bed stuffed with an entire household's belongings, it appeared, and had to wait for a chance to pass it. "But you seem to get along okay with him now."

"It took a while, but yeah. Things are fine, I guess. Sometimes I still feel like the new kid in school, you know? Like they're whispering among themselves, and when I come into the room they all stop and try to act casual."

"That's a universal at every cop shop, I think," Annie said. She seized a break in oncoming traffic and punched the accelerator, swerving into the other lane and around the truck, then cutting back in. As she slowed back to within a few miles of the speed limit, she was glad that she hadn't pulled that in Hidalgo County with a sheriff's deputy in the car.

"Probably. Anyway, I admit that I've been a little fascinated with the Raines family since I got here and found out how influential they are. And, like you said, a little strange. The family all lives together on the same street—I guess you could almost call it a compound, since no one else lives close to them. Even some of the houses they don't occupy anymore are still standing there, empty, but as far as I can tell they've never tried to sell them."

A small city emerged ahead of them, as if rising up out of the ground. Afternoon light slanted in from behind them, covering the city with a golden glow. "That's Douglas, right?" Annie asked.

"Right. Originally it had the smelters for the copper mine in Bisbee, but they've been torn down."

"Funny how you know so much more about parts of my home state than I do. I know a guy from around here—a sheriff's lieutenant whose son was killed in Phoenix, shot outside a nightclub—but I've never been down here."

"It's only because I've lived in Hidalgo County for more than a month," Leo said with a chuckle. "You have to explore pretty widely to find decent meals, movies, and so on."

"It isn't that bad," Annie insisted.

"No, but stick around awhile and you'll go a little stir-crazy, you wait and see."

"If I can't make some headway on Johnny Ortega's case, I just might."

As they entered the city, driving past a vacant car lot and an occupied jail, Leo told her where to turn. "We'll spend tonight in one of the West's grandest hotels, the Gadsden," he said. "You'd never expect to see it in such a sleepy little border town, but it's here and it's amazing. Then tomorrow if we're on the road by six or six thirty, I can still get to work on time."

Annie looked at the dashboard clock. It wasn't quite five. "Is there enough to do here for the rest of tonight?" she asked.

"You honestly think I'm even letting you out of the hotel room?" He squeezed her thigh. Sometimes, she thought, the transference of emotion could come in handy. If she hadn't been aroused before, his touch—Leo was more than ready for her—did the trick. Suddenly, hotel sex seemed like a fine way to pass the remainder of the day.

33

ANNIE got Leo home in time to change for work, then went back to her own place, where she napped for a couple of hours before a lunch date with Johanna Raines. She had almost forgotten about it, but when she got home she saw it penciled in on the seed company wall calendar that had been hanging in the kitchen when she moved in. About an hour before their scheduled rendezvous, she called Johanna and asked if she could pick the deputy up at home. Leo had made her curious about the Raines "compound," and that seemed like a convenient excuse to get a look at it.

Once she got Johanna's directions jotted down and checked a map to confirm where she was going, Annie realized that Johanna lived on the other side of New Dominion from her. There were hills on that side too—the New Dominion site nestled in a bowl of them, with the only open side the one facing the field of stones. But although it would only be a short hike over the hills, through New Dominion, and then over the far hills, on the region's indirect roads it would be a twenty-minute drive to Johanna's place. Annie took a shower, dressed, brushed her hair, and applied some minimal makeup, then got back in the car. Since moving to the country, it felt like she spent her life behind the wheel.

Leo had not exaggerated the strangeness of Raines Road, as it was called. It turned out to be within Drummond town limits, but just barely. From town, Annie had to follow a long, straight road with sharp dips and sudden rises for a few miles, then turn left on Raines Road. The road led into a kind of hollow that kept the Raines family homes hidden from the main road. Open fields surrounded the road, but tall trees encircled the houses, keeping them shaded and providing protection from the wind. The low hills Annie had expected hunkered to the west, with New Dominion on the other side of them.

The houses themselves looked as old as Leo had suggested. They were two-story structures made of logs—rare enough in this country where the only big trees were the ones the Raines family must have grown here—widely spaced, with stone-embedded mortar between them. Slanted roofs of gray shingles topped each house. Every driveway was flanked by brick gateposts decorated with bizarre statuary. On one stood a statue of something that might have been a dog, its front end low, mouth open in a stylized snarl, haunches raised and tail curled under. Across the driveway from it, eight feet high atop the post, was a misshapen human head crudely carved from a piece of gray stone, mouth and eyes wide open as if regarding something terrifying. At the next house, the statues were of a bundle of corn and a pig. Not the kind of thing Annie would expect to see anyone putting up by choice—maybe something kids would leave there as a prank on Halloween, after they took the property owner's real statues away. But it had been a long time since Halloween.

Johanna's house came after one that looked completely abandoned, its windows either empty altogether or boarded over, as was the front door. Even from the car she could see a gap in its roof, as if someone had dropped a bowling ball through it. Yet, as Leo had suggested, there seemed no attempt to repair it, or to put it on the market.

At Johanna's, Annie eased between the gateposts, which were so close together they might have been intended for horse-drawn wagons instead of automobiles. Johanna's posts were topped by sculptures of a raven and a sun.

Johanna came out her front door as soon as Annie entered the yard. She was off duty today, dressed in a long-sleeved black T-shirt and jeans, carrying a leather purse. Watching her cross toward the car, Annie realized that most of the houses had very few windows—Johanna's had two that Annie could see, on the ground floor, and only one upstairs. Where one of the windows would have been on an ordinary house was a painted circle with crossbars emanating from a solid inner circle connecting the four compass points. It might have been a representation of a wheel, or yet another very stylized sun.

"Now you know the Raines family secret," Johanna said when she climbed into Annie's car. "We've never read an issue of *Architectural Digest* in our lives."

"There is a certain similarity to the houses," Annie said. Mistress of the understatement.

"Family tradition. We come from Celtic stock. Our family's ancient homes back in Britain would have been round houses with thatched roofs. Not all that practical here, but the Celts adapted, and when our ancestors came here they adapted more. The houses now are meant to evoke the old ways without really being anything like them. But they're still not exactly Santa Fe style."

"Hardly," Annie said. She turned around and pulled back out between the posts, then turned left, headed back toward town. As she passed the "empty" house again, she noticed that behind it, in the shade of the trees and before the low hills began, a wrought-iron fence enclosed a small cemetery. "Greenfield's for lunch?"

"Is there anything else?"

"Not close by." She let Johanna chatter about her day for a few minutes, then interrupted her. "So, Johanna—are you related to the families that founded New Dominion?"

Johanna sat quietly for most of a mile. "Distantly," she

said. Annie could tell she had picked at a fresh emotional scab, but she didn't intend to let Johanna dodge the topic like she had before. "Just about everyone in Drummond—and lots of other places—are distantly related to them."

"What do you know about the settlement of the town? Why here, in what must have been the middle of nowhere. Apache country still, back then, right? Wasn't it dangerous?"

Johanna laughed. "I don't think Cochise himself would have wanted to meet a Celtic warrior in full battle regalia," she said. "He would be painted blue, naked except maybe for some jewelry, a torc around his neck, that kind of thing. He would be carrying a sword or spear and an oblong shield almost his own size, and when he went into battle frenzy he would look like he was possessed or deranged, banging his weapon against his shield, screaming, and charging fearlessly into battle. Celtic warriors didn't know the meaning of sur- render."

"But that was thousands of years ago, wasn't it?"

"Sure," Johanna said. She was resigned, but a note of pride sounded in her voice and simultaneously swelled up within Annie's breast. "Some of that spirit lives on, though. If there have ever been people more fiercely independent, I'd be afraid to meet them. The ancestors of the Raines family came to the U.S. to escape religious persecution in Great Britain. They settled in Virginia in the late 1700s, but then found themselves hounded out of there too. Over the course of the next hundred years, they made their way across the nation, trying to put down roots in various spots. Finally they wound up here, in a place that had been claimed by the Apaches and the Mexicans, and which the American gov- ernment really only wanted in order to keep it out of the hands of those others."

"So they finally found peace here?"

"At least for a while."

Annie remembered how vague the newspaper accounts of the town's demise had been. "Then what happened?"

Johanna shrugged. "They went their separate ways, I guess. Some founded Drummond. Others moved other places." Annie had slowed down through town, but she couldn't delay their arrival at the café indefinitely, and Johanna took advantage of that fact. "Look, here we are. You hungry?"

"Famished," Annie said. She killed the engine, and they went inside. It didn't sound like she was getting more from Johanna on that topic.

34

"I brought contraband."

"Contraband?" Annie echoed, pushing the door open for Leo to enter. "Ooh, sexy. Come on in."

He smiled and flapped a manila file folder at her. "You probably say that to all the men who come bearing gifts."

"Only if they're contraband." She pressed her lips against his in a long, lingering kiss, then led him to the kitchen table. He was proud of something, even a little full of himself at the moment. She had been sitting there going over her files on Johnny Ortega, looking for whatever she had missed—and she had missed something, she was convinced—when Leo pulled up outside in a sheriff's department SUV. He was in uniform, but he took his hat off when he sat down at the table. Annie closed up her files and took the one he offered. "So what is it?"

"The house was empty this morning, so I did some digging in the old filing cabinets."

"Did you find anything new on the Ortega case?"

"Not yet. But I did find something about your other current obsession—a copy of the report on the New Dominion investigation, from 1933."

"You're kidding."

"Take a look," he offered. "The copies are shitty, and I'm sure the originals are filed up in Lordsburg where we can't get at them. I mostly brought it for your amusement, because in terms of actual useful information, you might be better off just reading the Sunday funnies. Sheriff Jeremiah Raines ran the investigation, if you could call it that. If he'd written down what he didn't find out, it would have taken more space. Most of it is just a list of the names of the deceased, and the dates they died—which were all the same day, of course."

Annie flipped open the file and examined the report. As Leo had said, there wasn't much to it. On brittle, faded pages, she could barely make out the tight, scratchy handwriting of Jeremiah Raines. She scanned the list of names, seeing McKeens and Fryars, Raineses and Conways and Howells, Stones and Wellses. Whole families of them, from the looks of it. The date of death given for each was March 22, 1933.

"Jeremiah Raines being an ancestor of Martin Raines, no doubt," she said. "And these other Raineses, probably the same."

"That's my guess," Leo said. "But here's something weird. I also found a record of old Jeremiah's retirement, in 1938. But I couldn't turn up anything after that. I even called a contact in the county records office, and there's nothing there either. No death certificate, no certificate of burial, nothing."

"Maybe he's still alive?" Annie suggested.

"He was sixty-six when he retired. In 1938. I think if he was still around, at that age, we'd have heard about it."

Annie was still perusing the rest of the file, but it was disturbingly vague. "Yeah, I guess we would have." She closed it up, handed it back to Leo. "I was at Johanna's house today and saw a little cemetery back behind the houses. Maybe it's private, unofficial, and he's buried back there."

"That could be," Leo said. He rose from the table, tucked the folder under his arm. "I'll keep digging around, see if I can find out any more. But I thought you'd want to see this."

Annie stood up too and planted another kiss on his lips. "Thanks, Leo."

"No problem."

"And if you come across anything in your digging that pertains to the Ortega case . . ."

"I know. I'll keep you posted, Annie." He kissed her once more. "Annicka."

"Oh God, don't."

"What? I like it. Annicka. It's pretty."

"Pretty goofy. And whenever I hear it I think I'm in trouble with my dad."

"No dads here," Leo said. "But if you need a spanking . . ."

She shoved him toward the door, laughing. "Didn't you have to get back to work?"

"I'm going," he said, swatting at her ass. "Don't worry, I'm going."

35

"YOU know," Gary Raines said, "it's always been a guy, far back as I can remember."

"That's right," Martin said. They were cruising the dusty back roads of the county's southeastern corner, washboard hammering their spines with every revolution of the Tahoe's tires. The way to beat washboard was to speed up and flatten it out. But they had to go slow, so they could watch for the faintest signs of passage. Some UDAs knew to sweep across their footprints with branches, but they still left tracks at the edges of the roads, dropped trash or cigarette butts or scraps of fabric from clothing snagged on thorns. You couldn't see those things at thirty or forty miles an hour. "What about it?"

"I'm just asking," Gary went on. "Does it have to be? I mean, is that one of the rules?"

"It's the way it's always been done," Martin said.

"Right. But that doesn't always mean that it can't be changed."

Martin's patience was running shorter with each day that passed. "Tradition's important. What exactly are you getting at, son?"

"I've been thinking about that cop from Arizona. That ex-cop."

"O'Brien? The redhead?"

"I guess, yeah. Johanna said she keeps asking questions about New Dominion."

"She does?" Martin hadn't heard anything about that. Those two talked, though, Johanna and Gary. Talked all the time. Used to drive him nuts when they were growing up.

"That's right."

"She's supposed to be here trying to get Johnny Ortega out of prison."

"Well, that's a problem too, isn't it? I mean, if she can prove he's innocent somehow."

"She can't."

"But if she could."

"Well, then that would be a problem," Martin said.

"So what I'm getting at is . . . what if we could solve two problems at once?"

Martin stopped the Tahoe. A cloud of dust kicked up into the air and started to settle around them. "You know, Gary? Sometimes you do have good ideas."

"You think?"

"Sure do this time."

"What about tradition?"

"Tradition's important, I said. But sometimes it can take a flying fu— Well, you know what I mean. You know where to find her?"

"She had lunch with Johanna at Greenfield's. Johanna said she was going home after."

Martin started to work the big SUV into a three-point turn. "Then maybe we ought to pay her a visit," he said. Once he had the vehicle headed the other way on the dirt road, he gunned it, smoothing out the washboard just fine and spraying a plume of dust behind them.

THE phone rang a few minutes after Leo left. Thinking it might be him, Annie picked it up and said, "Hellooo," in flirtatious tones.

"I . . . um, I'm looking for Annie O'Brien," a male voice said. It wasn't Leo's.

"This is she."

"Ms. O'Brien, this is Harold Tsang, from Cenoba Labs. I'm sorry, I didn't recognize your voice at first."

"My bad," she said. Annie was surprised. It would take weeks to get DNA results, she had been told. This private lab wasn't quite as backed up as the Phoenix PD's crime lab, but there was a backlog just the same. "Is everything okay?"

"Oh, yes, there's no problem. It's just . . . well, when we were prepping the articles you brought in, it became apparent that not only was there no sophisticated lab testing done on them but not even the most cursory inspection was performed."

"What do you mean, Dr. Tsang?"

"Well . . . obviously the pockets were emptied of the larger items. Wallets, keys, and so on."

"Yes?" *Get to the point.*

"But in the right front pocket of the suspect's jeans—Mr. Ortega's, wadded up and deep in the corner, there was a piece of paper. A receipt, in point of fact."

"A receipt?" Annie repeated.

"That's right. A cash register receipt. Mr. Ortega bought a pack of cigarettes, two candy bars, and a Pepsi."

Annie shook her head. They missed a cash register receipt in his pocket? Just how incompetent could one sheriff's department be?

But the answer was, extremely, when it was run as a personal fiefdom, the job handed down from father to son for generations. No wonder the sheriff in Lordsburg had wanted to bring someone in from the outside.

"What's the date on the receipt?" she asked. If it was in the jeans Ortega had been wearing the day he was arrested, it could be significant.

Dr. Tsang read her the date. The twentieth of March, four years ago. The day of the murders. Her heart quickened. "And where's it from?"

"A place called Lonnie's Twenty-five-Hour Service and EZ Eats," Tsang said. "In Willcox."

"Willcox, Arizona?" She had driven past it on her way to New Mexico, and then again on the way to Tucson with Leo.

"That's right."

"Is there a time stamp on it?"

"Let me see. Yes, three eleven p.m."

For a few seconds Annie thought her heart had stopped. She couldn't catch her breath. "Are you sure?"

"It's pretty creased and faded, but yes, it's still quite legible."

"Please hang on to it," Annie said. "If you can get any fingerprints off it, that would be great."

"We'll do our best," he promised.

Annie hung up a moment later and almost danced for joy. If Johnny Ortega was in Willcox—the last city of any size in Arizona, on I-10, but still forty miles or so from the New Mexico line—at 3:11, then it was impossible for him to have killed two people in southern Hidalgo County, at least a hundred miles away, at 3:30.

This was the break she had been looking for, and it was huge. It was what was missing from the file, or what she was forgetting to look for—if Ortega wasn't the killer, where was he when the murders were being done?

Now she had the answer.

She put her files away, pulled on shoes, and grabbed her purse. There were water and tunes in the car, and she had a lot of miles to cover.

36

"THAT'S the place," Gary said.

Martin brought the Tahoe to a stop in the dirt driveway outside it. "I know that's the place," he said. "That's why I drove us here."

"I'm just saying . . ."

Martin wanted to snap at his son, but he was still pleased with the boy for having a good idea, and he didn't want to discourage him in case there was another such occasion in his future. "Come on," he said. "Let's get this done."

He got out of the SUV and unsnapped the strap that went across the butt of his duty weapon. "Miss O'Brien?" he shouted as he approached her front door. There was no car in the carport, which worried him. He knocked three times, hard. "Miss O'Brien, it's Sheriff Raines! You in there?"

Nobody answered. Gary stood in the sunshine, near the Tahoe, keeping an eye on the back in case she tried to go out that way. "I don't think she's home," Gary said.

Martin moved to one of the windows, pressed his hands against the glass to cut the glare and looked inside. The place was neat, if sparsely furnished. No sign of the woman, though.

"I guess you're right," Martin said. He went back to the door, tried the knob. It was locked. Probably not worth breaking in. If they didn't find someone else pretty quick, they might want to come back and try again, and it wouldn't do to tip her off.

It was a damn shame, though. Gary had been right—using her would have fixed two problems at once, in a very convenient way.

"Let's get out of here, son, and keep on looking. Eyes sharp, now."

"All right, Dad," Gary said. His voice dripped with disappointment, and Martin realized for the first time how much his son had wanted this to happen.

He just might turn out to be worth something, after all.

37

ANNIE inhabited a world somewhere between the one she had lived in for most of her life and the strange, fragile one she had discovered right after the explosion. The ringing in her ears was constant, though not loud enough to drown out any but the softest or highest-pitched sounds. At the same time, her empath powers were heightened but nowhere close to their peak.

As a result, she stayed close to Lonnie Briggs, touching him often as she pleaded her case, hoping to pick up whatever cues she could about how to proceed. It was not the most pleasant way she had ever passed some time. Lonnie was a beefy guy with dark curly hair, a heavy growth of beard shading his cheeks and chin, and a pungent odor. His T-shirt was red and stained, his pants khaki and held beneath his massive belly by a belt that should have been awarded a medal of valor.

"I don't know, man," he was saying. "Four years, that's a hell of a long time."

"I understand that it might be a long shot," Annie said,

brushing his furry arm with her hand. "But how far back do you keep copies of your surveillance videos?"

"Well, it's all digital, right? It backs up every night to a hard drive, and then there's a secondary backup to DVD. I gotta change the DVD three times a day."

"But it's all saved?"

"The hard drive is constantly overwritten," Lonnie said. "But DVDs are cheap. I just mark the date on 'em and toss 'em in a drawer in the back."

His place was a standard gas station/convenience store, just off the interstate in Willcox. Outside a series of gas pumps stood under elevated canopies. A couple of repair bays were open, one with a Buick up on the rack. Inside the shop, it was all neon and ugly black-and-white linoleum floors, shelves of foods loaded with sugars and carbs and high-fructose corn syrup, glass-fronted cooler cases containing beer and dairy products and sodas. There were probably a thousand places just like it along Interstate 10 between its terminal points in California and Florida. More.

But *this* was the one Johnny Ortega had stopped at that day.

Annie picked up a contradictory welter of emotions from Lonnie Briggs. He was single, which came as no particular surprise. He was lonely, and ditto. He liked working on cars better than running the shop—the grease under his nails would have told her that much even without her being an empath—but in the store there was at least the possibility of human interaction, so he hired mechanics and tended to the store himself most of the time. While Annie had been talking to him, he'd had only two customers, but there were things he could be doing other than talking to her: straightening up, restocking, paperwork. On the other hand, he didn't especially want her to leave.

She might hate herself for it later, but she had to play whatever cards she could. She put her hand on his shoulder and left it there, looking right into his brown eyes. She tried to send out the signal that if he did her this favor, maybe she would let him take her into a service bay and open up her hood. "Lonnie," she said. "If the disks are all back there, and dated, can't we just have a quick look?"

"They're not in any order," he said. "They're just all thrown in the drawer every which way."

"I understand that. I don't mind sticking around a while, if that's what it takes."

"Well . . ."

"If you have customers or something else you have to do, you can just leave me alone and I'll look," she said. "I mean, I understand if you don't want me in the back by myself, but I'm happy to do the digging."

It was so wrong to play him like that. But if there was a chance that Ortega had been captured on a surveillance camera, she had to know. And if her best shot was to promise to stick around, maybe flirt with him, then she would do it.

She knew he would come around even before he did. She felt his acquiescence, then saw it spread across his stubbled face. "Okay," he said. "There ain't nothing back there you could hurt, I guess. Just you be careful so you don't fall or anything."

"I'll be so careful," she promised.

"All right," Lonnie said. "I'll show you where they are."

THEY were, in fact, just thrown into a drawer. The only order to them was sedimentary—layered approximately year by year. She tried reaching down to the bottom of the big drawer (her wrists getting sliced up by the uncased DVDs as she pushed through), and found that the bottom ones were only five years old. She wondered if he had recorded to videotape before that, and where all his tapes were if he had. He didn't seem like a guy who threw much away. The back room was lined with shelves on which he kept supplies and stock for the sales floor, but she also saw mountains of used cash register tapes and faded boxes overflowing with old business records.

Finally she started pulling out handfuls at a time, skimming the dates scrawled on them and stacking them on the

back room's concrete floor. It took her half an hour to find
the right date—with Lonnie coming in every five minutes or
so to check on her progress. He happened to be there when
she found the right one. "This is it!" she said, waving it at
him. "Is there someplace I can watch it?"

"I got a machine in my office," he said.

"Do you mind?"

"It's right in here." He took Annie through the jumbled
back room and into a small office that made the back room
look organized. She was leery about sitting in his desk chair,
which tilted forward at a dangerous angle and seemed like it
had been used as a napkin, gum repository, and she didn't
know what else. But that was where the computer was, its
keyboard virtually submerged between papers, forms, greasy
sandwich wrappings, and other debris, so she swallowed her
concerns and sat, feeding the disk into the machine. Her own
laptop was in the car, but if this wasn't the right disk, or if
Ortega didn't appear on it, she didn't want to leave until she
knew.

Lonnie walked back and forth between his office and the
shop, keeping an eye on both. Annie fast-forwarded through
the hours of customers and the slow times between customers. At three, she slowed down, skipping ahead little by
little.

At eight minutes after the hour, Johnny Ortega walked in
the front door. Annie's heart skipped, as it had when Dr.
Tsang told her about the receipt in the first place. The
time/date stamp on the disk showed when he was in the store,
and a forensic technician could verify it.

She watched Ortega in real time, making his purchases—
a pack of Marlboros, a Pepsi, a Kit Kat, and a Nestlé
Crunch—and then leaving the store. When he was gone, she
ejected the disk.

"I need to borrow this," she said. "It's very important."

"That's what you said."

"Is it okay?"

"I don't need it. Not even sure why I save them. I guess if
someone robbed me and I remember having seen him be-

fore . . . other than that, they don't do me much good after a day or so."

"I'll get it back to you," she said. "But it's very important evidence in a death penalty case."

"Take it," he said. "Bring it back when you're done."

Not because he needed it, but because he wanted to see her again. That was okay. At the moment, she could have kissed him.

Well, almost.

38

A fierce wind had picked up, flapping Annie's hair in her face and tossing sand and grit and litter around Lonnie's tarmac, and she had to wrestle her car door open. She got inside, slammed it shut, and fished her phone from her purse. She dialed Jocelyn Moreno's office in Lordsburg, only to be informed that the prosecutor was at her Silver City office. Annie asked for that number, scrawling it on her left palm, then dialed it. A minute later she had Moreno on the phone, and she explained what she had seen.

"I'm just leaving Willcox, headed your way." Annie said, putting the Taurus into gear. Wind snatched at a sign duct taped to the convenience-store wall in front of her: DON'T SPIT IN MY PARKING LOT AND I WON'T PISS ON YOUR CAR!

"I'll meet you in Lordsburg," Moreno said. "And I'll round up a judge. If you have what you claim, then you're right, Ortega couldn't have murdered those kids."

"I have it," Annie said. "The receipt is safe at Cenoba Labs in Tucson, and I have a copy of the surveillance video with a time and date stamp. He was here."

"I'll see you in a little while," Moreno said. "Drive carefully—it's really blowing out here."

"Here too," Annie said. "See you soon." A gust hit the car and shuddered it, and a newspaper circular slapped her windshield before tumbling out of sight. She put the phone down and gripped the wheel with both hands, wrestling the vehicle toward the freeway.

The wind was blowing out of the southeast and heading into it was a struggle for every mile, like trying to drive underwater. Dust clouds billowed into the air; the late-afternoon sky took on a hazy, gray brown color. In Annie's mirror, the lowering sun slipped in and out of orange clouds.

Just across the New Mexico border, brake lights burned ghostly red through a thick cloud of dust. "Damn it," she said to herself, pounding the steering wheel in frustration. "Out of the way!" Annie tapped her brakes, approaching the twin lanes of stopped traffic cautiously, hoping the people coming up behind were paying attention too. She came to a dead halt and sat there, twisting uncomfortably in her seat. Didn't the people in her way understand her urgency? An innocent man was sitting in prison. Anything could be happening to him there.

She had a chance to do something good for someone, to correct a grievous wrong, and everything—weather, traffic, other drivers—conspired to slow her down. She fought off the impulse to lean on the horn, understanding that the vehicles blocking her way weren't sitting there by choice. She tried to focus on her music—Amy Winehouse, who sang like an earthbound soul angel and whose life made Annie's look conventional by comparison—and on the fact that she had managed to turn up the evidence that would spring Ortega.

In a pasture by the highway, dozens of cows had hunkered down, some lying on their sides to get out of the punishing wind. Annie didn't blame them—gusts battered her car as she sat there, making it sway as if on the deck of a ferry instead of a solid interstate.

Eventually, traffic began creeping forward. The flashing lights of emergency vehicles loomed out of the intermittent dust fog, and the two lanes of the interstate merged into one. Annie switched to an Indigo Girls CD. She crawled forward. She tried to call Jocelyn Moreno to warn her of the delay, but she had no cell phone service.

Finally, almost an hour after she had first seen the brake lights, she edged past a tractor-trailer that had been blown onto its side, blocking the inside lanes in both directions. Beyond that, traffic thinned out, although now she passed two lines of cars piled up heading west toward Arizona.

With the roadway clear at last, Annie gunned the Taurus as fast as she could against the wind. By the time she reached Lordsburg, the lights of the small city gleamed faintly through the haze as if enveloped in thick smoke, and a three-quarter moon was rising, fat and red as a blood orange. In town, buildings cut the wind and dust to some extent, and she raced to Moreno's office, half certain the prosecutor and judge would have given up on her.

But they were inside sharing a pot of tea. Jocelyn Moreno introduced Luisa de la Garza, the judge who had presided over Ortega's trial, and within minutes they were watching Annie's DVD. Outside, the wind howled like a pack of hell-hounds on the loose.

"Play it again," Judge de la Garza said when Ortega had vanished from the screen. Annie complied.

"That looks like him."

"It is him," Annie said. "There's no doubt. And even if there were, the receipt from that sale is at the lab in Tucson, where it was found in his pocket."

"Do you have any idea how much I hate being wrong? Or hate it when a jury is shown to be wrong?" De la Garza was in her fifties, squat and gray-haired, with energy to spare. She didn't so much sit in a seat as allow it to temporarily identify where she was, but by the time anyone had her pinned down she was shifting or standing or pacing, then alighting again, as briefly as a hummingbird on a branch.

"You're not the only one," Jocelyn Moreno said. "Sheriff Raines put together what looked like an airtight case."

"Airtight because Sheriff Raines left out all the things he didn't want anyone to know," Annie said.

"I'm not sure I like the suggestion that this was done intentionally," Moreno said, eyeing Annie sternly.

"I can't see any other reason for it," Annie said. "It was either intent or gross incompetence. I'm leaning toward intent."

"We'll have to look into that," de la Garza said. "In the meantime, Jocelyn, if I could use your phone, I think the governor will be interested in this."

"You're calling him now?" Annie had been sure this would only be a first, tentative step into a bureaucratic tangle as thick as the mesquite grove outside New Dominion.

"Watch me," the judge said, smiling.

Annie sat quietly, trying not to rejoice, while de la Garza spoke with New Mexico's governor. The judge explained in terse, specific phrases what she had seen on the DVD and what the Tucson lab claimed the sales receipt showed, then went through the other points Annie and Moreno had discussed. When she was finished, she answered a few yes or no questions, and listened. Then she thanked the governor and hung up. She swiveled in her seat and fixed her gaze on Annie. "He's making a phone call," she said.

"He is?"

"It's a ways down to the prison. If you want to be there to pick Mr. Ortega up, you'd better get going. I'd hate to wait for a cab on a night like this, if it were me."

"But . . . so fast?"

"One of the perks of working in a relatively small state, Ms. O'Brien. When we make a decision, we can implement it. Especially when there's been a serious miscarriage of justice. Nobody wants to see that poor man in prison for a minute longer."

"Thank you," Annie said. She shook the judge's hand, picking up enough from it to know that a combination of relief and anxiety filled de la Garza. "Thanks, Ms. Moreno."

"Go," Moreno said. "Park Mr. Ortega in a motel—you can forward me the bill—and let me know where. The state will want to officially apologize for our error."

"I'm on my way," Annie said.

"And, Ms. O'Brien?" the judge said. "Thanks for your persistence."

39

AT the prison, after another wearying hour behind the wheel, Annie had to wait while Johnny Ortega was processed out. While she sat in the wind-buffeted car, she called Morgan and told him the news.

"That's terrific, Annie," he said. "I knew I could count on you. We could—Johnny and I both. You've done really well."

"I'm just glad he's getting pardoned," she said. "The governor didn't waste any time."

"He's a good man," Morgan said. "Obviously you didn't waste time either."

Annie considered confessing her visits to New Dominion and the time she had spent researching the abandoned town. But she still wondered if there was a connection between New Dominion and Kevin Munson's murder. Had she found a link, the same result might have been achieved. Either way, Johnny Ortega would soon be a free man.

"I'm waiting for him now," she said. "The DA wants me to get him a motel room in Lordsburg."

"Let me know where," Morgan said. "I'd like to call him."

"As soon as he's checked in," she promised.

When Ortega emerged into the night, he carried a cheap suitcase and wore clothes that might have fit him before he went in, but he had bulked up in prison and they strained to contain him. Annie braved the wind and walked up to him. "Johnny," she said. "Congratulations."

He looked at her with hard eyes, as if trying to remember who she was and which side she had taken. "Thanks," he said.

She shook his hand. He was as emotionally blank as ever. She released it quickly, disturbed by the impression that getting out of prison meant no more to him than staying inside had. "How does it feel?" she asked.

"Fine."

"I found surveillance footage of you buying some smokes and snacks at the time you were supposedly killing those teenagers," she said, walking him toward her car. She thought the wind would blow her over, but he didn't even seem to notice it. "And there was a receipt in your pocket. Did you tell your defense attorney about that?"

"Don't remember," he said.

"Well, you're out now. I'd be glad to take you to a motel in Lordsburg. The district attorney who prosecuted you, and probably the judge who sentenced you, will want to talk to you tomorrow."

"Not the same one," Ortega said.

"Sorry?"

"I don't want to go to the same motel as before."

"No problem," she said. She couldn't remember the name of the place Johnny had checked into the day he was arrested, but she knew it was right next to the Kountry Kitchen. There were plenty of motels flanking the interstate, so she could find him a Best Western or something and put him there.

The drive to Lordsburg was quiet. Annie didn't think it would be polite to play music as loud as she would have ordinarily, and Ortega was no more talkative than he had been in prison. Once her few conversational openings had been rebuffed, they rode in silence except for the wind, which had lessened slightly but still made every effort to shake the Taurus to bits. By the time she had checked him into the Holiday Motel on East Motel Drive, she was fighting back yawns. All her driving back and forth through heavy wind had sapped her energy, and then some.

She parked in front of room 110, got out of the car with him, and watched as he swiped the electronic key card and opened the door. "Thanks," he said. Annie started to respond, but the door closed in her face.

"You're welcome," she said to the door. The rooms lined the sides of a big parking lot, in the middle of which sat an indoor pool and a kids' playground. There were no kids out now, though, and the lights were off in the pool enclosure. She went back to the car and sat there until she heard the TV blare and saw its sudden burst of light at the curtains. Then she called Morgan, telling him where Ortega was ensconced. Morgan thanked her again, complimenting her on her detecting skills.

When the call was done, she put the phone away and started the car. Another hour and she would be home in bed. Her temporary home, anyway. Her bed for how much longer? She'd have to figure that out, over the next few days. With Ortega free, her business in Hidalgo County was done. She could go back to Phoenix, knowing that she had done well and done some good in the bargain.

Or she could stay put. The factors that had driven her to seek solitude hadn't changed—her hearing had improved somewhat, but not completely, and the empathy wasn't altogether gone. Besides, in the short time she had lived there she had come to like the country life—the birds and wildlife and abundant, high-desert foliage, the clear, star-glutted night skies, the peaceful days. She had to consider Leo too. She certainly hadn't come looking to meet someone, but since she had, she should figure out how she really felt about him. He deserved as honest an assessment as she could make, whether she stayed or left.

She was thinking about him, not yet out of the Lordsburg phone reception sphere, when he called. "You've got to see what I turned up," he said.

"What is it?"

"Raines has a big old safe in his office. He doesn't always keep it locked, but there are usually people around so nobody can get at it. I was around doing paperwork after Rosemary went home, and June, the night dispatch, was late. Martin and Gary took off in a hurry for something, and Martin left it open, so I poked around and found an old leather-bound journal. It's my job if anybody finds out I have it—my job, and probably a prison term."

"Maybe you should just put it back, Leo."

"But it's important. Or I think it is, anyway. It might be. I don't think I can decipher it all on my own, honestly. I'm hoping it'll make more sense to you than it does to me. I have it on me now. Where are you?"

"Believe it or not, I'm just leaving Lordsburg, where I dropped Johnny Ortega at a motel."

"Ortega's out?"

"That's right. I was going to tell you when I saw you later. I am seeing you later, right?"

"I'll come by your place in a little while—maybe I'll even beat you there. You're going to want to look at this journal right away."

"I'll see you there," she said. "And hey—maybe there is something to that whole helping-people concept after all, justice and all that. I have to say, I feel pretty good right now."

"As you should, Annicka. You did a good thing. You drive carefully, okay?"

"Same to you," she said and hung up.

TWENTY minutes from home, her shoulders aching from the constant battle against the wind, so hungry she thought her stomach lining would eat itself, Annie was almost over-whelmed with anticipation. What could be in the journal Leo had found? Obviously it didn't pertain to the Ortega case, or Leo would have mentioned that. Something more on

New Dominion, then? If she decided not to stick around Hidalgo County, that mystery might just have to solve itself without her.

For the second time that day, emergency vehicles slowed Annie's progress. As she approached a bend, the flicker of lights strobed the darkness. Sheriff's vehicles and an ambulance were parked willy-nilly, mostly off the road but sticking out far enough to make her slow down. She would have anyway; the cop in her wouldn't let her go past such a scene, involving officers she knew, without stopping to help. She pulled in behind the other vehicles and stepped from her car.

An embankment fell sharply from the side of the road here, and a sheriff's Tahoe was on the ground at its base, upside down, illuminated by flashlights and a couple of floods that had been quickly set up. From the top of the hill there was no way to tell who had been driving the SUV, but whoever it was would have been lucky to walk away. As Annie started down the hill, Johanna spotted her and rushed over.

"No, Annie!" she called. She caught Annie, still at a half run up the slope, and gripped her upper arms. The emotion pouring from her and through Annie was almost physically painful in its intensity. "Don't go down there."

"Johanna, what's going on?" Annie asked. "Whose car is that?"

In the glow of emergency lights and reflected floodlights, Annie saw tears filling Johanna's eyes. "It's . . . goddammit, it's Leo. You can't go down there, Annie."

Hearing that, Annie couldn't *not* go down. The vehicle looked like it had rolled a few times on its way down, leaving a trail of crushed and uprooted foliage and torn up earth. She shook free of Johanna's grasp. "I've got to," she said.

"Annie, you're a civilian! This is our scene, and if you go down there, I'll arrest you!"

"Fine," Annie said. She continued her descent, picking her way down the precarious slope and trying to steel herself against whatever she would find at the bottom. *You're a cop,* she told herself, *you've seen everything.* "Where is he? Where's Leo? Is he okay?"

Johanna followed Annie, clawing at her leather jacket. "Stop," she said. "Stop, Annie!" She clutched at Annie's shoulder and arm, holding on with a ferocious grip, as sobs burst from her. "Annie, he didn't make it."

40

THROUGH misting eyes, Annie gazed up at the ambulance that sat on the shoulder of the road, then back down at the crash site. The Tahoe was oddly foreshortened from here, accordioned in on itself. The gas tank hadn't ruptured but the wind blew a sharp smell to her then whisked it away just as fast, the stink of motor oil and burned metal and death.

He *had* to have made it. She couldn't accept the alternative.

She didn't know if she loved him, had almost given up wondering if she was capable of love or if it mattered one way or the other, but she valued him and she wanted to hold him, talk to him, to watch his ready smile light his face up like neon.

"You're wrong," she said. Once again, she shook off Johanna's hands, wishing she could avoid the woman's emotional torment as easily. "You're wrong." She knew she sounded like everyone else, every survivor who tried to deny the death of somebody close to them no matter what the evidence showed. She was becoming a stereotype, an archetype. No longer Annie O'Brien, but everywoman, and losing her cop's objectivity along with her own identity. The kind of person every cop had to deal with at these sorts of scenes and learned to hate, to resent.

"Who is that?" Martin Raines called. He was standing near the crashed SUV, looking up, surrounded by men Annie didn't recognize. He held a Maglite in his hands and he played it toward Annie's face.

"It's O'Brien," Johanna answered. "I'm trying to stop her."

"Well, try harder!" Martin said. "Ms. O'Brien, you really don't want to come down here."

Annie struggled to find her voice. "Maybe not, but I have to."

"No, you don't, Annie," Johanna said. She followed Annie, so close that if either one slipped they'd both go down together.

"Yes. Yes I do. How did this happen?"

"We're not sure," Johanna said, sniffing back tears. "He was off duty. Not heading home, because he wouldn't have taken this route, but going someplace in a hurry. I guess with all the wind and everything he must have been distracted and just didn't quite make the turn. There's no guardrail here, and—"

"He knew the road."

"What?"

"There's no guardrail, but Leo *knew* this road. He wouldn't have just missed the turn."

"It's pretty treacherous out tonight," Johanna said. "There have been lots of accidents. None this severe locally, but in other parts of the county, there have been reports coming in all night. Lots of fender benders."

Annie barely heard her. She was trying to listen for signs of life from the wreck, but the wind howling through the trees and shrubs, the engine noise from the emergency vehicles, and the sound of conversation were all folding together in her ears and picking out anything specific was getting harder and harder.

She was almost at ground level now, and Gary Raines moved to block her progress. "I think you should stay back, ma'am," he said. "It ain't pretty."

"It never is." She dodged his hands, but not the blast of emotion that rolled off him in waves. Off everyone, in fact— intense, raw, feelings of sorrow and loss, and something else that felt like betrayal. Everyone had liked Leo. Annie found herself resenting them. She wanted to know her own sorrow, wanted that sense of loss to be hers alone, instead of having to share it. She had never hated being an empath, even on a minor scale, more than she did right now. She couldn't even be certain of how she really felt, and wouldn't be until she was alone again. "I've seen plenty of ugliness in Phoenix."

"I'm sorry, Annie," Johanna said. "You've got to stay back. We're working this scene."

As well as you worked the scenes when Carylyn Phelps and Kevin Munson were murdered? she wanted to ask. She almost let herself give voice to the question, then bit it back. From behind, she felt a hand on her shoulder. For a brief, glorious instant, she thought it would be Leo's, that he had escaped the vehicle after all and hid in the brush until she arrived, but it was only Johanna again. "Please, Annie, stay away from the vehicle for now."

Tears spilled from Annie's eyes at last. From here, she could see that the cab was almost flattened. She hoped Leo wasn't still inside, because they'd have to cut him out with torches. Maybe he had been thrown from it as it rolled. Maybe he had died quickly, suddenly, breaking his neck against an unyielding boulder. She was tired, weary from the long day and tired of fighting Johanna, and she stopped where Johanna indicated, stood there letting the tears flow and her stomach clench and churn.

He had come by here on his way to her place, she knew. He was bringing over that journal he had told her about, and he was hurrying to get there before she did, his mind wandering because of whatever he had found in its pages, and he had missed the turn and flown over the edge.

Which made it her fault.

If she hadn't become obsessed—*his word*—with New Dominion, Leo would be alive.

Wind lashed her hair into her face, and she wished it was leather whips, punishing her. She was selfish, caring only about what anyone could do for her, about what the world might deliver to her feet—men, interesting cases, mysteries to solve. A journal, a ghost town. She took and took and gave nothing back. Even getting Johnny Ortega out of prison was about her, about what she could accomplish, about how she was a better detective than those who had investigated the original crimes. Ortega was a prop; he could have been anybody. She had never cared about him for an instant.

But Leo—Leo, she had cared about. And he died trying to bring her something he believed she'd find interesting. *Important*, he had said.

If his death was not to be utterly in vain, she had to try to find that journal.

She rubbed stinging salt water from her eyes. He would have had it on the passenger seat, probably. Maybe when the SUV started to roll, it had flown free, even if Leo hadn't.

Keeping her gaze toward the ground and directed away from the vehicle, she started slowly walking a wide perimeter of her own. Broken glass glinted on the ground, and she saw a side mirror that had snapped off the vehicle, a bumper, a hubcap. Other parts too, once her eyes adjusted better to the darkness beyond the range of the lights. A ballpoint pen stuck up out of the ground as if it had been jammed there intentionally, like a knife. Annie recognized it as the type Leo kept in the breast pocket of his uniform.

She didn't get any closer to the wreck, but Johanna and the others let her roam outside their perimeter. She could tell they kept an eye on her, though. Finally, she heard wind fluttering something that wasn't desert scrub and saw a book, splayed open on the ground, its pages flapping as if it wanted to fly away.

She started toward it, but stopped, pretending she hadn't seen it. From the corner of her eye she watched Martin

Raines eyeballing her while he feigned checking the wreck-age. He was sly, but cops were often watched while they went about their business, and she wasn't fooled. She saw his gaze tick over to the book, then back to her.

It was a trap, then.

The book was almost certainly the journal, and Martin knew that Leo had taken it from his safe. He probably even knew where Leo was headed. If Annie went for the book, he would know for sure that the two of them had been conspir-ing together. She was outnumbered here, with Martin's son and daughter beside him, and the other officers under his command. They had the SUV surrounded but they didn't seem to be making a lot of progress at getting into it.

The cynic in her, the detective who viewed everyone and everything through a lens of suspicion, wondered if the whole thing was a setup. Did Martin know before the acci-dent that his journal had been taken? Was it an accident at all? Or had they murdered Leo for taking the book and were now just waiting to see if Annie was an innocent bystander or part of the plot before they decided what to do with her? Maybe that was where the feelings of betrayal she sensed came from—not that he had abandoned them by dying too soon, but that he had stolen from them and they had made him pay.

She couldn't grab the book, and she had to get out of here before they decided it was easier to do away with her than to wonder. She had the Beretta in the car, but hadn't brought it or her purse down here with her. If they wanted to kill her, they could do it easily enough and probably manufacture evidence suggesting she had been in the Tahoe with Leo.

As she stood there, silently debating herself, the wind snatched a page from the book and whisked it away. Another one was tearing, ready to go at any time. There was no way to tell how many had already gone.

Annie made an abrupt decision. She brought her hand up over her mouth, widened her eyes, made a retching noise, and dashed into the brush.

"Annie?" Johanna said.

"She's getting sick," Martin said. "Leave her be."

Annie crashed and stumbled through the underbrush, scanning for any telltale white patches catching moonlight. The seconds ticked by, and she knew that if it took too long, someone would come looking for her. When she caught a glimpse of a page impaled on the thorns of a mesquite, she stopped and faked vomiting, to cover kneeling down and grabbing it. She folded the page, stuffed it in her pocket. From that low angle she could see another one, a few feet away. She spat once and went to that one, pocketing it as well.

"Annie, are you okay?" Johanna asked. She was starting through the foliage toward Annie.

"Sick," Annie said. "I'm sorry—I didn't want to contaminate your scene, though."

"I understand," Johanna said. "Come on, let's get you out of here."

"I'm . . . I'm okay," Annie said. At a glance, she didn't see any more pages, and Johanna was too close now to keep looking. She kicked dirt over nothing, as if hiding a puddle of vomit, and headed toward Johanna. "I guess I should get home, though. It's been a long day."

"I'm sure it has," Johanna said.

"You'll let me know . . . about Leo? His funeral and . . . whatever?"

"Of course, Annie."

Annie let Johanna guide her back to the slope. Along the way she finally got a glimpse inside the Tahoe. Leo dangled upside down, still belted in, his face a mass of blood and raw meat. She almost genuinely vomited, but swallowed it back, tasting bile. "You sure you can get home all right?" Johanna asked.

"Yeah. I'm usually more . . . detached, I guess. But I'll be okay."

"Call me if you need to," Johanna said. She sounded sincere. Annie got the sense that she meant it. Maybe she didn't know what her father had done. Or if she did, she agreed that it was necessary, but she would still miss Leo.

"I will," Annie said, starting to walk up the embankment. "Thanks, Johanna."

Johanna waited at the bottom, watching her go. Making sure she went, more likely. Annie didn't disappoint. She got into the Taurus, rubbed her eyes some more, started the engine, and drove off, picking her way carefully around the emergency vehicles in the road.

41

BECAUSE he might have to be in a distant city on short notice, the Impressionist kept a private plane at his disposal. Even private planes had to file and follow flight plans, but most law enforcement officials—if they ever thought to look for connections between wildly disparate murders—turned first to commercial airline passenger manifests, not guessing that someone with the resources to own an airplane might be responsible.

Tonight he was glad he had one. He had received a phone call, and the instant it ended, he made a call of his own, ordering the plane fueled and ready to go. It was a short jump, less than six hours by car, but he didn't want to waste even that much time. He'd had to deal with Momma; a pillow held over her face had only set him back a few minutes, and he wasn't too concerned about leaving behind evidence at this point. Once he reached the airport, he was wheels up in twenty minutes and on the ground again, behind the wheel of a rented sedan, fifty minutes after that.

This night was too important to waste time. This night was the one he had been waiting for, the night everything he had worked toward would come to fruition. He had been a student, but this was graduation day, time to flip the old tassel to the other side of the mortarboard. It was late on the eve of transformation, when he would change from what he had been into the far greater being he would become. Any doubt at all had been blown away by that phone call. The pieces had fallen into place, just when he needed them to. That last piece, the one element not entirely within his control, confirmed that it was meant to be.

He drove from the tiny rural airport into the . . . well, *city* was too grand a word for it. Town. Into town. Not even big enough to get a decent rental car; he drove an old, beat-up junker that belonged to one of the airport's employees.

Just across from the railroad tracks he spotted the sign he was looking for. Illuminated against the midnight sky were the words HOLIDAY MOTEL. He pulled into the motel's parking lot, past RVs and a pickup truck with a tarp over the bed, one corner loose and snapping like a flag, past Harleys and a broken down Nissan Sentra and a customized VW, and parked next to a Dodge Dart badly in need of paint, or perhaps a trip to the junkyard.

Power flowed into him, through him, the power of a universe that had made its decision, chosen its champion. Before morning's first light, he would be another, and that knowledge almost made him giddy.

He walked up to the room with 110 on its door and knocked. When nobody answered, he rapped again, louder. From inside, he heard movement, rustling, muttering. Then the knob clicked and the door opened to the extent of the sliding bar lock. Johnny Ortega's dark, tattooed face appeared in the gap.

"You," Johnny said.

"That's right," the Impressionist said.

"You did it."

"I told you I would, didn't I?"

"I just didn't expect to see you tonight," Johnny said.

"Well, I couldn't wait, Johnny," the Impressionist said. "Aren't you going to let me in?"

"'Course." Johnny shut the door for a second, undid the lock, opened it again, wider. The room smelled like smoke. "Come on in, Mr. Julliard."

"Thanks, Johnny," the Impressionist said. "And please, call me Morgan. We need to get busy—we have a lot to do tonight."

42

A couple of miles from the crash site, far enough to know she hadn't been followed, Annie pulled over again, clicked on a map light, and fished the journal pages from her pocket. The paper was old and brittle and yellow, the ink purple with age. One of the pages had cracked along the lines of her fold, obscuring some of the text. Holes from mesquite thorns eliminated more of it. The other page held together, but it too was chipped and torn. Even what she could see, she couldn't always read—it was written in a stiff, old-fashioned hand, the letters formed in a way she wasn't used to, and the ink had blobbed in places, smudged, run together.

The first line at the top of one page said, ". . . ere one calls upon Asmillius, one must ensure that all preparations herewith set down are followed with care and precision, that no errors be . . ." The page had ripped there, and Annie had to hold the next section up, trying to piece together the rest of the line. She couldn't make it out. The next legible part said, ". . . and the conditions as described must be met in their totality, as to timing, as to participants, as to . . ."

After that came some blurred words. She skimmed the

rest of the page. It described preparations for a ritual of some sort and went into a fair amount of detail about required cleansing processes, although she couldn't determine the ritual's ultimate purpose.

The other page came from somewhat later in the journal. Running her gaze over the page, she saw the word "Asmillius" again. Below, another sentence caught her eye. "With the crucifixion sword gripped firmly in the right hand, the Magician shall touch the tip of the blade to the ground thrice, in such fashion; once to the East saying, From the East, I command thee, thence to the West, saying, From the West, I commend thee, finally to the North, saying, From the North, I summon thee. Only then must the blade be allowed to touch the . . ."

There it became illegible again, until farther down the page, when she found the phrase ". . . Blood spills upon the Earth, Earth drinks of Blood, Heaven dries the Earth but Blood soaks through to Hell and Heaven tastes not of its . . ."

Suddenly anxious, Annie shut off the map light. She sat in the darkness for several moments, trying to see beyond the windows of the car, looking for anyone who might be watching her. Satisfied that she was still alone, she put the car into gear and pulled out into the road again. She could continue trying to read the pages at home. She wished she had the whole book, but maybe she could find some other way to get to it.

Another thought struck her and she screeched to a stop in the middle of the street, thought about the best route, and then continued. Up ahead there was a dirt road that would connect with 338. She could take that toward Drummond.

With all the law enforcement Raineses at the "accident" scene, there might never be a better time, she had realized, to go back to the Raines family compound and have a look at that little graveyard.

When she turned onto the dirt road, it hit her like a hurtling brick in the gut. Leo was really dead. Her eyes filled again and a keening sob escaped her lips. Now, alone in the car, faced with her own unadulterated sense of loss, she ached. She had held something precious in her hands for a few moments and then lost it again, and the loss was all the greater for having known it was there so briefly. Not love, maybe, but a human connection with a decent person, and that was almost as rare.

Driving along the narrow dirt road, she wept, tears making everything liquid before her. The night and the wind threw obstacles in her path: an owl swooped at the upper edge of her headlights' glow, trying to gain altitude with a rat writhing in its beak; a tumbleweed leapt onto the hood and burst apart like one of those spun-sugar prop bottles from the movies; a plastic water bottle spun into the road, hit a tire, and bounced away.

All the while, her mind spun as crazily as the bottle. Leo was gone. That journal he'd found seemed to be an instruction manual for some sort of magical rite involving a crucifixion sword, whatever that was, and someone or something named Asmillius. Martin Raines kept it locked up in his safe, and he might have killed Leo over it. Did that mean he believed in it? Or was it simply a curiosity, an old book, maybe a family heirloom? But who killed someone over an old book?

At least Johnny Ortega was safely in Lordsburg. That was one problem off her mind.

43

THE Raines "compound" was mostly dark, with lights shining in only a few of the houses. Annie cut her own lights, pulled off the road before she reached the first house, and switched off the dome light so it wouldn't come on when she opened the door. Carrying a mini flashlight and her Beretta, she left the car as quietly as she could, even though the wind would mask most sounds.

The little cemetery was behind the house that looked abandoned, the one with the hole in the ceiling big enough for a small plane to pass through. It was the third house on the right, just before Johanna's. Old wood gleamed silver in the moonlight. Annie dashed carefully past the first two houses, trying to stay in the shadows of trees and gateposts. She waited until clouds crossed in front of the moon, high in the sky at this hour, then picked a path that took her close to the empty third house, since lights glowed in a couple of upstairs windows of the second.

No light spilled into the back, though, and with clouds still screening the moonlight, Annie raced to the wrought-iron fence surrounding the graveyard. It was just over waist-high on her. There was a gate, but when she tried it, a squeak she could hear over the wind's racket began to sound, so she released it and climbed the fence instead. The ancient steel wobbled under her weight, but held.

There must have been three dozen headstones, bearing dates ranging from 1891 to 1999. Annie didn't know from what stone they were made, but as she crouched among them, playing her light over their surfaces, she saw they had symbols of nature etched into them, snakes and plants, climbing vines and the like, and other shapes she couldn't identify, sensuous and organic. Celtic designs, she guessed.

Most of the names on the stones ended in Raines, although there were some women and children with different surnames—Raineses who had married into other families, she supposed. At first she jumped from one to another, scattered, her thoughts still whirling so fast she had a hard time focusing. But if she kept that up, she would miss something, so she went to one corner of the rectangular graveyard and started over, in sequence, right to left and then to the next row.

When she was finished, she had not seen a stone belonging to Jeremiah Raines. Starting over was out of the question—she had spent enough time here anyway. It was odd, though. If he had been sixty-six in 1938, then he couldn't possibly be alive. And the county had no death certificate, no burial information. So where was he? Annie couldn't help thinking he was key to everything that had happened in New Dominion—and therefore, by association, to Kevin Munson and Carylyn Phelps. Johnny Ortega was out of prison, so there was no urgent need for her to investigate further. But she couldn't let it go. Leo had died trying to help her figure this whole thing out. She owed him, if nothing else.

One of the graves had a crucifix engraved on it—it seemed out of place amidst the other designs, but it was one of the non-Raines surnames, so maybe that explained it—and Annie realized with a start what the journal entry about a "crucifixion sword" must have referred to.

She had once been in the morgue when the medical examiner and one of his assistants had started arguing about the actual, literal cause of Jesus Christ's death on the cross. The assistant, a guy who had tried to draw Annie into religious conversations before, had insisted that his death was the result of his heartache over his inability to minister any longer to the people of Earth—that while he knew he was ascending to Heaven, moving to a different state of being, and that his death and resurrection would be more powerful forces than his life could have been, he still mourned the loss of his personal connection to humanity. "The rest of it—the flogging, the weight of the cross, the blood loss from having nails driven through his wrists and feet, the loss of energy due to his inability to draw breath with his feet extended and secured—those were all factors, but ultimately, his heart failed because of his sorrow over that loss. That's the only explanation that makes sense to me."

The medical examiner had listened patiently, while using bone cutters to snip through the deceased's ribs (Annie had refused to prune her dad's roses for months after the first time she'd heard that, because just handling pruning shears reminded her of the loud snap each rib made). The ribs finished, he had put the tool down and smiled at his assistant. "You're forgetting one thing," he said. "I agree, as far as you've gone, except I think the cause of his heart failure was probably more mundane. Maybe he fell while trying to carry the cross, and he was crushed beneath it. Remember, it had to be heavy enough to support his weight, so it was a big honking piece of wood. But the Bible tells us he called out and then died in a relatively short period of time. That's because his heart was working so hard—trying to draw breath from an awkward position, as you suggest, on top of everything else he had suffered—but he didn't die of exhaustion or asphyxiation, because if he had he wouldn't have been able to cry out. No, the final straw was a rupture of the free wall of his left ventricular myocardium. And do you know what confirms that hypothesis?"

The assistant looked into the open chest cavity. "Not an autopsy."

The medical examiner laughed. Annie fought to keep down the yogurt and coffee she'd had for breakfast. "No. John tells us that after his death, a Roman soldier stabbed him in the side, and a mixture of blood and water poured out of the wound."

"But if he was already dead, he wouldn't have bled much, would he?" Annie asked. The whole scene, doctors talking religion inside a temple of science, struck her as vaguely surreal.

"You've been paying attention, Ms. O'Brien," the medical examiner said. He gave her two gloved, blood-spattered thumbs up. "That's good. And you are correct."

"But . . . blood and water?" the assistant asked.

"That's just the thing. The stress factors we've discussed would have elevated his pericardial fluid from the usual thirty cc or so to a hundred cc or more. The free wall rupture would have added a few hundred cc of noncoagulating blood, settling to the lower reaches of the pericardial cavity. When the sword pierced his heart, that blood flowed out, followed by clear pericardial fluid, which unschooled observers took to be water. *Et voilà*—blood and water."

The conversation had stuck with her, mostly because of how strange the whole thing was. Now it came back to her in a rush, triggered by that phrase—*crucifixion sword*. The sword that the Roman soldier stabbed Christ with? Why would there be a reference to that in an old journal from an empty corner of New Mexico? Surely an artifact like that would be stashed in some vault at the Vatican, wouldn't it?

Then again, how did she know the journal had anything to do with New Dominion? Leo had said so—or implied it, anyway—but the two pages she'd seen didn't give any such indication. Why else would Martin Raines have had it locked in his safe, though? Why else kill Leo to keep it a secret?

Well, she wasn't going to find anything out here. The cemetery was a bust too, at least in terms of trying to find what had become of Jeremiah Raines. Time to get out of there before someone spotted her skulking around.

She climbed the wobbly fence once more. As she came

down on the other side, she noticed the abandoned third house again. From the rear, in the moonlight, it looked like the empty wreck it certainly was. But she remembered noticing that from the front, although it was obviously vacant, it had been well kept, the yard neat. Almost as if someone meant to put it on the market, which Leo said was never done. Why the discrepancy between front and back? Now it looked more like she expected.

She started toward the shadowed, still, and silent house, swallowing hard, her throat so dry that it hurt, like trying to choke down something the size of a fist. She couldn't have said precisely why, but she needed to have a look inside.

44

LIKE the windows in front, the rear ground-floor windows were covered with sheets of plywood, warped by weather and time. Annie found one that had buckled, working some of its nails free of the wall, and managed to tug it away far enough to aim her flashlight's beam through the gap. The light reflected off jagged shards of glass, thick with dust. Heart pistoning, she shifted the light and found a space where the glass had been knocked clear, although she had to pull harder on the plywood to do it, and she was a little afraid she might yank it free altogether, at which point—one arm under the wood, holding a light—she would be unable to catch it and it would either shatter the rest of the glass or fall to the ground, either way making enough of a racket to bring some Rainses running.

If, that was, anyone could hear it over the wind that sliced through twin overhead power lines with a wail like a thousand mournful ghosts.

Annie's flashlight beam landed on a floor caked with dust and rodent droppings. Just what she would expect to find in a house that had stood empty for as long as this one apparently had. She trained the light up the far wall, exposing plaster that had fallen away, leaving a latticework of wood framing behind it. Below the wainscoting was wood paneling that termites and other vermin had feasted upon for years. She moved the light across the wall until it illuminated another doorway.

On its far side, her beam picked out a big leather easy chair, and then revealed an old man sitting in it. Annie caught her breath and her chest clenched painfully as she waited for him to react to the light. But the man didn't move. He just sat in the chair, his eyes halfway open, staring into the darkness of the house. Was he dead? That, or blind, she decided. Only one way to find out which.

"Hello? Sir?"

He didn't respond.

Annie's first instinct was to get out of there and call the sheriff's office to report a dead body. But every house around here was inhabited by the sheriff and his family, including his two top deputies. If there was a DB in their midst, the idea that they didn't know about it was pretty far-fetched.

Which meant calling in reinforcements from elsewhere—the real sheriff, Teller, from up in Lordsburg. An investigation would have to be launched into the whole Raines administration and Martin Raines's connection to Leo's death. Before she could set any of that in motion, though, she needed to make sure this geezer was really dead, and not just sleeping or comatose.

She had to get inside.

The front door was clearly visible from the street, and she had no guarantee that the law enforcement Raineses would stay away from home much longer. Still hoping to avoid discovery, Annie stayed at the back of the house, the side facing the graveyard, and found a doorway there with planks nailed over it. She didn't have anything like a crowbar, but when she pulled on one of the planks, it came away easily. The jamb it was nailed to had rotted, and the soft wood wouldn't grip the nails. Annie tore the board free and set it down on the dirt. The second one gave her more trouble, one of the nails squealing like brakes worn down to the metal, but she figured anyone who heard it would blame the wind. Four boards later, the door was revealed. It rested uneasily in its jamb, wind whistling through its gaps.

Annie pressed on the door, the weathered wood rough and cool against her palm, and turned the pitted brass knob. The door gave a groan that bled into a withering screech, but it swung open.

"Sir?" she said again as she entered a dark kitchen. Former kitchen, anyway. Its sink had been torn out and pipes jutted from the wall, rust stains trailing beneath them and scabbing the floor. Something skittered away from her and ducked under the baseboard, and rodent droppings were everywhere, small, hard nuggets beneath her shoes. The room had the smell of a place left to the elements, urine and mold and rot no doubt eating it from the inside out.

She followed her flashlight beam through veils of spiderweb to the room she had seen from outside. From there it was easy to find the old man, in a room across the hall from the one she'd been looking into. He still sat motionless in that chair. "Sir, are you . . . ?"

There seemed no point in finishing the question. Elvis, as they said, had left the building.

But as she trained the light onto his face, she revised her first impression. His face had a little color to it. He didn't seem to be breathing, but he didn't look like any corpse she had ever seen, except the very freshest. Had this guy died within the past little while, maybe as she'd been exploring the graveyard? A certain spooky irony there, if that was the case.

She touched his neck, looking for a pulse and not finding one. Finally, fighting down her distaste and wishing she had a pair of latex gloves, she pulled back his eyelid and shone her light in his eye.

The pupil contracted.

And Annie's world turned inside out.

45

THE old man was Jeremiah Raines. He was not dead, but he was not alive either. Someplace in between the two. Heaven didn't want him and Hell was too good for him, or something like that. In the briefest instant, Annie knew that and more. So much more.

The room fell away, then the closed, fetid house, the old man, everything. Annie stood in a grassy field on a long-ago March evening, with the sun at the brink of vanishing for the night and a fresh breeze lifting her hair. The sky was more clear than she had ever seen it, and a flock of birds that must have been miles long flew past, heading north.

Beside the field stood a church, its walls made of stone and mortar, a single tower piercing the dusk sky. A circle linked the arms and center post of the cross at the tower's peak. Off to one side, a bonfire blazed, with flames leaping a dozen feet into the air and galaxies of sparks swirling into the violet sky.

Jeremiah Raines and his wife, Mary, held court behind a table next to the church, handing out drinks of some rose-colored beverage in small earthenware goblets. It was not wine; Annie could taste the stuff on her lips and tongue, just as she could taste the sweat and grime on Jeremiah and the others, and a bit of blood where Mary had poked herself on a needle earlier and then put her finger in her mouth. The liquid had a sour tang to it, with a slightly nutty aftertaste. A long line of people stretched out from the table, people waiting their turns patiently, while those who already had their cups had scattered to the flat stones set around the field.

Each of the people standing in line held something in their hands. Annie realized they were small effigies, created in the shapes of animals and people from sticks and leaves. They reminded her of the ones decorating the shelf at Greenfield's, in Drummond. She watched the woman at the front of the line, barely twenty (Annie knew, somehow, that her name was Frances Conway, that she was a virgin, and that she was easily startled by sudden sounds), one hand clutching a twig deer, the other holding her skirts as she stepped to the table. Her lean face was taut, her cheeks sucked in, her pale blue eyes shifting between Jeremiah and Mary Raines and the cups they dished up from an open barrel standing on the ground below the table.

"Hello, Frances," Jeremiah said. He wore a white robe over his clothes, tied with a sash. A smile played about his lips. The ghost of one, really, something closer to the memory of a smile than a real one, and he pushed it away quickly. "Bless this day," he added.

"Bless this day," Frances echoed. She released her skirts and took the cup Jeremiah proffered in her left hand. She still held the effigy in her right.

"Drink it, dear," Mary said softly. Her voice was brittle, as if it might break at any moment. She was nervous, barely able to remain upright, and Annie realized that Jeremiah was handing out the drinks because Mary would have been sloshing them all over the place.

"Yes, Mary," Frances said. She was nervous now too, more so than she had been just moments before. There wasn't much liquid in the cup, so she raised it to her lips, tilted her head back, and let it pour into her mouth.

She choked on it, coughing and gagging, her eyes filling with water, but she got most of it down. "That's fine, dear," Mary said. "That's good. Now take your creature to the fire."

Still coughing, eyes watering so much she could barely see, Frances walked toward the bonfire on unsteady legs. She almost tripped over her long skirts as she approached the blaze. When its heat struck her, a sheen of sweat broke out on her face.

Behind her, the next person in line was drinking. Ahead of her, the previous one had already tossed his effigy into the flames. Frances forced her way closer to the fire, until it felt as if the smoky heat would singe her lungs, but she didn't trust her arm to throw the little wooden deer very far. When she was certain she could get it into the thick of the flames, she finally tossed it. The twigs sizzled, the sound barely audible over the roar and snap of the big blaze, and Frances hurried away, out of the nimbus of heat and into the cooler air beyond its fringe.

On her way toward the flat stones laid out in the field, her steps were faltering. She released her skirts again and put her hands out to her sides for balance. She walked like a drunk woman, or a dizzy one trying to counteract the spinning of the earth under her feet. When she reached an empty stone, she sat quickly, gratefully, holding on to its sides to steady herself.

Her eyes drooped closed. She lay back then, hands down, lowering herself carefully to the stone. She turned sideways, lying on her right hip and arm, curling her legs so that every part of her was on the stone's surface and holding her hands to her stomach as if to quell some turbulence there. Her face began to relax, her eyes fluttered, and a thin line of saliva escaped her lips, wetting the stone.

All around her, the same scene was being repeated and had been repeated many times. Those in line drank, threw their figures into the flames, picked a stone, and settled onto it.

As with Frances, within minutes after reaching the stone, they were still. Some went easily, others fought it at the end, gasping for breath, coughing, a few even trying to vomit out the liquid they had consumed.

It didn't matter. Easy or hard, they all slept.

Approaching the table, a man named Herbert McKeen fidgeted anxiously. When his turn arrived, Jeremiah Raines offered a cup and Herbert swore at him, batting the cup aside. He threw his stick figure at Jeremiah and broke into a run, heading for the low line of hills hemming in the valley.

"Stop him!" Jeremiah called.

Two men standing nearby with rifles at the ready chased after Herbert until they had passed the fire and the other participants and had clear shots. Herbert was scrambling up the slope, pawing at big rocks and jamming his toes into any foothold he could get. One of the riflemen dropped to one knee, the other aimed from a standing position, but both fired at the same instant. Annie couldn't tell which bullet hit Herbert—the other kicked up chips of rock a few inches from him—but he let out a screech and arched his back, then fell backward down the slope. He rolled and skidded and came to a dusty stop two-thirds of the way to the valley floor.

"We all have our part to play," Jeremiah called out when the echoes of the gunshots stopped resounding through the valley. "Better to cooperate and aid your community than try something like that."

The next man in line was anxious too, but watching Herbert tumble down the hill, he took the drink and downed it quickly, as did the woman after him.

The gunmen went to Herbert McKeen, who was badly hurt but not yet dead, and dragged him down the rest of the hill, holding his legs so that his head slid and bounced and scuffed behind them. When they got him to one of the flat stones, they hoisted him onto it. He whimpered and tried to claw his way down, so one of them hit him in the face with the butt of his rifle, and he went still.

Finally, there was no one else in line. Thirty or forty adults stood in the shade of the church, watching the scene with expressions either rapt or horrified. With them were a few dozen children. Most of those were crying but a few stood quietly, stoically observing the panorama. The field looked like a vast dormitory full of silently slumbering bodies.

Jeremiah filled one final cup from the barrel. "Mary, darling," he said. He took her trembling hand in his, held it, and whispered something to her. She tried to reply but the words caught in her throat.

"Never mind," he said. "Just drink, dear." He handed her the cup. Tears escaped from her eyes. "And bless this day."

"Bless this day," Mary managed, her voice cracking with every word. She downed the stuff quickly, then fell into Jeremiah's arms.

He draped his arm over her shoulder. "Come, Mary," he said, leading her out from behind the table and toward the bonfire. Weeping, she stumbled several times, but he kept her upright. Near the fire, he took the twig elk she carried from her and hurled it into the roaring flames. Then he helped her to an empty stone on the far edge of the field. By the time they reached it, her legs had almost given out altogether, and he stretched her out on the stone, positioning her so that her head hung over one edge, her brown hair touching the ground. Tears glistened in his eyes as he drew a large, straight-bladed knife from his belt. No, Annie realized, not a knife, but some kind of short sword.

"Bless this day," Jeremiah said again. No one answered him this time; all the people on the stones were beyond speech. Annie didn't know if they were asleep or half dead. Some of them stirred slightly, but none tried to get away. Jeremiah tapped the sword against the ground on the east side of the flat stone, and Annie recognized the words he spoke. "From the East, I command thee." Next he tapped on the opposite side, and said, "From the West, I commend thee." From there he tapped the earth on the north side, above his wife's head. When he spoke again, his voice broke mid-phrase. "From the North, I summon thee." At last, he raised the blade over his wife's throat and brought it down with a swift, slashing motion. As blood began to spurt from the wound, he let out a loud, barking cry.

But he didn't let his emotions stop him. He went to the next stone and did the same, shifting the person lying there so that his head overhung the side, touching the sword's tip to the earth, then cutting the victim's throat. Blood ran out onto the ground.

By the time he had slit the fifth throat, Jeremiah's hands were slick and red. He was having a harder time holding the sword, so he wiped them on his pants and continued. Every now and then he cried, "Bless this day!" before he cut.

The people remaining beside the church were weeping and wailing now, trying to control increasingly hysterical children. Some of the women gathered children into their skirts, hiding their eyes.

Still Jeremiah Raines slashed. He cut a stout woman's throat, and blood splashed his hand to the wrist. He brought the wrist to his own mouth, touched his tongue to it, then greedily lapped the blood off his hand. The next time, he intentionally put his hands in the flow, soaking them, and painting his face with the crimson fluid. He drank a little more and kept cutting. Before he was finished with a third of the slumbering victims, he was red from boots to hair, and had gone from crying softly to cackling gleefully and fairly skipping from one stone to the next.

Annie's stomach roiled and churned. She knew she wasn't really there on the spot—enough of her consciousness remained to reassure her that she was only observing the past from her position in the present. But it was more affecting than the most powerful movie, because she could smell and taste the blood as it soaked the earth and decorated Jeremiah, and she could hear the squishing sounds of his boots on the wet dirt and the sword slicing flesh and cartilage and veins, and the final gasps of the dying.

Almost as if the realization of her circumstance knocked her into a different time and place, she felt a moment's fresh dizziness, and when she regained her equilibrium, she had gone somewhere new.

46

JEREMIAH Raines sat in a chair covered in a homey plaid
fabric, facing an empty fireplace, in a room lit by flickering
incandescent lights. Blood had caked his once-white robe
and the clothes beneath it, his hair, his skin. He was not re-
laxed, but sat upright in the chair, his bottom barely touching
it, his spine well off the chair's back. His hands picked and
kneaded at the arms of the chair. Beads of sweat cracked the
blood in spots, and a rank odor rose from him. He was expectant, Annie thought, waiting for someone, or else for
something to happen.

Something not altogether welcome.

Looking at the wooden floor and adobe walls, Annie realized that the room was familiar to her. After another moment's closer examination, she knew why. Jeremiah was
inside her rented house. Not in her present, though, but years
before. The furnishings were all different, but the basics were
there, walls and floor and beamed ceiling all in place, just
decades newer.

Jeremiah heard—or *sensed*—something before she did.
She waited for it to reveal itself to her. After a few moments,

she heard a faint creaking noise. The house shifted slightly but noticeably, as a car does when someone steps in or out. A sharp, fiery smell tickled her nostrils, as if from a leaf pile burning someplace far away. All these things were subtle, but Jeremiah's reaction was profound. He let out a strangled cry of horror and the sweat that had been beaded on him beneath the blood suddenly unleashed in a river. Urine flooded his pants and the chair, adding its own acrid, ammoniac tang to the growing smells of smoke and flame. He stayed in the chair by force of will, but Annie could tell by his posture and the way his feet slid on the floor that he would rather have been running from the room.

He stayed, though. Was it courage or terror that kept him pinned in place? She couldn't be sure.

Then the house jolted from side to side as if an earthquake had struck, and it filled with bitter black smoke. Whatever old Jeremiah Raines was waiting for, it had arrived. He let out a strangled cry that degenerated into a wet, wheezing cough as he sucked smoke into his lungs. One more time, the house moved, almost knocking Annie off her feet (even though she wasn't really there at all). The smoke billowed, thick and greasy as an oil well gusher. When it dissipated, the house was no longer simply a house.

Jeremiah Raines still sat in his chair, holding on to the arms as if they were the only things tethering him to reality. But instead of facing a cold fireplace, he looked down a rocky tunnel. It seemed a dozen feet wide and miles long, stretching out forever, illuminated by spitting, smoking torches. There seemed to be as many torches as there were stars in the night sky, with the black smoke standing in for the open vacuum of space. The whole thing was impossible.

But no more impossible than what emerged from the tunnel. A dozen men emerged from the thick smoke. They were gaunt, with skin the color of saffron, dressed only in loose dark pants or open shirts that flapped around them as they walked. She had seen them before, in New Dominion, when she had opened her mind and touched a wall. Taking long, even strides, they swung gnarled hands tipped with sharp claws from side to side. They might have been brothers, all of them virtually identical in age and size, every head shaved, faces long and ending in equally pointed chins.

Jeremiah watched them pass in two rows of six, coming out of the tunnel and walking out of Annie's field of view, maybe out of the house.

Behind them came the torchbearers. Annie had thought the torches were held by wall sconces, but now she found that wasn't the case. Each torch was held by a woman, as identical to her sisters as the gaunt men had been to one another. She had seen them before too, their skin yellow, their heads bald, their breasts round and heavy and their hips wide. As she had observed on that occasion, the women were naked, and their yellow skin was marked by black tattoos or paint. Two-inch-thick lines rose up from hairless pudenda and crossed their stomachs. Between their breasts, the lines split into branches, one extending out to each breast and swirling around it to the nipple, creating a conical shape, while still others wrapped around the shoulders like straps, and thinner ones climbed their necks, marked their cheeks and brows and met on top of their heads.

At least a dozen of the women emerged from the tunnel into the space that still resembled the house's living room, but beyond that, more of them lined the sides of the tunnel, as far as Annie could see down it. When the women who came out had reached the room's end, they turned toward each other, stepping backward until their backs were to the walls. There they stopped, torches held before them, as still as statuary lining a wide corridor except for the flickering flames and the very slight rise and fall of their breasts as they breathed.

If not for that, Annie wouldn't have been sure they were alive at all. The spark of life that animated the eyes of almost every living thing was missing in these pale-eyed beings. None of them had spoken, or acknowledged the presence of either Jeremiah or Annie. The only noise they made was the soft shuffle of bare feet on wooden floors.

As weird as it all was, these yellow people were not who

Jeremiah was waiting for. He barely spared them a glance, and his anxiety increased, his fingers literally tearing into the cloth-covered arms of the chair.

No, these were heralds, Annie understood, announcing the imminent arrival of something else. Something Jeremiah Raines dreaded and longed for at the same time.

Asmillius.

The name came into her head, not spoken but somehow sensed.

Asmillius.

She remembered where she had seen it, in the scraps of pages she had found from the journal Leo had stolen for her.

Jeremiah Raines's journal.

Asmillius.

47

AND then Annie was standing in the abandoned house with the ancient Jeremiah Raines sitting in front of her. The other house, the gaunt men, the naked, painted women, the torches, all of that was gone.

Asmillius, the name, floated in her consciousness. But if Asmillius had come to Jeremiah that day, she had been snatched back into her reality before it happened.

"Raines," she said aloud. "What are you doing here? Who or what is Asmillius?"

Her voice rang in her head with an odd tone.

And she realized she couldn't hear the wind howling and clawing at the walls anymore.

She stamped her foot. Clapped her hands together.

Nothing.

Damn it! She tugged at her ear. Stone deaf again. The only sound penetrating the silence was the all-too-familiar ringing in her ears, and she was sick of that. She stamped once more, this time out of rage.

Jeremiah watched her performance without seeing it. At

least he wasn't passing judgment, she hoped, because she probably looked pretty lame.

And if she couldn't hear the wind, then she couldn't hear cars driving up to the house.

Jeremiah wasn't going anywhere, and he had stopped broadcasting on Annie TV. Annie wasn't sure she could take any more visions anyway—what she had already seen chilled her to the core. Whether she had been watching something that had actually taken place, or something from the darkest recesses of Jeremiah's mind (or her own—a nasty thought, but there it was), she couldn't know, but it was disturbing either way.

She had to get out before someone showed up and found her. She made her way through the kitchen to the back door. If anyone had come around that side of the house, they could hardly have missed seeing the boards set on the ground and the formerly sealed-off door exposed. She would have to be watchful on the way back to her car, not knowing if she had been discovered, if anybody would be waiting in ambush.

At the door she paused, steadying herself against the jamb and trying to peer out into the dark night. Normally she would have scanned for the slightest movement. But the wind hadn't suddenly quieted, which she had sort of been hoping for when the sound of it stopped reaching her ears. It blew in ferocious gusts, and everything outside moved, grass and leaves and branches alive and waving.

Instead, she looked for stillness.

Not much of that around. Moonlight showed her that the rusted iron fence around the little cemetery plot hadn't budged. The gravestones held steady.

A whole platoon could be hiding among the brush and trees and stones, though, and with the wind setting everything in motion she wouldn't know it until they struck. And they could be shouting to each other right now without alerting her. Not likely, but possible.

She just had to risk it.

Dizzy from the sudden deafness and the unexpected

whirlwind tour of Jeremiah Raines's past, Annie left the shelter of the doorway and dashed out into the yard. The wind buffeted her, whipped her hair, slapped her with dust and debris. She had to go between the houses to the street, then back to her car. Crossing the yard, she snapped her head around to check behind her. No one there. She faced front again, but her toe caught on uneven ground and she went down, catching herself on hands and knees.

Swearing under her breath, she stayed down for a moment. Breathed in and out, deep breaths, trying to fight the disorientation caused by the silence and the wind. From that position, she blinked grit from her eyes and surveyed her surroundings once more. All clear.

Annie got to her feet again and started for the gap between the houses. Still no movement that she could detect in the house that appeared occupied, and she had begun to doubt that Jeremiah Raines had left his chair in decades. She had almost cleared the houses, nothing but front yards and then the street ahead of her, when she saw headlights rounding the curve and heading toward her.

If she moved another step forward, she would be visible to anyone in the vehicle.

Instead, she retreated. She backed away the first few steps, then turned (half fearing there would be someone right behind her, creeping up on her) and darted between the houses again. She headed for the cemetery plot, vaulted the fence, and ducked down behind one of the larger headstones.

From there she could see portions of the street on both sides of Jeremiah's house. As the vehicle passed the first gap she saw that it was a sheriff's department Tahoe. At the second gap, it pulled to the curb and stopped.

Had they seen her? Instinctively she touched her hip, looking for a weapon that wasn't there. The passenger door of the SUV opened and she saw a flash of uniform leg, then Gary Raines stepped out. His father emerged from the driver's side. They both went around to the rear passenger door, on the side that Annie could see. Martin drew his duty weapon and stood back while Gary opened the door.

Gary reached inside and drew someone out of the back-seat, someone who moved in the uniquely awkward fashion of a person with his hands cuffed behind his back. He was shorter than either of the Raines men, probably not more than five-seven or -eight. Short black hair, olive complexion, dressed in tight jeans, Vans sneakers, and a nylon jacket with a soccer logo on it. Cops learned to make snap judgments, and this guy had undocumented alien written all over him. His head was lowered, chin almost sagging to his chest.

That didn't make sense, though. If they had run across a UDA, the right thing to do would be to call Border Patrol to come and pick him up. A second option would be taking him to the sheriff's department and putting him in a cell until the Border Patrol came for him. The absolutely most wrong thing to do would be to bring him back to your house in cuffs.

After another few moments, she was sure she hadn't been seen. They wouldn't simply ignore her, or let her see their prisoner. Cautiously, she left her spot behind the gravestone and stepped over the fence, then crouched low and rushed to the corner of Jeremiah's house.

From there she had a wider angle on the Raineses. With Gary holding one of the prisoner's arms, they marched him toward the house across the street from Johanna's. The wall of her house cut off Annie's view, and if they went inside and slammed the door, she couldn't tell. When they didn't reappear, she guessed they must have.

Annie waited another couple of minutes, still breathing heavily, then hurried back across the yard and down between the two houses again. At the far corner of Jeremiah's house, nearest the street, she stopped, waited, looking back toward the Tahoe and the house the Raines men had just gone into, then the other way.

No one in sight.

She didn't think she would get a better chance. On legs rubbery with nerves, she took off, running full tilt for her car. When she reached it, she yanked the door open, slid in behind the wheel, and tugged her Beretta from under the seat.

Its cold steel was comforting in her hands. She sat there for several moments, watching the road for signs that she'd been observed. Her heart thumped hard, her stomach was clenched like a fist. She had been in some hairy situations before, but this one—deaf as a post, with the wind kicking everything around her into motion and cops nearby who might have killed her only ally—easily jumped to the top of the list.

She couldn't stay here, though. With trembling fingers she inserted the key into the ignition and turned it. The car vibrated, letting her know that its engine had started. She hated not being able to hear it. Driving by moonlight, she put it into gear, executed a three-point turn to go back the way she came instead of passing the Raines houses, and stepped on the gas.

48

A mile away, she flipped on the headlights. The silent drive was as terrifying as running down the street past the Raines houses had been. Twigs and leaves flew at the car from nowhere, appearing suddenly in the cones of light before her, swatting at the windshield. A huge jackrabbit darted across the road. A semitruck would have been just as unexpected, since she wouldn't hear it coming either. She looked forward through the windshield, into the rearview mirror, the side mirrors, up ahead again. No chance to relax, not a moment that she wasn't watching for the flashing lights of a sheriff's car or the muzzle flash of a gun.

Finally she pulled over to the side of the road. Sweat coated her, almost as wet as if she had just stepped from the shower. Her hands wouldn't stop shaking. She sat with her head leaning against the wheel, gripping the plastic with both hands, drawing in deep breaths and blowing them out, willing her body to respond to her commands. It was as if the whole thing had rebelled against her, her hearing gone, her eyes refusing to see through the dark, her heart and lungs trying to quit altogether.

Only one thing could make it worse, she decided.

Going back to her house, the house where Jeremiah Raines had waited feverishly for . . . well, for what, she didn't know. Something preceded by impossibly gaunt men and lush-bodied women bearing torches. Something foul, she was sure. Something unnatural. Annie had given up doubting things like that, had let go of the rational world in which she had lived the rest of her life. The things she had already seen and experienced had shown her that she didn't know the half of what could happen in the world. Stranger things than her limited imagination could conjure up.

But she didn't want to go back to that house. Not now. Not when she was already so freaked, so on edge and off balance. She couldn't take that, couldn't handle walking through that door, wondering if this was the time her nightmares would come true, the time the living room would have turned into a pit, trying to suck her in. Or if the yellow men and women would be waiting for her, hoping to draw her into some sick ritual.

Anyway, she didn't think going back there would bring her closer to any answers. She needed answers now, needed to know what was going on in Drummond, what was so important that someone would kill Leo to protect it.

She was up against a wall, though. Leo had been her only shot, Leo and maybe that journal he'd found. But Leo was gone and Raines had the journal again, or whatever was left of it. All she had were scraps, a few names. Useless.

Sitting there in the car, her breathing beginning to steady, her heart rate normalizing, the comforting weight of the gun on her thighs, she realized she had two possible allies—only one of whom was in the area.

She dug her cell phone out and flipped it open. She couldn't hear to make a phone call, but she could still text. She composed a hasty message to Morgan, asking him to call Sheriff Teller's office and the New Mexico State Police and send them down to Drummond. Then she put the phone away and turned her thoughts toward locating her only remaining local friend.

Johanna Raines had been kind to her, even when the others might have had suspicions. Did that mean she wasn't part of whatever the Raines men were up to? Annie had had the impression that Johanna wasn't being entirely forthcoming with her, but every cop knew you couldn't trust anyone completely.

She had to try.

Driving more cautiously than before, still freaked by the silence engulfing her, she headed into Drummond and the sheriff's office.

A dispatcher she hadn't met sat behind the counter. He said something Annie couldn't hear. Annie figured she was a mess, hair blown to hell and back, clothes torn and dirty. She hoped she wasn't arrested for vagrancy or being a public eyesore. She crossed to the counter and mimed writing something, not trusting her own voice. The dispatcher spoke again, but he brought out a small pad of lined paper and a pen. For a small town dispatcher, a surprising sense of world-weariness hung on him like an old suit—if he hadn't seen everything, he believed he had, and her condition didn't particularly concern him.

"I'm looking for Johanna Raines," she wrote. She turned it toward the dispatcher. He read for what seemed an inordinately long time, then spoke. Annie shook her head and pointed toward her ears.

This time he got it. He took the pad back and wrote, "She's not on duty tonight."

"Thank you," Annie said, hating the way her voice sounded in her head. She walked out before the dispatcher could ask her anything. If he called to her on her way out, she couldn't hear—the only advantage to her condition that she could think of.

Next, Annie tried the site of Leo's death—the last place she had seen Johanna. The crews had gone, though, and Leo's truck had already been hauled away. Nobody lingered at the scene. Annie got out of her car briefly to see if there were any more pages of the journal around, but she couldn't find any.

Her last hope was Johanna's home. That would mean driving back down the street into the heart of Rainesworld, which was the next to last thing she wanted to do—close behind going back to her own rented place. Maybe the two were tied for first.

If she had another option, though, she didn't know what it was. She couldn't call Johanna. She assumed Johanna had a cell phone, but she didn't know that for certain, or know what the number was, so texting her was out of the question. She checked for any response from Morgan, but there was none yet.

Fighting to stay in control of her fears, Annie started toward Raines Road.

When she was a couple of miles from the Raines compound, she saw headlights spearing the sky, coming her way. She killed her own instantly, pulled as far off the road as she could, and shut off the engine. Crouching as low as she could and still see out, she waited.

A minute later, a sheriff's Tahoe sped past. Martin drove, a somber expression on his face. Johanna rode shotgun, looking equally grim. Behind, in the back with Gary, was the Mexican illegal she had seen before, but now he was slumped against the window. He looked unconscious or dead.

They hurtled past without slowing, some urgent destination clearly in mind. None of them seemed to pay any attention to the car beside the road.

Annie had to follow them. She wanted to know what they were up to with the illegal, and if it tied into whatever else was going on. Clearly Johanna was part of it, so Annie was glad she hadn't actually reached her.

Another three-point turn—she was getting used to whipping around quickly on these narrow country roads—and she raced after them. Without a lot of side streets, she didn't think she would lose them even though they had a good head start. And when they curved around to the west, making a turn onto the Cloverdale road, she suddenly realized where they were going.

Where they *had* to be going.

If she followed them on that long, straight road, they would certainly spot her. But there was another way.

She shot past the Cloverdale turn, headed toward home.

49

ANNIE didn't have to go inside her house, that was the good part.

From the outside, it looked just like it always had. She would have to go back in at some point, she knew, but not just now. Parking in her usual spot, she picked up the Beretta and flashlight and raced for the low hill behind the house, shoving the weapon into the waistband of her pants. Nothing had changed about the conditions—she was still deaf, the wind was still punishing—but taking some sort of action felt better than just being batted around like a leaf on the breeze.

She ran up the hill, scrambling when it got steep, close to the top. The wind carried the night scents of the desert to her but then snatched them away just as fast.

As she reached for a rock to use as a handhold, her sleeve drew back, exposing her wristwatch. In the glint of moonlight she saw the two hands together, pointing straight up. Midnight, then. March 21, the first day of spring. She noted it and then tucked it away.

At last she reached the top of the hill, crested it, and started down the other side.

Down toward the field of flat stones. Beyond that was New Dominion.

Moonlight limned the Tahoe, parked in the tall grass close to the field. Johanna and Gary Raines stood in the center of the field, still in uniform. Martin stood with them, but he had changed into a long white robe with wide sleeves, like the one Annie had "seen" Jeremiah wearing. He looked like a Klansman who had lost his pointy hood. They surrounded the Mexican man, lying on his back on one of the stones. He had been so trussed up with branches and leaves that he looked like a man inserted into a foliage burrito. He wasn't struggling or trying to move—between that and the way he had looked in the back of their vehicle, she suspected that he had been drugged, back at the Raines house.

Johanna and Gary stood relatively still, but Martin was engaged in some activity Annie couldn't quite decipher. He moved back and forth past the illegal's head, his own head bobbing, his arms waving. Sometimes he stopped and rocked back on his heels, throwing his arms toward the sky as if imploring the heavens. Then he bent forward, putting his head just inches above the bound man's face, and then the whole thing started again.

In his right hand he held a long knife. Its blade caught the moonlight and threw it back, giving the impression that Martin Raines gripped a stick of pure silver.

Annie had never been a very regular churchgoer, and the most complicated religious ritual she'd ever seen was communion. Martin Raines wasn't putting wafers on anybody's tongues or handing out tiny paper cups of wine or juice, but there was something of the same choreographed seriousness in his motions, the same number of steps to each side, precise movements of his hands and head in different directions.

If she could hear his voice, she would know for sure, but she suspected he was performing a ritual of some sort. What was that name she had heard at Jeremiah's? *Asmillius*? Did this all have to do with him or her or it? And what *was* Martin Raines, a sheriff or a high priest?

She picked up her pace going down the other side. So far

Raines had only brandished the knife, waving it above the man's head, but he hadn't actually threatened him with it yet. But she remembered Jeremiah's vision. She didn't intend to let it get that far, if in fact that's where this was heading.

As she worked her way down, she realized that she could hear the wind, faintly, as if through layers and layers of cotton. It had been an hour since she had touched Jeremiah Raines, maybe a little more. The deafness had come on abruptly, but at least it seemed not to be as long lasting as her original case.

She had made it a little more than halfway down the hill, her progress obscured by the noise of the wind and the Raineses' distraction, when Martin's body language changed. He had been making big, expansive motions before, but now he tensed up, his focus tight on the trussed up Mexican man. His grip on the knife changed at the same time—blade pointed down now, instead of up. He touched it to the ground on the east side of the bound man.

Annie couldn't wait any longer. And she couldn't trust her voice, not from here, over the driving wind. She stopped in place, turned off the flashlight and pocketed it, then drew the Beretta. Holding it out with both hands, left bracing right, she took a deep breath, blew it out, and squeezed the trigger.

The report was sharp, not loud, to her ears, but the muzzle flash was almost blinding in the darkness. Annie blinked, moved the weapon a couple of inches left to cover Johanna, and saw Martin Raines rolling on the ground clutching at his left upper arm.

Damn it. She had been aiming at his right. Showed what a few months away from the practice range would get you.

Johanna and Gary Raines couldn't know how far off she had been, though. She held her sights steady on Johanna. "Johanna, you and your brother lose those weapons," she said, hoping she sounded commanding. "Toss them aside, now."

Gary was already reaching for his weapon, but he looked at Annie, saw where her gun was aimed. Whatever else you could say about the Raines family, and at this point Annie didn't think all that kindly about any of them, they looked after each other. Gary's brotherly protection must have kicked in, because he did as Annie ordered, opening his holster carefully and pulling the weapon out with a finger and thumb, then throwing it away from him.

"You too, Johanna," Annie said. "Like Gary did."

Johanna glared at her. If they had been something resembling friends once, they weren't anymore and wouldn't be again. Johanna said something, but Annie couldn't hear. She could still barely hear the wind. She released her right hand and tapped her ear with her left, shaking again. "Deaf," she said. "Don't talk, just do what I say."

If she had been within range, Johanna might have bit her, that's how furious she looked. But Gary said something to her and Johanna tossed her gun aside, into the tall grass near one of the other flat stones.

Annie came down off the hill carefully, not lowering her weapon. Martin Raines rose to his feet, unsteady, bleeding profusely from through-and-through wounds on front and back. Gary and Johanna started toward him. "Hold it," Annie said. She really wanted to ask questions, to find out what they were up to, but that would have to wait until she could hear the answers. "You can help your father, but get rid of his weapon first."

She twitched the barrel of the gun to back up her demand, and Gary and Johanna both took a few steps back, Gary disarming and then assisting his injured father. "Farther," Annie said, and they complied.

She kept approaching the man on the stone, still tied up in leaves and branches. His bindings were held together with gourd vines, still showing their broad triangular leaves. The UDA was awake, but docile. She crouched beside him, keeping her weapon trained on Johanna. "You okay?" she asked. "Don't bother answering, I can't hear shit. Or speak Spanish. Can you move?" With her left hand, she yanked at one of the vines wrapped around him, tugging it aside. "Can you help me out here, pal?"

He just gazed up at her through bleary eyes. *Definitely*

drugged. "Come on, dude, you gotta do something here," she said. She snatched at his casing of plant matter, tugging what she could away from him. She needed two hands, though, and she couldn't risk lowering the Beretta. "Johanna," she said, "untangle this guy."

Johanna complained, or so it looked, but Gary said something to her and she shrugged, then approached the bound illegal. She set to work pulling the vines and branches away from him—not tenderly, but ripping and tearing, unconcerned with any damage she might be doing to the man. Annie figured it was better than having his throat sliced with Martin's big knife. Anyone crossing the border illegally had to expect to have a rough time of it, but he shouldn't have to expect to be murdered in some weird ritual by a sheriff's officer.

"That's good enough. Back off," Annie said when the guy was mostly unwrapped.

Johanna gave her the kind of look usually reserved for obnoxious motorists who cut you off in traffic, or people talking on cell phones during movies. Annie was glad the woman was no longer armed, because if she had so much as a pocket knife on her, Annie would probably be on the ground bleeding by now. But Johanna backed away again, joining her father and brother, glaring hatefully at Annie the whole time.

Gary might have charged her, but his father was slumping, held up only by Gary's arm around his middle. In the moonlight his face was pale and coated with a film of sweat. He was in bad shape, needing medical attention in a hurry. Annie wondered if she should kill the three of them outright.

If she didn't, she would spend the rest of her life looking over her shoulder, wondering when they'd come after her. Because they would. Cops were that way, and crooked cops all the more—once you stuck a weapon in their face, threatened or hurt their loved ones, they didn't forgive or forget.

But she wasn't a killer. In the line of duty, sure, if it was necessary, she could pull the trigger. Not this way, though. Not people who were unarmed and cooperating. Maybe she wasn't the best cop ever, but she was clean and she didn't murder people.

She had to make sure they stayed unarmed for a while, though. Keeping her Beretta trained on Johanna, she gathered up the guns they had thrown down, ejected the magazines and put them in her pockets, made sure there were no rounds in the chambers, and threw the guns as far as she could in three different directions. They would run for them as soon as she turned her back—maybe sooner, if they saw half a chance—but at least they would have to reload before they could kill her.

The hard part was still ahead. If she left the Mexican guy there, they would just kill him the moment she walked away, and then this all would have been pointless. He was coming around a little more every minute—trying to sit up now, moaning and holding his head in his hands. Annie couldn't tell how much of what had occurred he remembered, or if he had been so out of it that now he would wonder just what in the hell he was doing out in this field with all these crazy people.

She wondered about that a little herself.

The cop in her wanted answers. But the rest of her wanted to get away from there before Johanna and Gary realized that if they played it right, she wouldn't be able to shoot both of them before the other got to a weapon, or to her.

"Come on," she said to the Mexican guy. She reached her left hand out to him, and he grasped it, letting her help him to his feet. He was wobbly, but she got her arm under his (much as Gary was holding his father) and they started backing away, toward the hill. He was the first person she'd been close to since the encounter with Jeremiah Raines had brought back her empathy overdose, and the drugs that had knocked him out left him disoriented, and too numb to be feeling anything yet. Annie knew they'd have to move out fast, before she succumbed to the same sensations.

"I don't know what your deal is," she said to the Raineses as they left. "But I couldn't stand by and let you murder someone in cold blood. You're law officers, you figure it out.

If I were you, I'd turn myself in to the sheriff in Lordsburg, because he's going to hear about this and then you'll be going down for it anyway."

She didn't really know if they would or not. Maybe the sheriff was in on it too. Maybe all of Hidalgo County was, except Annie—all of New Mexico, even. The whole situation was just strange enough that she couldn't take anything about it for granted.

And even if they did come to trial, it would be their word against hers. No way would the UDA still be around to testify, not by then. He had been drugged, anyway, so any testimony he did offer would be useless.

And Annie had shot an officer of the law. Hell of a case. If Jocelyn Moreno didn't hate her before, she would when this landed on her desk.

Gary and Johanna both had what looked like some choice words for her as she and the Mexican guy started up the hill (walking backward up a hill, no easy task), but she didn't know what they were. She got the sense of it, though. They weren't serenading her with "Happy Trails."

Somehow, though, she and the Mexican got up and over. As soon as they topped the rise, Johanna ran for the weapons, and Annie and the Mexican guy broke into a mad dash for what she dearly hoped would be the relative safety of her house.

Time to go back inside, whether she wanted to or not.

50

THE house was fine. No open pit, no miles-long tunnel, just the house that Annie had seen so many times before. She blew out a breath she had been holding, only then realizing just how anxious she had been about passing through that door again.

Instead of shooting at them as they went over the hilltop, Johanna had gathered their unloaded weapons and then helped Gary haul Martin Raines to their Tahoe. The old man needed a doctor, and they must have recognized that going after Annie would steal valuable moments he couldn't spare.

So she was alone in her rented house with an undocumented alien who seemed to know very little English. "You speak English?" she asked him. His mouth moved, and she could hear faint sounds, but it was as if he was standing on the far side of a waterfall and whispering. No detail got through, not even enough to know what language he used. She did the old tapping her ears and shaking her head trick. "I can't hear anything," she said. "No hear." Because that was how you spoke to people who didn't understand English—in bad English, but a little bit louder.

He smiled and nodded, making Annie think that perhaps he understood. "English," she thought he said. Some girls she had known had been proficient lip readers by sixth grade; she, sadly, was not one of them. "English, yes." *Maybe.*

She found some paper and a pen and wrote, "Do you read and write English?" When she turned the paper to face him, he studied it intently, forehead furrowing, and then looked at her with a blank face and a little shrug.

She tried another tack. "You came across the line, right? And the sheriff grabbed you? Not Border Patrol." She touched her arm where the sheriff's patch was on the Raines uniform jackets, and then her chest, where they wore their badges. "Not *la migra*, sheriff?"

She thought she heard a faint *"Si, si."* Good enough for her. She continued with an interrogation that would never pass muster in court. She mimed being cuffed with her hands behind her back, the way she had first seen him.

"They cuffed you and took you to a house, right? *Casa*? The sheriff's *casa*?" She waved her hands around, encompassing the house they were standing in, to get the idea across.

He might have said something like, "Si, sheriff's *casa*." Or not. But he was smiling and nodding again, so she kept going.

"And they drugged you there?" She mimed a hypodermic needle, injecting something into her forearm.

"Si!" he said, loud enough that time for Annie to be sure about it. He drew back the left sleeve of his nylon jacket and showed her a pinpoint hole on his forearm, scabbing over now, with a little bruising around it. So they had drugged him. And they weren't even trained phlebotomists.

"Can you write down your name for me?" she asked. "And an address?" She racked her brain for the Spanish words for name or address, but all she could come up with was *"nombre."* But was that name, or number? *It's a good thing the Phoenix PD had plenty of other cops who spoke Spanish,* she thought, *because I'm useless in that regard.* The guy wasn't helping—as the drugs wore off, his confusion increased, and standing in the house of an apparently crazy woman with a gun who jabbered at him in English only made it worse. Which fed her own confusion, making it hard to focus.

When he just stared at her, she wrote down her own name. "Annie O'Brien," she said, pointing to the name and then to herself. "You?" She pointed to him.

He got it then. He took the pen and wrote down "Ramon Olivera Montalvo."

"Good," she said. "Good, Ramon. Now your address." She did the same thing, writing down the address of the house, then once again indicating it with her hands. "What is your address? *Su casa?*"

Ramon just shrugged. *Of course, he doesn't want to give me an address in the U.S., even if he has one. And he doesn't think there's any point to giving me a Mexican address.*

He was right. She was treating him like he was going to be a useful witness, even though she had already decided he wasn't. She needed to cut him loose and get to Lordsburg before the Raineses came for her. The crash from the adrenaline rush of confronting them in the field was starting to hit, made worse, she guessed, by the lingering effects of Ramon's tranquilizer shot, coursing through her own body as a result of her empathic connection to him.

"Go," she said wearily. "Just go home." She waved him toward the door. He nodded and took a couple of steps toward it when the ground shook with a deep rumble even she could hear. As the trembling slowed, bitter, sulfuric smoke filled the room.

It was her dream, and the vision Jeremiah had shared with her. Only it was real, and Ramon felt it too.

51

RAMON froze in place. Annie had an idea about what might be happening, and she didn't want him sticking around for it. She could already sense his panic building, panic that threatened to bubble out of her any second, and she needed to function. She put her hand in the center of his back and shoved. "Go! *Vamonos!*"

He rabbited without waiting around for a second invitation. *"Vaya con Dios,"* she almost said to his departing back, but she stopped herself.

She had a sick feeling that *Dios* wanted nothing to do with what was about to happen at her house.

Ramon bolted through the door at the same time that another shock wave shook it. Annie steadied herself against a wall. A crack formed in the ceiling, plaster flaking off and dropping like heavy snow. This time the shaking went on longer and the smoke got thicker. She realized Ramon had the right idea—she didn't think the house was actually on fire, but the smoke seared her nose and throat and lungs, and she didn't want to hang around there any longer than necessary.

She knew where the door had been a few minutes ago and she headed there, hoping whatever was happening to her house hadn't relocated it. She could barely see the floor through all the smoke, but as long as it hadn't opened up into a deep pit, as it had in her nightmare, she would be able to make it outside.

In fact, it hadn't—at least, not yet. But the floor was cracking open, like the ceiling. She rushed across it, unnerved by the way it moved, like snakes writhing beneath her feet. Her gun and flashlight were on the dining table, which trembled under her hands as she groped for them. Once she had a firm grip on both, she burst through the door and out into the cool night air. The wind had finally died down a bit. Annie kept going, running, coughing and gagging and spitting, until she was twenty or thirty feet from the house. There she stopped and put her hands on her knees, sucking in great lungfuls of fresh air. She felt like she needed a shower on the inside, to clean out all the smoke she had inhaled.

The earth continued to rumble, not just under her house but all around, and even through the darkness she saw plumes of smoke rising into the air, blanketing the stars. Most of it came from over the hill. From the field of stones and New Dominion.

Get in the car and drive, Annie, she told herself. *Phoenix isn't that far. You can be there in five hours, this time of night. Faster if the highway patrol doesn't spot you. Anyway, you've done what you came here to do. Johnny Ortega is out of prison.*

But with or without a badge, she was a cop, and she had internalized cop habits until they were part of her chemistry, genetic traits she had inherited from her dad and would pass on to her kids, if she found anyone insane enough to want to have them with her. She was a cop and she couldn't change that. Leo had been smarter than her all along; he had recognized that part of being a cop was having a desire to help people when they're at the worst moment of their lives, and as much as she had wanted to deny that her motivations had ever been so pure, maybe she had been wrong the whole time.

She wasn't sure who she would be helping if she went back over that hill. Not herself, certainly. But she had undeniably helped Ramon, and she had a feeling that something else was going on over there now, and she couldn't just walk away from it without having another look.

By now she knew her way up and down. The moon had moved west, behind her, so going up she would have plenty of light but the far side would be in shadow. She still had the flashlight and Beretta and, she realized, pockets full of magazines for the Raineses' guns. She tossed those to rid herself of the extra weight.

Wishing she'd had a different father, maybe one who sold shoes for a living—nice ones, Jimmy Choos, Manolos, that sort of thing, because what was the point of pointless fantasizing if you didn't at least get an employee discount on fancy shoes out of it?—Annie started up the hill again.

52

FROM the top of the hill, Annie could see that she had been mistaken. There was no smoke coming from the field. It all issued from New Dominion, thick roiling clouds of it. The town was burning down.

Except there wasn't much town there to burn in the first place, and she didn't see any flames, no light at all flickering through the dark of night.

She descended the hill, which turned out to be easier when you weren't shooting at one cop and holding a gun on two others, although the task was complicated somewhat by the occasional earthquake-like temblors trying to knock her down. The Raines family had gone, and the field of stones was empty. Walking past the stone where Ramon had been, still covered in greenery from his vegetative bondage, she felt a chill tickling her neck. Unless Johanna or Gary had grabbed Martin's knife, it was still around someplace. The idea that she had interrupted a human sacrifice had not really sunk in before—the way she had viewed it at the moment was that she was interrupting a homicide. But when it was combined with Martin's strange behavior, what she'd read in the journal entry, and—it just now occurring to her—the vernal equinox, that all added up to the idea that there had been an element of ritual sacrifice to the whole thing.

Murder, she was as used to as a sane person could be. This was something else entirely, something that creeped her out.

It didn't help any that the ghost town nearby was burning without being on fire.

She reached the end of the field and started toward New Dominion, picking her way through the mesquite thicket. The smoke from the town wafted over her, and for once she wished the wind was still there to dissipate it. It had the same acidic stink as the smoke back at the house, and she felt like she had just begun to recover from that.

Annie worked her way past all the growth and into town. She held her trusty Beretta in her right hand and waved the flashlight in front of her face to try to blow away the smoke, but there was still no sign of fire, no heat or light, and if the distinctive crackle of flames was there, she couldn't hear it.

Walking through New Dominion, peering through billowing, biting smoke that stung her eyes, she couldn't quite get her bearings. The ruins of the church were right where they had always been, at the side closest to the field. But something looked different about it all and she couldn't tell if it was just disorientation from the smoke and everything she had already been through, or something else.

The earth jerked beneath her as if someone had snatched a rug out from under her feet. She went down hard, landing off balance, sprawling and flipping onto her back as the ground continued to rock. The flashlight rolled away from her. Sitting up slowly, ready to be knocked flat again, she was looking back the way she'd come, and as smoke drifted by she saw that the church she had just passed was bigger than it had been only moments before.

Bigger, and better preserved. Newer. Its adobe walls were clean, its wooden beams fresh. She pawed for her light, played it around the building to make sure she wasn't dreaming it. *Impossible,* she thought. *Just fucking impossible.*

Another jolt came. Already sitting down, she rode it out.

Then from just over her left shoulder came a grinding roar so loud that it hurt even her half-deaf ears. Annie screamed and jerked around to see a wall shooting up out of the ground—no, not just a wall, an entire house, once sunken and eroded, but now whole and new, the stones making up its walls sharp-edged, the mortar crisp and white.

She was glad there had been no one around to witness her screech, because it would have been humiliating. Shooting Martin Raines, holding the others at gunpoint, rescuing Ramon—that was cop work, and it brought a charge of adrenaline, but it wasn't truly terrifying.

This was, however. This was not natural. This couldn't be real. Had she hit her head when that big jolt knocked her down? Was she hallucinating this whole scene? She pawed at the earth under her palms, cool and crumbly, with embedded stones in it and twigs and leaves on top. She breathed in the air, filled now with other scents that mixed with the sulfur stink carried by the smoke. These reminded her of graveyard earth, of decomposing corpses, as if by churning up the earth, the newly risen house had released the smells of the buried dead.

Down the road, other houses did the same thing, rising up, sloughing off the overgrowth that had concealed them for so long, knocking the decades of caked-on dirt from the walls. She sat on the dirt roadway, unable to move.

But she didn't have to, because the world was moving for her, vibrating like one of those chairs at fairgrounds that you put a quarter in, and throwing in the occasional bigger jolt along with the steady buzz. A sound like heavy rain came from all the debris being shaken off the restored buildings. Even the road widened as foliage that had encroached upon it over the past decades shrank away.

Tears filled Annie's eyes as she watched the inexplicable occur all around her. New Dominion, forgotten by time and by practically everyone in the world, except perhaps for the residents of Drummond, was being reborn. It couldn't happen . . . but she couldn't deny her own senses.

She turned over, got her hands and knees under her, and

pushed to her feet. The steady motion of the earth made standing difficult, and the overwhelming smells and the smoke that continued swirling around her were dizzying. She hadn't realized what she was in for when she had come, but now that she knew, she didn't want to stick around any longer than she had to. New Dominion was an impossible place, and Annie O'Brien was a rational being. The two were water and oil.

Running was out of the question, though. She would fall if she tried; one of those powerful jolts would hurl her down. Instead, she walked fast, trying to escape a town that had, within the last few minutes, taken on the appearance it must have had when it was new and occupied by the people who had died that spring day that Jeremiah had shown her. Houses were whole, ready for occupancy. Streets were wide and hard-packed. Public buildings and shops waited only for people to put them to use, to stock them with merchandise. She almost expected costumed employees to step out of hiding, as they did at those tourist attractions masquerading as frontier settlements—except these would probably be silent, somber people with hairless, yellow skin.

When she passed the church again, its adobe walls were bright, spotless. The heavy wooden doors were wide open and her light showed her rows of pews inside, an altar beyond those. In spite of the voice in her head screaming at her to get the hell out of Dodge, she wanted to take a closer look.

At first blush, the building looked plain and simple. A plank floor, white walls, wooden pews. She moved in farther, playing her light around.

Then it landed on the wall behind the altar, where she would have expected perhaps a large crucifix or something of the sort.

Instead, the wall had been carved with dozens of niches, and from each one, a white, grinning skull stared down at her.

Annie gasped and almost dropped the flashlight. When she caught it, its beam traced across the altar itself. She had thought at first that it was made of wood, oak branches, perhaps, but now she saw that it was bones, thousands of them massed together.

Trembling, unable to quite conceive of what sort of church would be decorated in this way, she kept going, working her way behind the altar to see what other horrors awaited. She wanted to flee, but an awful curiosity wouldn't let her go. Not just yet. She had to play this out to the end.

The floor was as clean as if someone had just swept it out. The bones of the altar and the skulls were white and fresh. The only thing she saw out of place was a wooden box, about three feet long and a foot wide. Its lid had been removed and put back hastily, so the corners didn't line up right. Annie took a deep breath, held it, and kicked the lid off, beaming the flashlight inside.

The box was largely empty. Something had been there, sitting on a bed of soft fabric, but whatever it was had left, or been taken away. Unless, of course, the box had only held the velvety black stuff, in which case it was still there and she had no idea why anyone had filled it or opened it.

And who could have opened it? The last time she'd seen the church, it had been rubble. If the town had only started to restore itself in the last few hours—probably less; she suspected it coincided with the earth tremors and unexplained smoke—then there hadn't been anyone around, that she had seen. The Raines family, but she didn't think they'd had much time here, and the town hadn't really started coming back until after they had left the field.

There was nothing else to see here. Nothing else Annie wanted to see. Her impulse back at the house had been the right one after all. Get in the car and drive. Don't even look in the mirror. This sort of thing didn't happen in Phoenix.

Or if it did, she didn't know about it, and that was just as good.

After the church, nothing stood between Annie and her car except that damned empty field of stones and the little hill.

But the field was no longer empty . . .

53

THE things Annie had seen, in the category of what should not have been possible, were already so numerous it made her head hurt to think about them.

But what she saw next was *so* not possible that she stopped cold, rubbed her stinging eyes, blinked away tears, and looked again.

What she saw hadn't changed. If her eyes weren't deceiving her and she hadn't gone insane, then the only remaining option was that the scene before her was real.

The moonlight was still bright enough to reveal Johnny Ortega, dressed as he had been when she had dropped him at the motel in Lordsburg. He walked toward the field with a person draped over each shoulder. The people were limp, not struggling, but they looked like full-sized adults and he carried them as easily as if they were no heavier than forty-pound sacks of dog food. Off to the side of the field, not far from where the sheriff's department Tahoe had been parked, sat a dark sedan with the trunk open like a dark, gaping mouth. The Raineses must have knocked down a section of fence, Annie guessed, and this car had used the same path, getting much closer to the field than she had ever driven.

And Johnny must not have wasted any time getting there after the Raineses left, because he had already made a couple of trips from the car. There were four people stretched out on the flat stones. Someone worked over another one, his back to Annie. Nobody had seen her yet, so she risked moving closer, clicking off the flashlight and using the mesquite thicket for cover.

From there she had a better angle on the people on the stones. Two of them were already dead, their throats slashed. Blood, black with white highlights in the moon's silver glow, trickled into spreading pools that soaked the earth beside their stones. Annie's stomach tightened and she tasted bile. She had saved one life tonight, but doing so had drawn her away from the scene and allowed others to die.

She couldn't have known, but that didn't stop guilt from snaking its way under her skin.

The man went from the person he had been crouched over, toward the one on the next stone. Too late, Annie saw the short sword in his hand—a different weapon than Martin had used—its blade dripping. He moved with precision, and even as she raised her weapon, looking for a decent shot through the low, sturdy branches of mesquite, she saw two things that hit her like a battering ram to the gut.

The man sliced the final victim's throat with a smooth, practiced motion, and the person, already unconscious, offered no resistance. She strained to see the cutter.

It was Morgan Julliard.

54

ANNIE stepped from the trees, batting branches away with her left arm, oblivious to the thorns snagging at her.

"Morgan!" she called. "Drop that sword!"

He lowered the sword to his side but didn't release it. She recognized the weapon, now that she got a better look at it—the same sword Jeremiah Raines had used on New Dominion's citizenry in the vision she had seen.

Seeing it, she remembered the scrap of journal she had found, with its reference to a "crucifixion sword."

Its blade was about twenty inches long, tapering to a sharp point at the tip, and with a distinct depression, kind of a waist, about two thirds of the way to the hilt. It looked like a vicious weapon, good for thrusting or cutting. The only thing Annie knew about Roman weapons was what she had seen in sword-and-sandal flicks like *Gladiator*, but it wouldn't have been out of place there.

But Morgan? Oh, was he ever out of place.

He smiled at her. It was his usual smile, friendly, slightly paternal, as if they had just run into each other on the sidewalk outside the courthouse. She didn't understand how he

could do that, could act like he hadn't just murdered four
people. Blood painted his face, streaked across his forehead
and down both cheeks.

Behind him, Johnny deposited the pair he carried on two
more stones and started back toward the car.

"I've been wondering if you were still in the neighborhood," Morgan said. The combination of improved hearing
and lessened wind meant she could just barely hear him
across the twenty-yard gap separating them. He twitched his
head toward Johnny. "Frankly, I hoped you weren't, but
when I got your text message I figured you probably were.
That was great work, by the way, getting Johnny released.
Just in time too. If it had taken any longer, I'd have had to
rely on a contingency plan, or done all of this manual labor
myself."

"I'm sure you had a backup ready, just in case," Annie
said.

"Of course. You know me. Just like the Boy Scouts. Be
prepared."

Annie's mouth was dry. The last time she had heard that
was from Nanci Keller, in an entirely different context. In
what felt now like a different lifetime. "I don't think Boy
Scouts spend their camping trips murdering people."

"You never know," Morgan said. "They're a diverse bunch
these days."

"Drop the sword, Morgan."

"You don't know what you're mixed up with, Annie. I
love you like a daughter. And I appreciate the hell out of all
you've done to help out here, really I do. But your part in it's
done, slugger. Pack up and go home."

Life was funny. She had considered that very option
several times over the last couple of hours. Now the man who
had sent her here in the first place made the same recom-
mendation, and she couldn't bring herself to take it. She was
in it now, committed to staying until there was an end to
it all.

Especially if she had helped, however unknowingly. She
couldn't walk away from a situation she'd had a hand in

causing. "It's a little late for that," she said. "Why don't you tell me what's going on?"

"If you want," Morgan said. "You've already been to New Dominion, it seems. I'm sure you've already pieced most of it together."

"Morgan, just tell me." Her patience had run out. "And drop that sword, for the last time, or I'll shoot you where you stand."

He jammed the sword down into the earth in front of him, handle up. He could still grab it quickly, but she didn't intend to get within striking distance of it. And she had her Beretta, which she had already used tonight and was starting to think would get some more use.

The car at the edge of the field started up, its headlights flaring on. Johnny was leaving. Annie wondered if she should try to shoot out a tire or something. But it seemed apparent that Morgan was the brains and Johnny the muscle—as long as she had Morgan on ice, Johnny would come back. And if she divided her attention, focused on Johnny, Morgan might come at her with that wicked blade.

"I didn't think you'd help me if I told you what I was up to," Morgan said.

"You were right about one thing, at least."

"More than one. I was right to trust you to spring Johnny in time. You do know that it's the vernal equinox, right?"

"I figured that out."

"The beginning of spring. Season of rebirth and renewal. The season when crops are planted, with prayers for a bountiful harvest come the autumn. The people of New Dominion didn't want to count on those prayers by themselves, though. They had a special arrangement, one that not only predates the founding of New Dominion, but predates the so-called discovery of America by Europeans. Back in their ancestral homeland, in the bogs of northern Great Britain, after a few disastrous years, the forebears of this community struck a deal with a demon—"

"Asmillius?" Annie interrupted.

"Oh, you are good," Morgan said, smiling again. "Your dad would be proud."

"I'm not so sure."

"You're right, anyway, Asmillius was his name. Not just any old demon, either, but a prince of Hell."

"Sounds a little grand."

"I know, but there it is. He's one of Hell's most powerful badasses, and you wouldn't want to mess with him. Anyway, for the price of one sacrifice a year, on the vernal equinox, he would ensure the vitality of their crops and livestock and would otherwise leave them alone. It seemed like a win-win, as we say these days. But if they missed a year, he would come for them, one and all. And while Asmillius is good with things like nurturing crops and livestock, that's not his real nature, and every year that went by his rage and hunger would grow. If they ever flaked out on the agreement, it wouldn't be a pretty sight. It was a risky deal, made in risky times, when another crop failure could have wiped them out anyway. So they agreed.

"The thing is, when you make a deal like that, word slips out. Not everyone in any given community is going to get on board, especially when it's their son or daughter or lover who goes under the knife. When word spread, persecution began, and our friends had to move out of their homeland. By then America beckoned, and they booked passage to the New World, where religious freedom was guaranteed. Or so they thought."

"There are limits," Annie said. "Human sacrifice is one of those lines that isn't supposed to be crossed."

Morgan settled down on one of the stones. Annie was conscious of the weariness of her legs, the multiple trips over the hill, but she couldn't sit yet.

"For most people, yes," Morgan agreed. "But you're trying to apply modern rules to an ancient culture. And they had already made the deal. If they backed out, they were screwed. Asmillius would tear them apart in the most painful ways he could imagine. And he has one heck of an imagination."

"I'm not sure I'd feel too bad about that."

"Maybe not," Morgan said. "But then, you're not one of them, are you? By now generations had passed. The people who had to carry out the sacrifices weren't the ones who had made the original agreement, or even their sons and daughters. They had moved to America, where rich fertile soil was everywhere, unlike in their bog-soaked lands back home. They didn't feel like the crops were in danger, but they couldn't stop sacrificing to Asmillius. And again, people heard about it, and they had to move.

"This happened over and over, pushing them ever further west. They tried to stay ahead of the bulk of the population, but the country spread west, too, and then leapfrogged over much of the desert southwest to the West Coast. Even today, the interior west is one of the least populous regions of the country, although some of the northern plains states rival it."

"And Hidalgo County's population is tiny," Annie noted. "A few thousand people, a third of those in prison."

"Exactly. It's been a nearly ideal place for them. *Nearly* ideal. They came here, they built New Dominion, they grazed cattle and planted some crops."

"And they kept killing people."

"One a year. A small price to pay, many would say, for the prosperity and security of their community. Even so, it didn't sit well with some of them."

"Glad to hear they grew a conscience."

"Some did. It was mostly an old guy named Jeremiah Raines who decided to fight back."

She remembered the vision. Jeremiah feeding almost the entire population some sort of drug or poison, then cutting their throats with what looked like the same sword stuck into the dirt in front of Morgan. That didn't seem like fighting back to her—it seemed like giving in.

"We've met," she said. "Jeremiah and I, we're old acquaintances now."

Morgan laughed. "Oh, Annie, you are the best."

"Don't mention it," she said. "Really."

There was much she didn't want to think about right at

this moment, and her part in whatever was going on—falling for Morgan's lies, working so hard to free Johnny from prison—was at the top of the list.

She had screwed up, big time. Most mistakes could be put right, and she would try her best to fix this one. But she had a feeling this mistake was for keeps.

55

MORGAN pushed back the cuticles on his left fingers with his right hand. He looked utterly casual, at ease.

It was all Annie could do not to shoot him. But she needed to hear the rest, to find out if there was a way to undo what she had inadvertently done.

"Jeremiah killed most of the town," she said. "He ended New Dominion on a single day."

Morgan nodded, giving her an impressed look. "That's true. New Dominion was getting some heat on it, even though the area was so sparsely populated. And like I said, he wanted to fight back. He knew the cost would be high, but if he could break the contract, it would mean freedom from the threat of Asmillius, not just for his generation, but for all that followed.

"Jeremiah was a sheriff. Ordinarily this sort of thing is left to priests or kings, but they were in America now, and the Raines family had led the clan for generations. They continued to do so, but wearing the vestments of authority that their new country recognized. He studied and worked and came up with a plan to defeat Asmillius once and for all."

"So he got to kill just about everybody else, making them pay the price for his plan?" Annie said. "And then it didn't work anyway?"

"First time you've been wrong," Morgan said. "It did work, but only to an extent. And the highest cost was the one he bore."

"Explain."

"As you said, slugger—and I'm dying to find out how you know this—he killed almost everyone in town, leaving a select few behind to carry on the clan. He did it on a vernal equinox, when the usual sacrifice would have been held. But he combined it with a different ritual—one intended, along with the mass sacrifice, to summon Asmillius to Earth and to bind him here. Jeremiah Raines made the ultimate sacrifice, giving up his body to possession by the demon. And it worked.

"Where the plan broke down was that he intended to be able to control the demon, but he couldn't. Asmillius couldn't get much use out of him, either. Jeremiah effectively died, or went into a state you'd think of as suspended animation, coma, something like that. Asmillius was still around, so the deal held—it's just that he was here on Earth instead of in Hell, trapped in Jeremiah's slowly rotting, not-quite-dead corpse. The sacrifices went on as usual, and slowly the clan grew again, settling the town of Drummond."

He rubbed some of the blood on his cheek, getting it onto his fingertip, and he stuck that finger in his mouth, tasting it. "And that pretty much brings us up to date," he said. "The sacrifices continued every year, here at the spot that had become hallowed ground to the new, unimproved Asmillius. Until this year."

"When I interrupted the sacrifice and shot the sheriff."

"Precisely."

"Which means what?" she asked.

"Well, it would mean bad news for Drummond, New Mexico," he said. "If I hadn't been planning my own little ritual anyway."

"So I see," Annie said. "Is that really the sword that stabbed Christ in the heart?"

"It is indeed," Morgan said. "Impressive, isn't it?"

"Doesn't look like all that from here."

He reached toward it. "It's really quite special. May I?"

"Carefully," she said, training her flashlight on it. "No sudden moves, and drop it when I say so or I'll put a cap in your skull."

"No sudden moves," he promised. He stood, crossed the couple of feet to the sword, and drew it from the ground. Blood still dripped from its blade. "Just a sword, you're thinking?"

"Looks like it to me."

"But watch." He wiped the blade against his jacket, cleaning the blood from its length. Then he extended his arm, holding it out toward Annie. As she watched, more blood appeared on the blade, and it started dripping again. "That's the blood of the son of God," Morgan said. "It never stops flowing. Cool, huh?"

56

IN a night full of the impossible, this was the most miraculous thing Annie had seen yet. She couldn't deny what she saw, and Morgan's explanation made as much sense as any other. Sure, the whole thing could have been some parlor trick. She would have preferred that. Then she wouldn't be dealing with an unsettling sensation of awe that made the fine hairs on the back of her neck stand up.

"That's the genuine crucifixion sword," she said. "And you just happen to have it."

"I've made a lot of money over the years, Annie. A lot. You'd be surprised how much a cop can earn if he's willing to look the other way once in a while. Then as a lawyer, and running a big nonprofit . . . a lot of money, that's all I'm saying. I've spent most of it, learning about the sword and what it's doing here and how to get to it. But the being I'm about to become doesn't need nice cars and gold-plated faucets and Picassos. That sword has been here all along. Inside the church. It's just that since it collapsed the night of Jeremiah's summoning, the church has been . . . shall we say, inaccessible. Until tonight. The other sacrifices, since Jeremiah's day, have had to settle for being killed with more standard-edged weapons."

His entire statement was stunning, but there was one part Annie couldn't get past. "You were a dirty cop?"

"I didn't hang with any who weren't. Why do you think your mom ate your dad's piece? She figured out what was going on. She knew he'd snuff her himself if she tried to turn him in. She was a babe, but your dad wasn't the kind of guy who'd let a piece of tail compromise him."

Annie swallowed bile. Her stomach was flipping around like the tossed coin at the start of a sporting event. She recognized what Morgan was doing; skells did it all the time, trying to make their arresting officers or interrogators feel like the whole world was as filthy as they were, like nothing short of a forty-day rain or nuclear annihilation would clean it up. But that didn't mean his words didn't carry the ring of truth—truth that perhaps she could have tested, if she had dared get closer to him. She had inherited all her father's possessions when he died, and he only had four thousand dollars in the bank and a couple hundred in cash. But he had never gone wanting for anything, and he had taken annual vacations to Las Vegas or Hawaii.

"How would something like that get way out here?" Annie asked, in order to take control of the conversation again. "Shouldn't it be in a museum, or hidden at the Vatican or something like that?"

"Remember, slugger. The Roman soldiers who crucified Jesus weren't convinced that he was anything special. A troublemaker, a rabble-rouser, but not necessarily the son of God. They had no idea of the impact he would have on the world. The soldier who stabbed him didn't think it had turned his sword into a museum piece or a religious artifact. It probably started bothering him that the blood wouldn't stop running, if that even happened in those days, and after a while he'd have ditched it, or he died. Someone else took it, maybe knowing its history and maybe not. It remained in use as a soldier's weapon, and went with Roman legionnaires into Great Britain. At some point, the soldier carrying it lost a fight, and Celtic warriors took it. Certainly they had no idea of its provenance, and it probably wasn't until much later that the clan heard stories about the sword and realized what they had. By that point, they didn't intend to give it back. It came across the Atlantic with them and stayed with them until Jeremiah realized how handy such an artifact would be in his ritual to summon Asmillius. When that ritual was finished, it went back into its hidey-hole inside the church, where it was when the town collapsed after Asmillius was imprisoned inside Jeremiah Raines."

"And the rest of them kept up the sacrifices," Annie said, "even though Asmillius had possessed Jeremiah." That was a sentence she hadn't expected to ever speak in her life. This whole conversation was like that, wandering over intellectual territory she had never before had reason to consider.

"They had to. Asmillius hadn't gone away. He was closer than ever. He probably wasn't happy about being trapped in Raines, but a deal's a deal, even to a demon. He kept looking after the livestock and crops and they kept appeasing him with their annual sacrifices. Different members of the Raines family took over as sheriff, and as the county grew—not a lot, but some—the rules changed and a Raines lost the election. But they managed to convince the elected sheriff that nobody could handle this end of the county except a Raines, and that situation has held for the last couple of sheriffs. So Martin, who you shot earlier this evening, is the current regent of the clan."

"I think I get it," Annie said. "But here's what I don't get. What's your connection to all this? Why spend all that time and money tracking down the sword?"

Morgan drove the sword back into the ground and took his seat on the stone again.

"I've been studying death for decades, Annie. My whole life, pretty much. Learning about it, exploring it. You would call me a serial killer, I'm sure, and think of me as some sort of monster. I prefer to think of myself as a student of philosophy, a student of life, which we can only truly know by understanding death. Unfortunately, the puzzle of death has always been hard to unravel because we don't find out the real answers to our questions until it's too late to pass them along. In any way that's meaningful to the public at large, of course—there has been communication across the veil forever, essentially, but it's never been widely accepted as legitimate. And it's hard to tell with whom one is in contact, or what lies they might be telling.

"So I've been researching the subject as well as I could from this side. That, of course, entails dealing out a lot of it. Being present as people are dying, causing their dying, experiencing the dying in every possible way short of actually dying myself. It has been an often grisly, discomforting, and sometimes painful course of study, but always fascinating and quite edifying."

How could someone talk about a lifetime of murder like it was no different from studying urban planning or American history? Or was the more germane question how could she have known him for so long and have still believed that he was a human being? She had thought she was beyond surprise, when it came to the depths to which people could sink, but sadly it seemed that she had far underestimated the extent of human depravity. Even when she had been with him in his office, or walking beside the lake, she hadn't picked up any of this, just a kind of facile, shallow gregariousness.

"Through my legal work, I've come to know a great many cops and killers," he continued. "Sometimes they're one and the same. At any rate, I've been able to get access to case files, murder books, internal reports, and so on. Because I understand the nature of death and killers so much better than most police, I've been able to make a lot of intuitive leaps that they can't. I knew, for instance, that Johnny Ortega wasn't guilty of the murders he went to prison for—but also that there were plenty of others, in other states, that he had done. In the particular case for which Johnny was convicted, I'm sure the killer was Martin Raines himself. He hadn't found that year's sacrificial victim—usually an illegal immigrant, I believe, found crossing the border country but who no one can legally trace to this area—by the equinox, so he picked a local punk he didn't think would be particularly missed. Just bad luck that the punk had a girlfriend with him when they pulled him over.

"Johnny was actually headed into the area on my behalf, to observe what took place here at this time of year, because my research had shown that there were forces at work here that might be used to further my goals. But he was also a handy fall guy for the local law—not very bright and obviously guilty of so many crimes he couldn't really offer a convincing defense. The locals probably made him the second he hit Lordsburg, and when Raines knew he would need someone to take the heat for killing a pregnant teenage girl, he zeroed in on Johnny. Johnny went down for it, but that was okay because I wasn't quite ready to act anyway. I knew that when the time was right, a smart enough investigator could turn up the evidence to spring him. Operation Delayed Justice has done a lot for my researches, and it's also taught me that an innocent person can be cleared if someone's just willing to make the effort. It probably wouldn't surprise you to learn how many of the innocent people we've freed are neither white nor wealthy—those people can mount adequate defenses in the first place."

"No, it wouldn't," Annie said.

"Now, though—thanks to you—all the pieces are in place." He waved a hand at the bodies lying on the flat stones. "Johnny's going house to house, bringing me people I can sacrifice in this hallowed place."

"But why? You're not part of this community. What's it to you?"

"I should have thought that would be obvious by now, slugger. I intend to draw Asmillius out of Jeremiah Raines and into me."

57

ANNIE hesitated, not trusting her own voice. Apparently Morgan was still capable of shocking her. "You sure you want to end up like Jeremiah?" she asked after a moment. "He's not exactly having the time of his life."

"He didn't know what he was getting into," Morgan said. "I do. I'm prepared. He thought he would be able to control Asmillius, but I *know* I will. I know I'm ready to understand death from a more elevated perspective—to have the power over life and death. I told you, Asmillius is a badass. I'm about to take on power unimaginable to most human beings, but I've studied and prepared and I'm ready."

For the first time since she had seen him in the field, Annie felt sorry for him. Nobody could be ready for that, ready to be possessed by a demon of such tremendous abilities and appetites. "You think so." She left out her unspoken follow-up—*you're absolutely bugfuck crazy, Morgan. You're a murderous son of a bitch and a complete wack job all at once.*

But then, was she any better off than he was? She had been starting to believe in things like "justice," only to find out that she had helped a murderer get out of prison so that

he could take part in many more killings. She had relied on
her imperfect empath powers to let her know if people were
lying to her, instead of trusting the instincts honed through
years of police work. The fact that both Morgan and Johnny
had been able to play her testified, she suspected, to the fact
that both men were sociopaths with no sense of guilt, no
consideration for anyone but themselves, and probably no
other emotions she would recognize as human. She should
have known better, should have taken that into account, but
she had let a supernatural phenomenon that she couldn't control take the place of judgment and experience. Other people,
innocents, had paid the price for her shortsightedness. Morgan Julliard and Johnny Ortega were emotionally vacant,
with lumps of coal where their hearts should have been, and
the wires that were supposed to connect their brains up were
shorted out, melted, fused together in ways that even the best
brain surgeon couldn't untangle. No wonder she hadn't been
able to read them.

"You don't think I can pull it off," Morgan said. He
blinked into her flashlight's beam. "I can't see your face that
well but I can tell that much."

"I don't know if you can or not. I just don't think you
really grasp what you're in for. But if you wind up in a coma,
well, that's fine with me."

"I won't," Morgan assured her. "I've done the research,
Annie. I've studied this. I know as much about Asmillius as
anyone else on Earth, and I'm as ready as can be. Everything's right on schedule—the return of New Dominion and
the opening of the church so I could claim the crucifixion
sword are signs that events are moving along as they should.
Soon the rest of the ritual will come together and I'll be un-
dergoing the transformation I've worked toward all this
time."

And you're screwed, Annie thought. *Because Jeremiah
Raines waited in my house for Asmillius to come, and you're
on the wrong side of the hills.*

As if in response, another low rumble came from the town.
Annie turned around to see if she could tell what new changes

were occurring there. But in the few instants her back was turned, Morgan snatched up the sword. When she turned back, he had already reached the next unconscious person Johnny had deposited on a stone and was drawing it across that person's throat.

"Drop it, Morgan!" she commanded.

Morgan stopped what he was doing and looked at her. He still had that smile on his face—no hint of guilt or remorse. He'd been caught with his hand in the cookie jar, nothing more serious than that. She should have just shot him, instead of warning him. Next time she would.

"Just give it up, Morgan," she said. "You're in the wrong place, your stupid ritual won't work, and you're either going to prison or I'm going to have to kill you. Either one is fine with me, honestly."

"The wrong place?" Morgan echoed. "Are you sure about that?"

The rumbling from town continued, and she risked another glance in that direction.

And there, on the edge of town, where before there had only been a thicket of mesquite shielding the ruins of New Dominion from this field, stood her house. Its doors and windows were open, and yellow sulfurous smoke billowed up from them. As she watched, the front wall vanished, and behind it was a long, rocky tunnel, lit from within by flaming torches.

Asmillius was coming after all.

58

MORGAN moved fast. While Annie's attention was riveted on the unexpected appearance of what had been her rented house, on the wrong side of the hill, he scooped up the sword and lunged for her. If he made any noise, she didn't hear it, but she swiveled around and caught the rush of motion toward her.

Instinct took over. She squeezed the Beretta's trigger. The muzzle flared, the gun boomed, and Morgan let out a grunt of pain. He continued on course, slamming into her. They both went down, Morgan on top.

Annie shoved him off and scrambled to her feet. He stayed on the ground, moaning and clutching at his side.

"I hope you don't think I feel bad about shooting you," she said. She found her flashlight again and played the beam around the grass until she located the sword he had dropped. She picked it up and hurled it out of sight. "I ought to put one in your head." She pointed her weapon at him, giving it serious consideration. "What happens if Asmillius comes and you're already dead? What does he do then?"

Morgan moaned again, but managed to sit up against one

of the stones. The bullet had passed through his ribs. She couldn't tell how seriously wounded he was, but he looked bad. His face was pale in her flashlight's glow (considerably weaker than it had been when the evening started), his voice raw. "Not *if* he comes, but *when*," he said. "He's almost here. And when he's drawn out of Jeremiah Raines, he'll come to the last person who touched the sword. Now that you fucking threw it away, that makes it you. You sure you want that, slugger?"

If blood could spontaneously freeze, Annie's would have. "I've seen Jeremiah," she said. "I'd kill myself before I'd let that happen to me."

"Save a bullet," Morgan said.

"First I'll use them on him. How can he be killed?"

"He can't. Either he picks a host or he goes back into his previous host until someone else suitable comes along. If he's deprived of a host entirely, he goes back to Hell, or whatever passes for it." He took a few ragged breaths and went on. "And until then, his heralds will scour the Earth, bringing to it the bloodshed and chaos on which an unchained Asmillius thrives."

"You pick the nicest friends, Morgan," Annie said. "But I might have another idea." She drew in a deep breath, held it, focused on steadying her hand, and pulled the trigger again.

Her round made a neat hole in the front of Morgan's head, just above the left eye, driving chunks of brain and skull and wet stringy matter out the rear. She didn't hang around to admire her handiwork or to mourn his passing. If he wanted to study death, he could look at it from the other side.

Instead, she set off running—not over the hill toward where her place had been (she wondered briefly if her car was still sitting where she had left it, outside the house, and what was next to it), but toward the other hill. The one separating the field and New Dominion from the Raines compound.

As she ran, she holstered the Beretta and pawed her cell phone from her pocket. Her hearing had been steadily improving over the last hour or so. No signal on the way up the hill, but when she reached the top she acquired a couple of bars. She dialed Johanna's house.

Johanna picked up on the second ring. "Johanna, it's Annie."

"You shot my father, you dirty *bitch*!" She had quite probably never uttered that word before in her life, and therefore had to spit it out so that it would land as far away from her as possible.

"I know," Annie said. "I had to do it. Listen to me, Johanna, this is important. I'm heading toward your place now."

"You better not let me see you," Johanna said. "Or anyone else in my family, because we'll kill you in a heartbeat. We need another sacrifice, and right now you're at the top of that list."

"It's all gone past that, Johanna. You've got to check on Jeremiah, make sure he's still in that chair—"

"How in the heck do you know about—"

"Never mind, just do it. Make sure his status hasn't changed."

"I don't think I want anything to do with—"

"Just do it, Johanna!" Annie snapped. "There's no time to fuck around. We're only gonna have one chance to stop Asmillius from claiming another host."

She thought Johanna had been on the verge of hanging up, but suddenly the tenor of the other woman's breathing changed. "What do you want me to do?"

"Just make sure he's still like he was, that's all. If there's any change, call me. And don't let him leave!"

"Okay," Johanna said.

"Go now," Annie said. "I'll be there in a little while."

She shoved the phone back into her pocket. She had almost reached the street. The Raines houses loomed ahead. The moon was almost gone, balancing on top of the hill to the west, and within the next short while it would slip away altogether. Soon, dawn would gray out the eastern horizon.

She clicked off the flashlight. The darkness wasn't complete; some of the houses had lights burning, and the sinking moon still cast a wan glow over everything, for the moment. She couldn't risk carrying a light; there were no doubt Raineses who, as Johanna had said, would love nothing more than to take her out. For all she knew, Johanna had raised the alarm as soon as she hung up her phone. And if Annie was killed, who would stop Asmillius?

Assuming that even she could, of course.

She didn't want to think about the alternative.

She was thirty yards from the first house when she heard gunshots.

59

SHE had been staying off the main road, trying to keep yuccas and mesquites between her and the houses. At the first gunshot, Annie threw herself to the dirt. She landed on a mesquite branch, its inch-long thorns jabbing up through her jacket and shirt, but she didn't cry out, just rolled back and peeled them out of her.

She heard more gunfire, individual pop-pop-pops. A revolver, she thought. Muzzle flashes strobed, lighting up the nearest of the Raines houses.

Whatever someone was shooting at, it wasn't her.

She cautiously shifted her position, lying flat on the ground, able to look both ways down the road by moving only her head.

Toward the houses, she saw three figures, each carrying some kind of firearm.

The other way, approaching quickly, she saw the gaunt men.

The heralds of Asmillius.

Their loose clothes flapped as they passed Annie's hiding place, like flag bearers on the march.

The men at the house opened fire again. Bullets whined through the air and slapped into the gaunt men. Annie waited for them to drop, to cry out.

They didn't. They kept advancing. The men swore. One of them called for help. Guns fired again, flame blooming from their barrels, reports echoing off the houses and the hills. The gaunt men kept coming, close enough now that Annie could see their placid faces and yellow skin. Bullets tore into their clothing and flesh, puffing out behind them, but didn't slow them down.

Then they were upon the Raines men. Their movements had been steady, measured, up to that point, but as soon as they reached the men they became a blur of motion, a whirl of long limbs and fluttering cloth. The men made wet, whimpering sounds. In less than thirty seconds, they were down, and the gaunt men continued into the Raines neighborhood as if they had never been challenged.

Farther down the street, more voices called out. More guns fired. Nothing slowed the gaunt men.

Were they heading for Jeremiah? For Asmillius?

She needed to get there first. All attention was focused on the gaunt men now, so Annie risked abandoning her hiding place. She darted toward the houses. The moon was almost gone. She left her flashlight off and aimed for the house lights.

This time she didn't bother with the back door. When she reached Jeremiah's house, the front door was wide open. Yellow light shone from the back room where Jeremiah sat.

"Johanna?" Annie asked. If it was anyone else, she was in trouble.

"In here," Johanna's voice replied. Annie let her shoulders relax and walked into Jeremiah's room.

Johanna was alone with Jeremiah. An overhead light glowed.

Johanna pointed a shotgun at Annie.

"Whoa," Annie said. She raised her hands away from the weapon holstered at her hip. "You can lower that weapon, Johanna."

"I'll decide that," Johanna said.

At the sound of a chair creaking, Annie looked away from her, toward Jeremiah. He had been absolutely still, comatose, if not deceased, when Annie was with him only hours before. That had changed.

He rocked slowly in his chair, forward and back, almost to the point of tipping out of the chair and then settling into it again. His mouth moved as he did, and soft moans issued from it. His hands were in constant motion, too, held out before his chest, grasping and closing over empty air.

"How long has it been since you've seen him like this?" Annie asked, gesturing toward the old man. The shotgun wasn't forgotten, but it paled in significance compared to Jeremiah's sudden resurrection.

"Never," Johanna said. "He hasn't budged since I've been alive."

"That's what I thought," Annie said. "Things are happening tonight, Johanna. Bad things. I don't think it's too late to stop them, but it will be soon. If Asmillius takes a new host . . . well, let's just say we're all lucky he's been penned up inside Jeremiah, here."

When Johanna answered, her voice quaked with fear. "I don't know what you're talking about."

Annie took a step forward. "There's no time for lies, Johanna. Give me the shotgun."

Johanna twitched the barrel at Annie. Her eyes gleamed with madness and barely restrained tears. "You stay back. What you did to Dad—"

"I know all about what's been going on, Johanna. I know about the sacrifices, the deal with the demon, and what happened to Jeremiah. I've just come from New Dominion. The town is back. Like it was brand-new. Whatever you've seen in the past is nothing like what's going on tonight. Asmillius's heralds are outside—that's what all the shooting and screaming out there is about. They're going to keep killing until . . . well, honestly, I don't know what's going to stop them. But I think they're headed here, looking for Asmillius. I may have shot your dad, but I didn't kill him. There are other members of your family dying right now, though. Unless you give me that shotgun and get out of the way, more of them are going to die."

Jeremiah rocked in his chair, dangerously far forward and then back. Spittle bubbled up from his mouth, glistening on his chin, wetting his lap. His aged fingers clutched at something that eluded them.

Johanna's hands shook, making the shotgun barrel quaver. Annie was afraid she would forget she held it, or her hand would spasm—either way could splatter bits of Annie all over the decaying walls of Jeremiah's room.

"Come on, Johanna. Give it to me." She held out her hand. Johanna drew back, giving Annie a defiant look. She managed to hold it for almost ten seconds, and then her face crumpled like crepe paper wadded in a fist and she released the weapon with one hand, extending it toward Annie with the other.

Annie took the shotgun. "You should go," she said.

"No." She barely managed to get the word out, but the way she said it left no doubt that she meant it.

"Then look away," Annie said. "Don't watch."

Johanna turned toward the wall, moving like someone only partially awake. By the time this night was over, they would all wish they'd been dreaming.

She moved behind the old man, raised the gun, and waited until his head came toward the back of his chair. When it touched the steel opening of the barrel, she squeezed the trigger.

The boom was loud in the small space, and it echoed off the walls and rang in her still-recovering ears. As it started to fade she could hear the wet patter of blood and brain dripping from the walls and ceiling. Johanna's back heaved as she wept silently, her hands over her face. Annie started toward her, reaching out to put a hand on her back, but the ground heaved and rumbled and she had to fling it out to balance herself instead, catching the edge of Jeremiah's chair. When the earth stopped moving, she let go. Gore coated her hand.

"Let's get out of here," she said.

Johanna didn't move. Annie touched her shoulder with her clean hand, wiped the other on her own jeans. "Let's go, Johanna."

Johanna nodded and allowed herself to be directed toward the door.

Outside, people stood in the road, guns at their sides. There was no sign of the gaunt yellow men. *It must be working,* Annie thought. *Without Morgan as a host, driven from Jeremiah, with his precious field of stones empty of live host possibilities, Asmillius is losing his grip on this world.*

Unless he chooses me, *that is.*

60

THE moment of relief didn't last long.

Annie had been pretty sure that no one alive remained in the field. But then she remembered that Johnny Ortega was on his way back there, probably with more sacrificial victims. He couldn't know she had killed Morgan. If he or one of his would-be sacrifices touched the sword and was there when Asmillius emerged, presumably from her rented house, then the demon would have a new host in spite of her efforts. Johnny had plenty of blood on his hands, he was young and strong, and Asmillius would probably find him malleable and appealing.

She had to deprive him of every possible host. "I have to go," she said. "Do you have the keys to a car on you?"

Johanna was beyond arguing. She dipped into her jacket pocket and held out a key ring. "Department vehicle," she said, her voice flat. "In the driveway of my place, next door."

"Take care of your dad," Annie said. She grabbed the keys and took off at a run. The road would get her there faster than climbing over that hill again. She was tired, nearly exhausted from the emotional whirlpool and the running around, but as long as the threat of Asmillius remained, she couldn't sit out the fight. She had done too much to set things in motion, and now it was up to her to halt them.

Johanna spoke, but Annie couldn't make out her words. She was already racing out of the house and across the yard, gripping Johanna's shotgun. She dashed across the yard toward the Tahoe in the next drive. Voices were raised as she passed but no one moved to stop her. She guessed Johanna had said something to them, given some signal.

When she reached the vehicle she backed out of the driveway and sped out the way she usually came in. The wind that she had thought was gone for good was picking up again, and the pavement had cracked under the earth's violent paroxysms. Driving was treacherous once more, especially in the unfamiliar SUV. Annie kept the accelerator as close to the floor as she could and held on tight. The dark countryside flashed past, her headlights skimming across now-familiar fence posts and tall, many-stalked yuccas and pastures with cattle standing close to the road as if to watch the cars go by, rural mailboxes leaning this way and that on stands of wood or wrought iron or stone or block, and power poles with lines that sang in the wind, poles on which during the daytime, raptors perched like hunters in their blinds, watching for prey to scamper or slither down below.

When she was almost to the gap in the fence she saw the car Johnny had been using earlier. Her headlights glossed it briefly, and it looked like Johnny at the wheel, with two or three other occupants lolling unconsciously in the seats. He was ahead of her, coming from the other direction, just passing through the downed fence to head cross-country back to the field.

She had to stop him before he reached it. She stomped on the gas and the vehicle surged forward. Going through the same gap would eat up too much time, so Annie steered straight into the barbed wire, aiming between two fence posts. The wire resisted only briefly, then snapped, strands of it whipping back into the windshield and tearing at the vehicle's sides. Annie heard the boom of a tire being torn open.

The steering wheel tried to spin out of her hands. She kept her grip on it, muscled the car back on course, and headed overland toward Johnny's ride. The SUV bounced across the uneven ground, headlights stabbing dirt and lancing sky, but it moved faster than the sedan Johnny drove.

And they were on a collision course.

The Tahoe hit the sedan on the front right quarter panel, going just over thirty-five. The sedan was coming out of a shallow depression and the SUV was moving across the upper ridge of it and when the two vehicles slammed together it was as if someone had struck Annie with an ax handle. She jolted forward, her head whacking the wheel hard, then flew back against the seat. The seat belt bit into her chest, as if trying to cave in her ribs and lungs.

She didn't realize she had passed out until she opened her eyes again and felt blood stinging them from a cut on her brow.

61

ANNIE released the seat belt, flipped open the SUV's door, and tumbled out. Her chest ached and she was going to have some bad bruising, maybe a scar on her brow. But she was alive.

For now. If she couldn't keep Johnny away from that field, then all bets were off.

And not just for her.

She had only been unconscious for a few seconds. When she spotted him again, Johnny was running toward the field, full tilt, with bodies slung, once again, over each shoulder. Annie leaned back into the Tahoe and pawed out the shotgun. "Johnny, stop!" she shouted when she had it in hand. "Freeze!"

He didn't freeze, just kept running away from her.

From this range, she realized, the shotgun probably wouldn't stop him at all. And she would be pelting the people he carried with lead shot for no reason.

She dropped the shotgun and drew her Beretta.

Johnny ran through the darkness, eighty yards away. Annie was still shaky from the collision, tense and anxious. She sighted down the top of the barrel, aiming at a spot midway up Johnny's back.

When she pulled the trigger, the report was loud but the wind snatched the sound away. Johnny kept running. Annie aimed again and fired three rounds in quick succession. A tight grouping.

Johnny pitched forward, arms outflung. The people he carried crashed to the ground around him.

Annie scraped up the shotgun and took off at a sprint.

As she got closer to the field of flat stones, the wind picked up even more, whipping her hair into her face, slashing at her with tall grasses and spiny limbs. The ground rumbled and shook as if it wanted to knock her down. She stumbled but kept running, passing Johnny Ortega's still form and those of the people he had dropped.

When she reached the edge of the field, she slowed to a walk.

Across the field, her house stood open, its wall still gone and the tunnel inside it lit by guttering torches held by two ranks of voluptuous nude women. The gaunt men filed between them, back into the cavern.

Was it over, then? Had Asmillius given up?

Annie heard a crashing noise, behind her, and spun around.

No such luck.

62

ASMILLIUS had skin as yellow as the heralds and female torchbearers who served him. Like the women, he was naked and painted in black bars and swirls, lines and boxes and zigzags. But unlike them, he was tall, eight feet, Annie guessed, or thereabouts, and as gaunt as the heralds, emaciated, with long gangly arms and legs. His face was almost skeletal, the ridges of bone and stringy muscle clearly etched beneath tight yellow flesh. His eyes bulged from that drawn face, black and merciless. His ears were large and tapered to points at top and bottom. His mouth hung open, giving Annie the impression of a slack-jawed mouth breather. No one had ever claimed he was an intellectual giant, though, and one didn't need to be smart to wield immense power. There was no hair on him anywhere, just those tattoos or paintings.

He walked rapidly toward Annie, his intent clear.

She stood between him and the house, the tunnel that would allow him to return to whatever Hell he had come from.

She had been the last person to touch the crucifixion sword.

And there was plenty of blood on her hands. Just tonight she had killed Morgan Julliard, Jeremiah Raines, and probably Johnny Ortega. Given the circumstances, she couldn't even say that she regretted having done so.

If Asmillius was looking for a killer to inhabit, his search was over. Morgan might not have completed his ritual, but she didn't know how much of one was required since she had blown his host body's brains out.

"Nobody wants you here anymore!" she said. Wind smacked her in the face. "Just go home!"

Like she was talking to a stray puppy. Or Ramon, the undocumented alien, who she figured was already back in Mexico by now, counting his blessings that a crazy lady had rescued him from the crazier cops.

Asmillius gave no indication of having even heard her. He saw her, that much was certain; his bulging black eyes were fixed on her and he walked straight toward her.

She still had the shotgun in her hands. When she raised it, the fury of the wind grew, trying to rip it away. "Beat it!" she shouted.

Asmillius kept coming.

She pulled the trigger. The gun roared. Shot tore through his yellow skin, but as she watched, the holes it made closed up again. Within seconds, they were gone, leaving behind no marks.

She threw the gun away and drew the Beretta. Emptied the clip into him.

The result was the same. None whatsoever. He kept coming.

She didn't know what it would feel like to be taken as a demon's host body. It had done Jeremiah no favors beyond keeping his body upright long past the time it should have rested. She wondered if it would climb in through her mouth, snapping her jaw, stretching the skin of her face to the breaking point. She anticipated incredible pain, starting on the outside and running all the way through her, to her very core, and she guessed that the pain would never, ever end.

She held her ground, and Asmillius came closer. Five

yards away now. She could smell him. The stink reminded her of the rankest Phoenix alleyway she had ever been in, behind a restaurant where chicken parts had been left rotting inside a Dumpster in the summer sun, and three people had died in a knife fight, their bodies undiscovered for most of a day, and the usual alley smells of garbage and piss had been made worse by the bodies cooking in their own feces and blood. Asmillius smelled like that alley, only worse.

Blood from the cut on her head stung her eye. She wiped it away.

And she thought, *Blood*.

Blood.

He was ten feet away when she moved.

She hurled her empty automatic at him. It bounced off his bare chest. He kept coming.

But she was running, leaping over the flat stones, dodging around them.

Looking, in the faint light cast by the dying torches of the naked women, for the sword she had cast aside.

She knew about where she had thrown it. It had hit one of the stones and clattered away into the grass.

She threaded between the stones, shuffling her feet, hoping she would kick it if she couldn't see it.

Finally, she spotted the glint of its blade.

Asmillius had increased his pace. He was almost upon her again, his legs scissoring with inhuman speed, his long arms reaching out for her. His face had changed a little, his mouth closing most of the way, eyelids hooding his eyes just a bit. His expression had become one she could only describe as expectant.

Or maybe hungry.

She bent down and picked the sword up, getting a good grip on its handle.

"You really think you want a taste of this?" she asked.

"The question is," Asmillius said, his voice rasping like the lid of a stone sarcophagus being slid aside, "do you truly believe that which summoned me would drive me away?"

"Look, it speaks," Annie said sarcastically.

"When I have something to say."

"Well, I don't know if this thing can hurt you," she said. "But I'm willing to give it a go."

"Be my guest. But when you fail, you will be mine, Annie O'Brien. One with me, now and forever."

"I don't think so."

"The choice is not yours to make."

"There's always a choice."

He drew closer and Annie slashed out with the sword. She caught only air, but she had struck too soon. He didn't flinch away from it.

He kept coming and she did it again. This time the tip scraped across his belly, cutting a line in his flesh that healed up again as soon as the sword point was past it.

She had hoped there was some miraculous power in the sword that would frighten him off or destroy. But he was right—the sword had stabbed Christ, ending his life. It was, if anything, an unholy relic, not a holy one.

Just the kind of thing that would appeal to Asmillius.

But the blood on the blade's edge . . . that was holy, if Morgan's story was true.

Annie backed away, wiping her hand across the blade. It came away bloody. She rubbed the blood—not the blood of the sacrificial victims, but the blood of God's only son—onto her face, still backing away from Asmillius. Toward the house and tunnel, the heralds and torchbearers, but she couldn't let that worry her. Keeping out of Asmillius's reach, that was the main thing.

More blood had appeared on the blade. She wiped it off, wiped it onto herself. Then she took the blade and rubbed it directly on her, smearing her exposed skin, her clothes.

She saw Asmillius's step falter.

"You don't like that, do you?" she asked. "Not so sure how you'll take me over when I'm covered in holy blood."

"Give up while you can," Asmillius said. "Make it easy on yourself, Annie."

"I don't think so," she said again. She rubbed the blade against the back of her head. "How you plan to get in?"

"I have my ways," he said. Once again, he lunged, faster than any human could. This time sharp-edged claws tore through her jacket and shirt and into her flesh, and the force of his charge bowled her over. His breath was foul, gagging Annie as he exhaled into her face. Razor teeth snapped and gnashed, inches away. The pain was excruciating, as if he had held his claws over a fire before attacking her.

She held on to the sword, though. She touched its blade against herself everyplace she could reach, wiping more blood off it.

He released her shoulder, grabbing at the hand that held the sword. The motion caused blood to flick off the blade. A drop landed on his face, just beneath his left eye.

He screamed and shrank back from it. He moved the hand that still held her down, closing it around her throat, claws and skin like sandpaper cutting the tender flesh there.

The world began to turn black, as if the early morning darkness was wrapping around her like a shroud.

She had only one advantage, and she had to make the most of it, before he finished her. He wouldn't let her die, she knew, but he would take her over and use her as his vessel.

Annie flicked the sword at him again, intentionally this time. Blood splashed into his face. It sizzled and he gave a piercing wail. She reached a hand around his neck and drew herself close to him, letting her blood-painted body touch his.

Asmillius let her go, bucking away from her. The blood was poisonous to him, painful. She rubbed the flat of the blade against him. His skin sizzled beneath it, and he tried to swat it from her hands. His swing was too weak, and all he did was get Christ's blood on his hand. The sword was necessary for the ritual, Morgan had said, but it was never meant to come into contact with the demon.

She swiped the blade once more across her face, then dropped the sword and lunged for him.

If it was a mistake, she would know in a second.

He tried to back away, raising his hands to ward her off. But she broke through his defense, wrapping her arms around him in a crushing bear hug.

Making sure the blood of Christ was pressed against him.

Asmillius screamed and screamed.

He fell down, with Annie on top of him this time. On the ground, he thrashed and tried to roll away. She held on. He grew hot, uncomfortably so, then burning hot, as if she grappled with one of the flaming torches.

Still, she refused to release him.

The demon bucked and kicked and squirmed. Annie's grip loosened, and she realized he was getting smaller, shrinking from the contact with the blood.

Then he wriggled free, out of her grasp. He jumped to his feet and raced toward the tunnel. As he ran, he batted at his own smoldering flesh.

The gaunt men were gone, but the torchbearers remained. Annie thought she saw, on faces that so far had betrayed not the slightest hint of expression, traces of surprise, of bemusement.

He would be a long time living down this humiliation, she suspected.

When he had disappeared into the tunnel's depths, the nude women followed him, their torches nearly out of fuel. The tunnel glowed brightly for an instant, then went dark.

The wall of her house returned to its proper place.

The wind died, the earth stilled. All was quiet.

On her hands and knees, watching her displaced house, Annie laughed and wept at the same time.

Epilogue

ANNIE slept there, on one of the flat stones, exhaustion sapping every last bit of strength from her. When she woke again, not more then twenty or thirty minutes later, the eastern sky was slate gray, with a faint pink band at its lower edge.

Johanna and Gary Raines were walking toward her, accompanied by other family members she had seen around these past weeks. Gary's face was grim and clouded with rage. Johanna waved him off and approached Annie alone.

"I think it's all over now," Annie said. She sat up.

Johanna nodded toward New Dominion. Annie followed her gaze. The town was gone again, nothing but ruins mostly hidden behind the thicket of mesquite. "It's over," Johanna said. "For now."

"What do you mean?"

Johanna sat down beside her on the edge of the flat stone. Annie looked around. She could see Morgan's body, and Johnny's, and those they had sacrificed to Asmillius. Some of the Rainses helped the survivors to their feet. They were unsteady, still drugged or only semiconscious after whatever Johnny had done to make them compliant.

She didn't trust her own limbs yet. She remained on the stone, next to Johanna.

"For this year," Johanna explained. She tried to sound reasonable, but she was squeezing her hands like a barmaid trying to wring every last drop of dishwater out of an old rag. "Next year, it'll start over. We'll have to find someone else to sacrifice—an illegal, most likely, that's what we usually use—or the demon will come back. That's the deal, and whatever happened this year doesn't put an end to that. We make the sacrifice, Asmillius helps keep our livestock healthy and our crops growing. We fail to, and he comes for us. It's not a good deal and we're not the ones who made it, but we keep up our end."

"But . . ."

"Nothing you did here changes it, Annie. You freed Jeremiah, which I appreciate. But you also shot Dad, and you mixed into things that are none of your concern. Next year at this time a Raines will still be sheriff around here—probably Gary, although I'm thinking about making a play for it myself—and we'll be in charge of finding the sacrifice, making it, and keeping it quiet. Days gone by, it was the king, or a priest who stood in for him, but now it's the sheriff, and it's always been a Raines. I were you, I'd be gone by this time next year, because there's already talk that you'd be a sacrifice that would make Asmillius happy as can be. For that matter, there's actually talk about taking you now and keeping you on ice till then. So I were you, I'd probably want to be gone before breakfast."

"I can do that," Annie said. "Not that I think folks around here aren't hospitable, but I don't think I'll be investing in any retirement property in the neighborhood."

"That's for the best."

"Sounds like it."

"You think we're racist because we mostly sacrifice Mexicans. Don't try to deny it, I saw it in your eyes when you looked at me a few minutes ago. That's not it, though. They're just passing through. No one's looking for them, no one can trace them here because they're trying not to leave tracks. It's convenience, not hate. You, they hate. We hate. The only reason you're not dead right now is that too many people know you're here—the prison staff, the warden, the district attorney, and the people from that organization that sent you here. You're fortunate that you've made a big splash in this little pond, Annie. Swim away, and do it fast."

"You killed Leo," Annie said, stating it as a fact rather than a supposition. "Why didn't you use him?"

"We might have, but he ran," Johanna said. "Lost control of his vehicle. He was dead when we got to him."

Annie let it drop. She felt a little numb about Leo at the moment, which she attributed to Johanna's presence.

She wondered if Johanna was right about Asmillius coming back next year. She thought maybe not. The fight had shrunken Asmillius, weakened him. She figured those curvy torchbearers were still laughing at him, even now. Maybe the gaunt men were too. She thought it might take a few years before he would regain the strength he'd once had, if he ever did. And he would think twice about returning to New Dominion, to this field of flat stones, knowing that he'd had his ass kicked here.

By a human, at that. By a girl. She didn't know demon psychology, but she knew men. He wouldn't get over that for a good long while.

"All right." Annie forced herself to her feet. Her legs were unsteady, but they held her. "Your Tahoe's over there," she said, pointing. "Keys are in it. I fucked it up on the fence."

"I'll take care of it."

"I'd say thanks, but . . . forget it." She had nothing to be grateful to Johanna for. The woman had wanted her dead, probably had some part in Leo's murder, and who knew how many others in her lifetime? She had seemed friendly, but that was just to keep tabs on Annie. "Forget it," Annie said again. She walked through the field of flat stones and started up the hill on the far side.

Over that hill, she supposed, her rented house had been restored to its previous location and condition. She didn't plan to spend much time there, just enough to grab her stuff and pack the car. New Mexico was beautiful, but if she never came back to this part of it again, that would be soon enough for her.

As she climbed, emotions whirled within her. Disappointment at the idea that Asmillius's defeat might only be temporary. Betrayal by Johanna, compounded by shame that she had been used so thoroughly by Morgan and Johnny. Deep, abiding sorrow over Leo's death. Pride that she beat back a demon and lived, and prevented what could only have been a dangerous merging of him and Morgan. Wonder at the miraculous aspects of her world she had never before known. Curiosity at what tomorrow would bring, and the next day, and the day after that.

She tried to still it all, to put it out of her mind. She listened to the calls of the morning birds, to the sounds of distant voices, to the clatter of rocks sliding down the hill beneath her feet and the chuff of her own breath. Emotions whirled within her, but they were real, and they were hers, and instead of pushing them away she pulled them to her, embraced them, and they were clean and true and honest, and really, it didn't get better than that. She was Annie O'Brien, a cop and the daughter of a cop, a woman, a person, the sum of her aches and pains, longings and desires, sorrows and joys and regrets, hungers and thirsts and lusts and loves. That was all she would ever be, could ever be, but that was just fine, it was enough for her.

It was enough.

At the crest of the hill, Annie laughed out loud, and then she started down the other side.